W9-BJL-921

CAROLINA MOONSET

BOOKS BY MATT GOLDMAN

Carolina Moonset

Nils Shapiro Novels
Gone to Dust
Broken Ice
The Shallows
Dead West

CAROLINA MOONSET

MATT GOLDMAN

A Tom Doherty Associates Book / New York

This is a work of fiction. All of the characters, organizations, and events portrayed in this novel are either products of the author's imagination or are used fictitiously.

CAROLINA MOONSET

Copyright © 2022 by Matt Goldman

A Forge Book
Published by Tom Doherty Associates
120 Broadway
New York, NY 10271

www.tor-forge.com

Forge® is a registered trademark of Macmillan Publishing Group, LLC.

Library of Congress Cataloging-in-Publication Data

Names: Goldman, Matt, 1962– author.
Title: Carolina moonset / Matt Goldman.
Description: First Edition. | New York : Forge, Tom Doherty Associates, 2022. |
  "A Tom Doherty Associates Book." | Identifiers: LCCN 2022000560 (print) |
  LCCN 2022000561 (ebook) | ISBN 9781250810120 (hardcover) |
  ISBN 9781250810144 (trade paperback) | ISBN 9781250810137 (ebook)
Subjects: LCGFT: Novels.
Classification: LCC PS3607.O45454 C37 2022 (print) | LCC PS3607.O45454
  (ebook) | DDC 813/.6—dc23
LC record available at https://lccn.loc.gov/2022000560
LC ebook record available at https://lccn.loc.gov/2022000561

Our books may be purchased in bulk for promotional, educational, or business use. Please contact your local bookseller or the Macmillan Corporate and Premium Sales Department at 1-800-221-7945, extension 5442, or by email at MacmillanSpecialMarkets@macmillan.com.

First Edition: 2022

Printed in the United States of America

0 9 8 7 6 5 4 3 2 1

For my brother, David.

Catcher of chameleons. Slapper of sunburns. Big Man posting up in Nerf Basketball. Gulper of Horseradish.

I would not have survived our many moves without you.

CAROLINA MOONSET

1

When I saw my first palm tree, I almost died of disappointment. It wasn't on a tiny island. It didn't have coconuts under its fronds or monkeys clinging to its trunk. That palm tree failed me.

The tree lived in Beaufort, South Carolina, in my grandparents' backyard, and the letdown I felt over its lack of picture-book clichés is my earliest memory of that place. I must have been three or four. It was the same trip I met the ocean at Hunting Island State Park. I waded into the salt water. Tasted it on my fingers. Scanned the surface for sharks. Thought every dolphin and hunk of driftwood was a shark, which sent me screaming and splashing back to the beach.

I spent languid afternoons with my sisters catching chameleons. We put the lizards in a box and named them. Took the box inside to show the adults. And under strict and often shrieked orders, carried the box back outside to let the creatures go. The chameleons turned brown on the palm tree's trunk or green if set on a leaf. I was determined to bring one home to Chicago and set it in our snowy backyard to see if it would turn white. But my sisters told my parents of my plan, and the chameleon was freed from my suitcase.

That's when I learned I could not trust family.

"Remember that time, Joey, when we came down to Beaufort to

visit Grandpa and Grandma?" My father spoke in a South Carolina drawl, a melody he'd reclaimed since moving back to the place he grew up. He'd always been loquacious, but his lyrical cadence had lain dormant for half a century until the salt air brought it back to life. "You couldn't have been more than three years old. Grandma took you kids to the strawberry farm, and you went row to row picking strawberries and putting them in your little basket. Then Grandma picked a berry and added it to your basket. . . ." My father began to laugh, the memory vivid to him like film. ". . . And you said, 'No! Joey's basket!' And you dumped all your strawberries in the dirt. . . ." My father laughed so hard he listed, held up by his shoulder strap in the back seat.

I didn't remember the strawberry farm. The incident happened over forty years ago. Forty vacations ago. Although trips to visit family don't qualify as vacations. Families have pecking orders, and each gathering is an opportunity to shift the hierarchy—that hardly creates an atmosphere for relaxation.

My mother sat in the passenger seat. She responded to my father's story with a tragic smile. Carol Green had aged in the last six months. Aged fifteen years by the looks of it, her face now drawn and pale. Her gray hair dull. She'd had it cut short. Not cute short but surrender short. She could no longer deal with something as trivial as hair. She'd lost weight. It looked like her bones wanted to push their way out of her skin. From her cheeks, her shoulders, her wrists, and her knees.

She was only seventy-three.

My mother used to sparkle. She'd had the social calendar of a debutante. A champion pickleball player, she and Judy Campbell ran the table at the tournament out on Fripp Island. But age had caught up to her. Passed her even. My sisters had each visited to give her a break. Now it was my turn. My parents had picked me up at the Charleston airport. Such expectation and excitement on the faces of Carol and Marshall Green. It's a thing with relocated retirees. They're eager to show you their life of leisure the way children are eager to show you the fort they built.

"What color is your suitcase?" My father stood at the carousel excited for the responsibility of spotting and retrieving the bag. The challenge of lifting it. He was surrounded by septuagenarians like himself, most picking up their children and grandchildren who'd flown down to visit for spring break, the beginning of Beaufort's bustling tourist season.

"Navy," I said. "It's a roller with a green bandana tied to the handle."

"Green bandana for Joey Green. Smart." He smiled, entertained by his observation. Brown eyes squinting behind trifocals, the old kind with visible lines, his eyebrows creeping over in need of a trim.

My mother pulled me aside and lowered her voice. "I want you to drive back to Beaufort, Joey. Your father's sense of direction is . . ." She shook her head and pressed her lips together. "And he doesn't like it when I drive. He complained the whole way here." My mother sighed. "We were at the neurologist this morning. She changed the diagnosis. I haven't even had a chance to tell your sisters yet."

My father turned around and said, "Hey, Joey. What color is your suitcase?"

"It's navy, Dad. A roller bag with a green bandana tied to the handle."

"Green bandana for Joseph Green. Good thinking." He gave me a thumbs-up, turned around, then walked toward where the conveyer belt spit the bags onto the metal merry-go-round. He moved with small, slow steps, like a cartoon old person. Shoulders stooped. Suspenders holding his jeans on his slender hips. Bent forward as if he needed the tilt to maintain inertia.

He was only seventy-five.

I wondered when my father had started wearing suspenders and if I was too old to be embarrassed about it. And I wondered when I'd started associating the word *only* with *seventy-five*. Maybe it's because my father's parents had lived into their nineties. I looked at my mother and said, "Dad has Parkinson's and Alzheimer's, right?"

My mother shook her head. "That's what they thought, but the neurologist and internist discussed Dad's symptoms. Now they think he has Lewy Body Dementia."

"What's that?"

My father got halfway to the end of the carousel then stopped and turned to show us a most confused expression. "Carol?"

"What, Marshall?"

"What are we waiting for?"

"Joey's bag."

"I'll get it. What does it look like?"

I told him. Again. As if it were for the first time. As if my father were a small child. I had last seen him at Thanksgiving in Chicago—that's when I first witnessed his disease while driving to a restaurant in Evanston. He had said it looked like rain and we should go back to get umbrellas. I told him I'd brought umbrellas. Then five minutes later, he said it looked like rain and we should go back to get umbrellas. I said, "Dad. You just said that. I have umbrellas." He apologized. Said he was getting old. Said something about how it was going to happen to me, too, one day. We laughed it off. Then a few minutes later, he said it looked like rain and we should go back to get umbrellas. I caught my mother's eyes in the rearview mirror. She was crying.

At the Charleston airport, my mother said, "We'll talk more about it when we get home. And there is a silver lining. Dad's long-term memory isn't affected. He won't forget me. Or you. Or your sisters or his grandchildren. He's been talking nonstop about growing up here. And about when you and the girls were little. Your father has loved the simple pleasures in life, and to hear his stories about the old days, it's really quite sweet."

My mother's words were hopeful but her eyes betrayed her. She was moving forward in time as my father moved backward. She was losing her companion of fifty-one years. An hour and a half later, my father laughed at the strawberry farm story he'd just told. "Oh, you were mad Grandma put that berry in your basket!" He laughed until he cried as I drove into Beaufort's city limits.

Beaufort County is a delta of sorts comprised of the Sea Islands bordering the coast. The town is rich with antebellum charm, but much had changed since my father grew up there, and his lack of short-term memory made it seem like a tidal wave of new development had hit every time he left the house.

"Would you look at that?" he said, shaking his head. "Hammond Island has three construction cranes. I'll be damned."

I kept my eyes on the road and asked what they were building.

"I don't know," said my father. I would soon learn this was his go-to response. He was resigned to his moth-eaten memory. I wondered how that worked—how he could remember that he couldn't remember.

My mother said, "They're tearing down the resort and building a gated community of luxury homes."

"On Hammond Island?" said my father with disgust in his voice. "Who would want to live on Hammond Island? You can only get there by boat."

"No. Remember, Marshall? They built a bridge last year." She looked at me and said, "We all voted against it, but the powers that be won the day."

"The powers that be," said my father. "Those Hammonds are nasty sons a bitches. Every one of 'em. Stole that island from the blacks. When the Union Army came through, they gave black people their own land. Gave 'em a chance. And it worked, too. The people prospered. Until the goddamn Klan took over and redistributed the land." My father had venom in his voice. "Redistributed the land with guns and knives and ropes and trees. I wouldn't live on Hammond Island if you paid me a million dollars. Hope a hurricane wipes it off the face of the earth."

"Marshall, you don't mean that," said my mother.

"The hell I don't."

My mother looked at me and shook her head, as if to say *he doesn't know what he's talking about.* I checked the rearview mirror to see my father scowling at the construction cranes.

When my sisters and I were young and still lived at home, we played a game called Divert Dad. The object of the game was this: if our father got onto a topic any one of us didn't care for—say, government public health policy, pharmaceutical companies, or worst of all, one of our social lives or academic missteps—we would introduce a new topic he couldn't resist commenting on. One thing about our father: if he could make his point using ten words, he'd use a hundred. By the time he finished saying what he had to say on our interjected topic, he'd have forgotten what we distracted him from.

There was only one rule to the game. The rule was that neither my father nor my mother could know the game was being played or that it even existed. Divert Dad was a game for three players and no spectators. My oldest sister, Bess, invented it when I was about eight, and we have played it, on and off, ever since.

The game grew more intricate over the years. We could earn bonus points for working in obscure vocabulary words, or by trying to get him to say a predetermined word like *mozzarella*, *tomfoolery*, or *bunion*. But the one rule has remained—the game is between us three and for our amusement only. If that rule were ever violated, the game would be forever ruined. Therefore, a competent player must have (1) a good poker face, (2) a vast knowledge of distracting subjects, and (3) an understanding that Divert Dad is a team sport. Sure, you can rack up impressive personal stats, but we never competed against each other. For example, if our father was lecturing me over my C in physics, I couldn't be the one to divert him onto another topic. That would have been too obvious. One of my teammates had to do it.

But today, with my sisters home in Chicago, I was the only player. My father glared at Hammond Island. It upset my mother. Therefore, it fell upon me to Divert Dad.

"Dad, looks like the White Sox pitching staff is in trouble. Two starters out with injuries."

In the rearview mirror, I saw him look away from the construction cranes, but instead of launching into a diatribe on the White

Sox front office, he looked blank and then sad. He sighed and said, "I don't know anything about it."

Divert Dad was going to be a lot harder now. I said, "Well, the days of 2005 are long gone. Hey, remember José Contreras's start in game one of the World Series? When Guillén pulled him in the seventh?"

"Oh, hell, that was great," said my father as if the game had been played last night. "Guillén brought in Jenks in the bottom of the eighth to face Bagwell. Struck him out with a hundred-mile-an-hour fastball. High heat. I've never seen anything so beautiful."

"Eh-hem," said my mother.

"I stand corrected," said my father. "The most beautiful thing I've ever seen is Konerko's grand slam in game two."

My mother laughed and said, "Oh, Marshall! You're terrible!" as I pulled into the driveway behind the big white house.

2

I was born and raised in Chicago like my mother. She met my father while attending the University of Illinois when she was an undergrad and he was a medical student. She loved his South Carolina accent, though my father worked hard to lose it, and was attracted to his altruism. My father passed on lucrative offers in private practice to open a free clinic on Chicago's South Side, where he worked twelve hours a day, six days a week, until he turned seventy.

My friends' parents all told me how great my father was, putting the less privileged before himself. I thought, what about me? I'm the one who has to wear clothes from Sears. I'm the one who's allowed only one week of summer camp. I'm the one with the bedroom that's not the size of a closet but an actual closet without windows and a lofted bed so my dresser could go underneath. What about my sacrifice? Where's the praise for me?

Then, the day he turned seventy, a switch flipped in my father. He'd had enough. Of medicine. And sacrifice. And Chicago. He retired, convinced my mother to do the same, and begged her to move to South Carolina.

My mother would later tell me, "It was as if he didn't have a choice, Joey. Your father had to return to Beaufort, like he was programmed that way, like a salmon has to leave the ocean and return to the stream where it was born. He just *had* to."

I parked my parents' car in the garage, went around to the tailgate, and removed my bag. The air smelled of the sea, heavy with salt and humidity. I took a deep breath and inhaled forty years of pleasant memories from this place I loved.

My father saw my bag and said, "Hey, a green bandana for Green. I like the way you think!" That big grin again. "So good to have you here, Joey." I put an arm around him. He felt old. More bone than muscle. And up close, I saw he'd missed a few spots shaving, silver patches of stubble where there should have been none.

My mother said, "Oh, Joey, I forgot to tell you. Dad hired the guide to take you two fishing tomorrow."

"I did?" said my father.

"Yes, Marshall. And it was very nice of you. You and Joey will have some good father-son time on the water."

I said, "It'll be just like old times, Dad. You can untangle my line and buy my patience with candy bars."

"Aw, Joey. You were always a good fisherman. Even when you were tiny you were fascinated by what you couldn't see below the surface. That's what fishing is all about. Curiosity and the patience to learn."

I only fished with my father. I tried to get my kids interested because I appreciated the bond fishing provided between me and my father and hoped the sport could do the same between me and my kids. They didn't take to it, which was fine. We bond over other things. I didn't love fishing, but I did it for my father. To spend time with him doing something he loved. But I took his compliment as we walked into the backyard I had known since I was a boy, back when the house on Craven Street belonged to my grandparents. It was built in 1853 and had white clapboard siding and a red tile roof. Verandas out front on the first and second floors. The house rested on pilings eight feet off the ground to allow flood waters from hurricanes to pass underneath.

My grandfather was the only one of his siblings to have children. My father was never a wealthy man but inherited money from his parents, grandparents, aunts, and uncles. It wasn't a fortune, but it was something, and it included the house on Craven Street.

We walked through the backyard where my father's boat sat covered on its trailer, out of commission without its skipper. We passed a bed of roses and a small orange tree, its branches bent by heavy fruit. The old palm tree was still there, the kind that had a thick trunk and wasn't too tall, its bark woven like a basket. I checked it for chameleons, a habit I couldn't break, but saw none. Of course with chameleons, that didn't mean they weren't there.

My father said, "Remember, Joey, we were visiting Beaufort and sitting on the back porch, you were just a little guy, and you said you had to go inside to use the bathroom. Do you remember that?"

I reached for my phone and started the voice memo app. Greta, the younger of my two sisters, had asked me to record our father's stories. I said, "I don't remember that."

"I told you, 'Joey, we're men. And the best thing about being a man is if you got to go, just find a tree in the backyard.' So you went down the stairs and a few minutes later rejoined me on the porch. I didn't think anything of it until a couple hours later when I was taking the trash out back and saw that right there, at the base of that palm tree, was a human shit." Laughter seized him. I thought he might topple over. My father said, "I assumed you had to go number one. But no, sir. You just laid one out in the backyard!"

For a parent, there is nothing better than watching your child laugh. But watching your memory-impaired, stoop-shouldered father laugh is pretty damn close.

I said, "I might take a dump out here during this trip."

My mother laughed. "You'd better not, mister!"

My father took off his glasses to wipe away his tears and catch his breath, then he climbed the back steps at inchworm speed. Held the railing tight. My mother walked behind him, as if she could catch him if he tipped backward. I set my bag on the back porch then descended the stairs and took her place.

Two fighter jets roared overhead, and my father said, "You know what they call that, don't you, Joey?"

I knew but said, "No, Dad. What?"

"The sound of freedom."

He'd been saying that since I was a kid, and him repeating it had nothing to do with cognitive impairment. He just liked to say it. A lot of people in Beaufort did, the Marine base at Paris Island a source of hometown pride.

The old house looked like it had when it belonged to my grandparents. Plaster walls painted in solid colors. Blue, peach, green, yellow, depending on the room. High ceilings. Floors of heart pine. The windows extended nearly from floor to ceiling, which let the sea breeze push through the house before the invention of air-conditioning. The kitchen, however, had been remodeled into something that functioned without hired help.

We were greeted by a dear family friend. Ruby was dark-skinned and thin and had relaxed-straight hair that followed the contour of her face and stopped short of her shoulders. She had started working at the house on Craven Street for my grandparents when she was just a girl, like her mother had.

Ruby's family, the Wallaces, and mine, the Greens, had leaned on each other for generations. I wouldn't exist if it weren't for the Wallaces. In the 1940s there was a great migration from home births to hospital births. My father was slated for the latter. The first and only child of Julian and Ida Green was to be born in a modern hospital that was sterilized and full of life-saving doctors and equipment. Their child in utero had other ideas. While Julian was in Atlanta buying wares at a trade show, the soon-to-be-named Marshall Green made his appearance a full month earlier than scheduled.

Ida woke up in labor, her sheets wet with amniotic fluid, and a great pressure on her cervix. She could not get down the stairs to phone for help. By the time Ruby's mother, Ella May Wallace arrived to work, my grandmother's contractions seemed continuous.

Ella May had served as midwife for dozens of mothers and knew there was no time to call for help. She delivered my father, and most likely saved his and my grandmother's lives.

Ruby had stopped working as a domestic thirty years ago to start her own bakery, but still had a key to my parents' house. The bakery was two blocks away, and when my parents were out of town, Ruby took in the mail and watered the plants—she knew the old house as well as her own.

When we entered the back door, she pulled her head out of the pantry and said, "There he is. Joey Green. Still a little boy to me."

When I *was* a little boy and wouldn't sit still with my sisters, couldn't sit still, unmotivated by coloring books or Go Fish or cat's cradle, it was Ruby who'd walk me down to the waterfront. We'd watch the boats and pelicans and throw bread into the air dense with gulls. Ruby let me expend my boy energy, which my parents had deemed misbehavior in the wake of two well-mannered daughters. She'd push me on the swings and time me running around a circle of palms at Waterfront Park. I'd cross the finish line, look at her with expectation, and wipe the sweat out of my eyes. Ruby would glance at her watch, announce my result, and say, "I think you can do better." It was a perfect symbiosis. Ruby stole a few precious moments off her feet and gave me a few precious moments to move mine as fast as I could.

I hugged Ruby tight and said, "I smell praline cookies."

Ruby said, "I tried to sneak in here and drop them off like your fairy godmother before you got to the house, but you caught me in the act. There is no way I am going to let you visit Beaufort without baking a big old tin of my cookies. A boy's got to eat. And the part about me getting caught in the act? Well, that's just a big fat lie. I couldn't wait to see my Joey Green. Lord, look at you. Must be fighting off the ladies with fly swatters. And how are those babies doing?"

"Great. They're on spring break with Cheryl."

"Bring 'em next time. That's an order. And you'd better come visit me at the bakery."

There is no way I'd visit Beaufort without setting foot in Ruby's bakery. But I said, "You still baking elephant ears?"

"Sure am."

"Then I'll be there."

"Elephant ears, my backside. You're coming to see me and you know it."

Ruby left, and my father helped himself to a cookie before excusing himself to take a nap. A minute later the old wooden staircase creaked under his slow climb. My mother went to the refrigerator, retrieved a pitcher of iced tea, and poured two glasses.

She said, "I don't know who's happier you're here, us or Ruby."

"Well, based on this tin of cookies, I'd say Ruby."

My mother managed a smile. "She was so good to you when you were little. And she's right. Next year, you'd better bring my grandkids here." She had wanted to sound playful—I could hear it in her voice—but the idea of next year pained her.

I changed the subject and said, "What was all that in the car about Hammond Island? I haven't seen Dad get angry like that in a long time."

"Dad and the Hammond brothers didn't get along when they were boys. Now that your father only thinks about what he can remember, those old feelings surface more often than they used to."

I felt I already knew that, but wasn't sure how. I started to wonder but was distracted by the cookies, which tasted of pecan and molasses, a recipe that came to the house like Ruby had, with her mother and grandmother. I had half a cookie in my mouth when my mother said, "Oh, before I forget . . ." My mother opened her purse, retrieved a key, and handed it to me. "I'm worried Dad will wander off and get lost so I had the deadbolts switched to the kind that need a key from the inside. Here's yours. Keep it with you and please make sure the doors are locked. Dad can't go outside without one of us."

"He can't even go for a walk?"

"Not alone, no. He gets disoriented easily. Sometimes the locks make him mad, and he'll yell about them being a fire safety issue, but it has to be this way. Oh, and we bought Dad a special life vest for fishing. His balance isn't what it used to be, and I'm worried he'll fall off the boat. Promise me he'll wear it?"

"Of course." I sipped my iced tea. It tastes better in the South. And it wasn't even sweet tea. "Does Dad know about his diagnosis?"

"Yes. And he gets upset about it. He says it's not fair because he's taken such good care of himself. And he's right. It's not fair. He's scared to death he'll end up in memory care at some assisted living place. That he'll forget everything and everyone."

"But you said it's only his short-term memory that's affected."

"So far. Yes. Thank God."

"It's weird. He seems kind of happy."

"He is most of the time. He doesn't get frustrated with politics or his sports teams because he has no grasp of current events."

"That would make me happy."

My mother sat down next to me and said, "It's like when a person loses their sight, their hearing improves. Except with Dad, he's lost his short-term memory, and his long-term memory has improved. He tells stories I've never heard before."

"That's no small feat for a guy who hasn't stopped talking since he was one."

She sighed and smiled a sad smile, reached over, and placed her hand on mine. Her hand belonged to an old woman, spotted and bony. She had a younger woman's hands last time I saw her. "It's such a relief for me to have you here, Joey."

"Why don't you take a break, Mom?" I said the words as I thought them. No filter. No editing. "Go somewhere and relax for a few days."

She shook her head. "That's sweet, Joey, but I can't leave him."

"You're not leaving him. I'm here. I won't lose him."

"You lost Steve." She smiled.

"Steve was a hamster. And yes, I lost him. When I was six. I've matured since then. A little. And I wouldn't mind the one-on-one time with Dad."

"Really?" She handed me a second cookie, insisted I eat it.

"When Cheryl and I split up, I got less time with the kids, but it was better time because it was just the three of us. I got to know them in a different way. It's been the best thing about the divorce. No offense, but I'd love some one-on-one time with Dad."

My mother thought a moment, then said, "Well . . ." She sighed. "No . . ."

"No what?"

"Judy was heading down to Jacksonville tomorrow for a pickle-ball tournament, but her partner sprained a knee. Judy asked if I could sub in but I told her I couldn't. I have to stay with Dad. So she's looking for someone else."

"Mom, if Judy hasn't found anyone, you should go. What's it, two days?"

"Three. Joey, I can't. But I'll play with you while you're visiting."

"Pickleball?"

"Yes. Why not?"

"I think, legally, I'm too young to play. It's out of my hands."

"Oh, poo," said my mother. "Everyone is playing pickleball now. People your age, kids—it's not just for retired people. You'll love it. It's like a cross between tennis and Ping-Pong. I'll buy you a paddle as an early birthday present."

"Mom, I promise to play pickleball with you sometime. But you need a break. From the house. From Dad. Even from Beaufort. You need to have some fun. There will be plenty of time to kick my butt in pickleball when you get back. Please. Call Judy. See if she's found a partner."

My mother nodded and began to cry, a leak to relieve the pressure.

"This is good, Mom. You deserve it."

She nodded and said, "Will you please get Dad's life vest now so you don't forget it tomorrow?"

I unlocked the back door and walked outside past the orange tree and my father's covered boat and into the garage. His workbench—my father tinkered in retirement—held his fishing gear. He had always been meticulous. Neat and clean and organized. But like his memory, his organization and cleanliness had deteriorated. Fishing rods lay across his workbench at odd angles like pick-up sticks. Bait casting reels, their lines loose, tangled with one another. Tackle boxes sat open, their lures bound by intertwined treble hooks. A can of WD-40 on its side, its red plastic spray straw a foot away. A hammer on a dry sponge, rusted on the side where the sponge had been wet. Screwdrivers scattered pell-mell. The socket set case open, sockets missing and nowhere in sight.

The father I had known was fading. I wanted to call my sisters back in Chicago. The three of us had to do something. Get our mother more help. Insist she and our father move back to Chicago where we would be close. Something.

I spotted my father's new personal flotation device hanging on the pegboard, reached for it, remembered something, and stopped.

The pistol.

My father had always kept a pistol in his old metal tackle box, the tackle box pocked with rust, its paint eaten away decades ago. The revolver had been in the family forever, but my mother and sisters didn't know about it. As my sisters grew older, they and my mother lost interest in fishing. By the time I was ten, spending the entire day out on the water had become an exclusively father and son activity. That's when he showed me the pistol and swore me to secrecy, knowing that if my mother and sisters found out he owned a gun, he never would have heard the end of it.

For as long as I'd known the gun existed, my father had kept it locked in the tackle box, hidden in a canvas sack. But I found the old metal tackle box out in the open, unlocked. I opened it, and its levels of storage compartments stretched out and up like a staircase. My father had always kept the pistol in the bottom level. I removed lures, boxes of hooks, a decade-old jar of pork rind frogs, lead weights, pliers, sunscreen, a fillet knife. But the gun was missing.

I sifted through the mess on the workbench, lifting up rods, tools, an unopened package of paper yard waste bags. No gun. I looked below the workbench, pulled out half-spent cans of paint, extra tile from a bathroom remodel, a bike tire pump. But I couldn't find the gun.

My father's old fishing vest hung on a nail near the new life vest. I took it down, searched its pockets, and found a small box of ammunition—.32 shells. The shells fit the gun, but the gun wasn't in the fishing vest. I opened the box of ammunition—it was about two-thirds full. I pocketed the shells and took a cursory lap around the garage, lifting up bags of potting soil, pushing aside an edging tool, tipping over the old lawn mower, which was no longer in service since my parents hired out for lawn care over a year ago. The gas can was empty. I flipped through folded lawn chairs as if they were files in a filing cabinet.

No gun.

Marshall Green wasn't mentally sound enough to have access to a gun. If it was in the house, my mother would have found it, and if she'd found it she would have asked me about it. *Asked* probably isn't the right word. Freaked out is more accurate. The good news was my father was no longer permitted to leave the house unaccompanied. He was locked inside without access to a key.

I started to walk away but stopped. I didn't know why. I had no reason to stay in the garage, having decided that the gun presented no danger to my father nor to anyone else because he had no way to get at it. Besides, the old pistol had probably rusted into futility, wherever it was, buried in the natural decay of the neglected garage. And yet the revolver pulled at me. At least its image did, which was burned into my memory, or perhaps a memory of my memory, for a reason I couldn't explain.

After a minute of standing still, inhaling the mildewy air that's ever-present in the unkempt corners of a seaside town, I remembered my mission, grabbed my father's new life vest, and exited the garage.

3

I took my father's new life vest into the house and learned that Judy Campbell had not found a replacement pickleball partner so my mother took the spot. She'd leave for Florida early the next morning. My father had woken from his nap, and was sitting in the kitchen eating one of Ruby's praline cookies. He approved of my mother's trip and said, "We've always been surrounded by women, Joey. Your mother and sisters, God doesn't make them any finer, but there's nothing wrong with a little man time."

My parents lived downtown, a couple blocks from the water, where the commercial district met nineteenth-century homes and trees draped with Spanish moss, and horses pulled carts of sightseers. The tourist season had commenced. The three of us walked the old, fat sidewalks toward the Beaufort River and chose a restaurant for dinner. My father told stories of his childhood when, on hot summer days, he'd disappear at sunrise and be home by noon with a stringer of fish and baskets of shrimp and crab. This was before the commercial fishermen had emptied the Atlantic, he said, his mouth full of halibut. He started in on relocated New Englanders who had come in hordes, creating traffic problems that hadn't existed before.

I said, "You were gone for fifty years. You're kind of like a transplant."

"No, I'm not. This town is my birthright. When I was a teenager I worked at that marina right there, tying up boats for tips. I'm third-generation Beaufort. Living in my parents' house. Your mother and I didn't change the footprint of this town one inch when we moved down here. The construction cranes you see— they're not our fault." He looked around the restaurant. "Where's that waitress? I want a beer."

"She just brought you one, Dad."

My father looked down at a full pint of pilsner and said, "Our waitress is sneaky."

He laughed, and we laughed with him, ignoring the elephant in the pint glass.

After dinner, we walked along the waterfront to watch the boats come and go. It reminded me of when I was a kid, and my great-uncle David took us out and taught me how to throw the shrimp net. Folded it just so. Held one part in my mouth, the rest in my hands, then Frisbeed it out above the water so it spread like a parachute. The net landed in tiny splashes. I pulled it in. The shrimp were hopping mad and clear like glass. We took them home, where my mother, grandmother, and aunts peeled and deveined them on the kitchen counter. Popped their heads off and served them for dinner with grits and sweet tea and vinegar slaw.

Locals and tourists crowded the waterfront. Boats filled the docks. Sailboats, cruisers, and yachts, some from as far away as Halifax on their journey south through the Intracoastal Waterway. I read the boat names embossed on their sterns. *The Netty Professor*, a shrimp boat. *One Cocktail if by Land . . .*, a yacht. *Reason for Divorce*, a cigarette boat.

"Hello, Carol."

"Leela," said my mother. "Nice to see you."

A woman, who I assumed was Leela, walked toward us. She wore a white sundress and had big amber eyes and shoulder-length dark hair pulled back into a ponytail. Her face had freckles on pronounced cheekbones over bronze skin. She walked with two girls, the three of them eating ice cream from paper cups. The

kids looked a couple years younger than mine, in their early teens,
I guessed. They walked ahead when their mother stopped to chat.

My mother said, "This is Joey. Joey, this is Leela, Ted and Kajal's
daughter. She's visiting from Boston."

I said hello. Leela smiled and said, "Very nice to meet you,
Joey. I'm looking forward to tomorrow night." I smiled and nodded, though I had no idea what she was talking about. Leela
said, "Girls, not too close to the water," then she said goodbye
and walked away.

My mother said, "Isn't she nice?"

I said, "What's tomorrow night?"

The sun touched the horizon and ignited the marsh with pinks
and golds. A white crane rose into the air, its legs dangling like
forgotten appendages.

"Ted and Kajal invited you and Dad over for dinner."

"She's pretty," said my father. He looked at me and smiled. "I
wonder if she's married."

"Not anymore," said my mother.

I said, "I smell a setup."

"Oh, quit your complaining. It doesn't hurt to meet people."

I did not protest. My mother's matchmaking was as innocu-
ous as when she gathered us all for a family portrait—her joy out-
weighed my annoyance and discomfort. Besides, I was more than
intrigued by Leela. She had an intelligence in her eyes. A confi-
dence I found attractive. I will admit I saw my trip to Beaufort as
an obligation. My father's dementia had put its foot on the gas. My
mother was his full-time caretaker and needed relief. It was spring
break for most, but not for me. Running a company and parenting
two teenagers was easier than parenting my parents. Being set up
with Leela felt like a welcome distraction.

The sun disappeared before we meandered back to the house.
My mother retreated upstairs to pack for her early-morning depar-
ture. My father excused himself to use the bathroom, and I waited
for him in the front foyer next to a painting I'd known all my life.

Beaufort is full of art galleries—local artists love to paint its old buildings, its oak trees that form tunnels over country roads, Spanish moss hanging from branches, the boats coming and going, the rich landscapes and seascapes. My parents owned dozens of paintings by local artists, but the one in the foyer was the only one that depicted night. And it's the only painting I remembered from my childhood. The others felt interchangeable.

It showed the dark marsh in heavy brushstrokes. A sprawling oak in the foreground framed an expanse of reeds. A tidal creek snaked through the reeds. The tide was out, and the creek's muddy bottom reflected the moonlight. A clump of more oaks in the distance, and behind those oaks, the dark shadow of an immense home, no light in the windows except for one on the second floor.

The marsh is beautiful during the day, changing colors with the angle of the sun. But it's eerie at night. Too many secrets hiding in its vastness and in its crevices. The sea comes in and the sea goes out. Only it knows what's hidden in the marsh.

The painting was signed in the lower right corner, but the signature was illegible. A small brass plaque was affixed to the frame, not much bigger than a dog tag. It was engraved: CAROLINA MOONSET. The painting terrified me when I was a boy. I had too good of an imagination back then to let its darkness go unexplored. Every time I visited my parents, it commanded me to stop and pay my respects. To walk back in time so it could make me feel small and frightened.

My father returned from the bathroom. We went into the den and found the Duke-Clemson game on TV.

"You been watching much basketball this year, Dad?"

He shrugged. "I don't know." He was matter-of-fact about it. He really didn't know. That was his reality. "But I enjoy it. The score is always on the screen so I don't have to remember it. And I like watching Coach K on the sidelines. He's a legend."

"He sure is."

"So glad you came to visit, Joey." He nodded and smiled. My father seemed to have a nearly perpetual smile in Beaufort. He loved the place where he grew up. The salt marsh. The history.

The old house. The Union Army burned its way south but they spared Beaufort. They knew this place was worth preserving. "Ah, Joey, I loved watching you play. No one ran an offense like you."

"I wasn't great, Dad."

"You sure were. Best point guard in the conference. You could have played college."

"Maybe D3."

He threw up his hands. "Nothing wrong with D3. And you could have walked on D1. Doesn't matter how tall a team is, how fast they are, they need ball handlers. Some of the best shooting guards in the country can't handle the press, but you could. Always. If you had played in college, I would have come to every game."

He would have. My father loved ball sports. He had tried with my sisters, too, but they had shown little interest in ball sports. I was his first and only son, and he was determined I would be different. But like Bess and Greta, I disappointed him by favoring more individual sports. I had surpassed him in height when I was thirteen. At six feet one, I am, according to him, the tallest Green in history, and he made no secret about wanting to see the tallest Green in history on the hardwood and the diamond.

We were different, my father and I. I preferred running shoes and personal records to packed gymnasiums and "hey batta hey." But I tried, at least with basketball. It was a winter sport and kept me in shape between cross-country in the fall and track in the spring and provided us at least one overlap in our father and son Venn diagram.

My father's attention shifted back to the TV. He, like my mother, had aged exponentially since I'd last seen him. But unlike my mother, he had also developed a childlike facet. That's how he looked sitting in his recliner, dwarfed by the big chair, feet up as if the novelty of using the footrest were a special treat. I had a conscious thought to remember that image of my father—the supply of images wouldn't last forever.

I said, "So what time are we going fishing tomorrow?"

"We're going fishing tomorrow?"

It was hard to get used to my father's lack of short-term memory. It left so many topics off-limits. Like plans for tomorrow and what we'd just eaten for dinner. I said, "Yeah. Weather looks good. I bet the fish will be biting."

"I hope so."

I wanted to ask him when he last fished, but knew it was pointless. He wouldn't remember. I wanted to walk him out to the garage and show him his workbench, the condition and circumstance in which I found his gear. But I feared confronting him with such a stark display of his cognitive decline would devastate him.

A beer commercial came on TV. My father laughed. I envied people who laughed at beer commercials. So much free entertainment for them. Then he laughed at an insurance commercial. This had nothing to do with his memory loss—my father had always laughed at beer and insurance commercials. But seeing each one as if for the first time made them that much more funny to him.

And then my father stopped laughing, turned away from the TV, pointed to an empty armchair, and said, "Hey, Trip. What are you doing here?" His voice was friendly. Happy and surprised. "Would you look at that, Joey. Trip Patterson is here."

I glanced at the empty armchair, then back to my father. He saw someone who was not there. I felt like a parent whose child was talking to an imaginary friend, only with children, you feel excited about their imagination. Their creativity. It is something to be encouraged. When a parent talks to an imaginary friend, excitement does not best describe the feeling. The words *fear* and *shock* are more on the mark. But all I said was, "Yeah . . ."

"Trip. Sure is good to see you. Long time, old friend." He stopped talking and nodded toward the chair. For half a minute, at least. Then he said, "I know, Trip. That was sickening." Again, he stopped to listen. "No, no, don't say that. It wasn't your fault. And you know that's true because you know whose fault it was. It's a shame. It really is. That poor girl. That poor, poor girl." My father returned his attention to the game, "Ha! Look at Coach K. He's letting that ref really have it. Boy, he's mad!" He laughed. "Give 'em hell, Coach!" He kicked back in his recliner.

I had never heard of my father's imaginary friend. I Googled Trip Patterson on my phone. There were dozens of Trip Pattersons. I added Beaufort, SC, to the search and found Pattersons, but no Trip. I knew Trip was a common nickname for someone who was "the third," as in the son of So-and-so Patterson, Jr. I found Patterson Road. But no Trip Patterson.

When I looked up from my phone, my father had fallen asleep and was snoring in his recliner. I left the den, double-checked to make sure the front and back doors were dead-bolted because my mother had put the fear of God in me, then went upstairs and found her folding and refolding her athletic wear on the bed, a teenager's glint in her eye.

She said, "Are you and Dad enjoying the game?"

I said, "We were. But he fell asleep."

She smiled, "It's the medication. It wears him out. But chances are he'll wake up at midnight and roam the house for an hour."

"Something kind of strange happened before he nodded off." I told her about my father talking to the invisible Trip Patterson.

Dread replaced the glint in her eye. "Oh, no." She leaned to look out the bedroom door, as if she wouldn't have heard her husband creaking up the old staircase. "This happened once before. We were in the car. I was driving, and your father turned around and talked to Grandpa in the back seat. It was as if Grandpa was really there. Your father would talk. And then he'd listen. The listening was the strangest part about it."

"Yeah. Same thing just happened downstairs."

"I called the neurologist right after. It's one of the reasons she changed her diagnosis to Lewy Body Dementia. Hallucinations are a common symptom."

I sat in a lounge chair and said, "What did Dad say to Grandpa?"

"It was the weirdest thing. Your dad said he had wanted to go to the University of South Carolina in Columbia like everyone else in the family. Of course, I only heard one side of the conversation, but from what I gathered, Grandpa told Dad he couldn't go there—he had to go north. And stay north. Dad was so hurt. But he didn't argue with Grandpa. Dad was respectful with a lot of *yes, sirs* and *no, sirs*. You know how they talk down here." She picked up a sweater and put it in her roller bag.

I said, "Who's Trip Patterson?"

She shrugged. "A boyhood friend of your father's."

"It was strange, like when a street person talks to no one."

My mother's whole body slumped. She removed the sweater from the bag and said, "He's hallucinating, honey. I can't go to Florida."

"Sure you can."

"I don't want to burden you with that."

"It's not a burden. He's my dad."

She considered this, returned her sweater to the bag, and said, "What did he say to this Trip Patterson?"

If I told her the truth, my mother wouldn't go to Florida. Just like if I had told her about the pistol's existence and that it was missing from the tackle box. She needed a vacation. Desperately. For the exercise. For the sun. To reconnect with friends. So I said, "Not much. Just that it was good to see him."

My mother knew I was lying. She always knew. She was about to say something when her phone lit up. "Oh, hey," she said, "this is interesting."

4

Fifteen minutes later, I stood in front of the house and watched Leela Bellerose walk toward me under a proscenium of Spanish moss. Leela had released her dark hair from the ponytail she'd had when we met on the waterfront, but still wore the white sundress, a tan sweater draped over her shoulders.

Her mother had texted my mother to say Leela was headed out for a walk and in need of company. *In need.* It was 9 P.M. on a Thursday night—our mothers had conspired like a couple of Cold War spies. It was awkward and delightful.

I extended my hand and said, "Hello. My name is Joey. I don't believe we've had the pleasure of being railroaded into a date before."

"Hello, Joey. My name is Leela. I'm the only child of parents whose greatest fear is I won't get remarried."

"But husbands are so overrated. At least that's what I'm told."

"I couldn't agree more. Looks like we already have something in common." She smiled and said, "Maybe a short walk to someplace we can get a drink?"

We started toward downtown and filled each other in on the basics. It was my ex-wife's year to have the kids for spring break. Emily was sixteen. Hank was fourteen. I showed her pictures on my phone, as if my children could somehow vouch for my legitimacy as a human being, and she complimented their looks the way you do when someone shows you pictures of their kids. But I believed she meant it. Leela's kids were twelve and fourteen. I had already seen them on the waterfront, so Leela kept her pictures to herself. She and her ex-husband, instead of trading off every other year for holidays and vacations, split each one. Leela and her ex had flown down together from Boston. She took the kids for a few days while he vacationed on Hilton Head. He had just picked them up for a trip to Orlando's theme parks and chain restaurants. They'd fly back to Boston together next week.

I said, "That sounds civilized."

"We've had a friendly divorce," said Leela. "As far as divorces go. It helps when no one is in love with the person they married or anyone else. Kind of just makes you face the hard truth that it's over. No one did anything terrible. We just grew in different directions, like those trees with split trunks. Eventually, the separate trunks get so big and heavy and far apart that the tree splits in two."

The intelligence I'd seen in Leela's eyes earlier that day showed itself. I felt like skipping but restrained myself and said, "A botanical analogy. I like that."

She smiled at me under dappled streetlamp light and said, "What about you?"

"We were a couple of vines who got entangled and pulled each other out by our roots."

"Sounds unpleasant."

"It was for the best. She's a good person. And a great mom. Everyone's happier now."

The air had cooled and hung damp and motionless under the magnolia trees. Leela didn't respond for a good ten steps, then said, "I'm sorry about your dad."

"Thank you. It is strange. And sad."

"I bet he's thrilled to have you here."

"I think he is. My sisters are better at staying in touch."

"Yeah, it's a girl thing. One of our many talents." We crossed

Craven Street and cut through a parking lot toward the commercial district. Leela said, "So what is your source of income, young man? Any prospects?"

We'd only walked a block and I already liked Leela. My mother had tried to fix me up a few times before with not great results, but I wondered if she and I got lucky this time. I said, "I steal the allowances of tween girls."

"I'm intrigued. Go on."

"I'm a principal in a costume jewelry company. We sell shiny and dangly items that are only available at the finest retailers: Claire's Boutique, Walmart, Target, and, sorry to get all braggy, Walgreen's. We're one of the world's leading contributors to garage sales and landfills."

"You're just trying to impress me."

"Play your cards right and you could end up with a necklace made of genuine plastic emojis. I might even put a poop emoji on there to impress your friends."

Leela said, "Don't say things like that. I'll get my hopes up."

She said it as if she meant it, and all I thought is I'd better not get my hopes up. "And what about you? What keeps you in sundresses and freckled cheekbones?"

She looked at me and smiled, showing the same delighted surprise I felt. "Clinical psychology."

"Psychologist or patient?"

Leela laughed for the first time that night. A birdsong in the salt air. "Psychologist. I see patients and teach a little at BU. It's not as lucrative as undertaking or plastic surgery, but I get a steady stream of customers. Hey, there's a good bar at an inn on Bay Street. Want to go there?"

The inn looked similar to my parents' house, at least to my northern eye. A white clapboard multi-story affair with up and down front porches but on a larger scale. We found a bistro table in the bar and ordered mint juleps to honor the South. Leela's face glowed in the soft light of the hurricane lamp on our table.

She said, "This feels like high school when I'd go on vacation with my parents but had no interest in spending time with them." She rested her right hand on the table, displaying slender fingers free of nail polish and jewelry. "I would just hope to meet someone my own age."

I said, "I'm forty-six. How old are you?"

"Forty-five."

"Look at that. Dream come true."

Leela's eyes shined but she said nothing.

I caught a curiosity in her expression and said, "What?"

Leela said, "I would like to propose an experiment."

"You're a woman of science. At least behavioral science. Please do."

Leela lit up and said, "This is a social experiment. Here are the constants: our parents set us up on this date, hoping we'd hit it off and live happily ever after."

"The bastards."

"But I live in Boston. You live in Chicago. We both have kids and jobs rooted in our respective cities."

"No one likes changing jobs or kids."

"Exactly. And even if one of us wanted to uproot our kids and move, our exes would have to okay it and that is highly unlikely. So the possibility of us hitting it off and living happily ever after is statistically zero."

"Your math is correct."

"Now," she said, "I've been divorced for five years so I've been dating a while. Is that also true with you?"

"Yes. Three years."

"Perfect. So another constant is we've both been out in the world dating."

"This is very scientific. We should be wearing lab coats."

"And eye protection," she said. "Okay. So with those constants in place, I'm going to throw in a variable."

"Can we call it x?"

"Yes. Thank you. We'll call it *x*. And for *x* we'll substitute this: you and I have a five-day relationship. This is our first date. We'll break up when I go home to Boston."

I felt my life taking a hairpin turn. I'd flown to South Carolina to nurse my ailing father but found myself sitting across a bistro table from the most intriguing woman I'd met in years. All I wanted in that moment was to keep Leela Bellerose smiling. I said, "Excuse me. Are you asking for my hand in flingdom?"

"No, no. This is all hypothetical."

"In the name of science."

"Yes," she said. "In the name of science. Now, here's the experiment that will take place during our hypothetical first date."

"Which we're on right now."

"You're a quick study," she said.

The server brought our mint juleps. We clinked glasses and I said, "To our experiment. Whatever that means."

She smiled. "To our experiment. You're about to find out."

"Please proceed, Doctor."

"Thank you." Another sip and Leela said, "So, let's say we were going to date for real."

"You mean have a relationship longer than five days?"

"Yes. Ordinarily, if this was our first date, we'd both present the best sides of ourselves. In other words, we'd present ourselves as fairly well adjusted adults with promising futures and little baggage."

"We sure would."

"And after presenting the best sides of ourselves, we'd want a second date. And a third. And before you know it, we'd enter into a committed relationship."

Just her suggesting the idea of a relationship with me broke my heart a little because geography made it impossible. I said, "We'd become an item."

"Yes. We'd tell our parents and friends and eventually our kids. Then we'd meet each other's kids. And right when we'd be really intertwined in each other's lives, we'd get tired of presenting our best selves, and our true selves would emerge."

"That is exactly what would happen," I said. "And I have the emotional scars to prove it."

Leela lowered her mint julep and set it on the table, her amber eyes twinkling in the candlelight. "So here's the experiment: you and I, tonight, let's do the opposite of what happens on first dates. Let's tell each other the absolute worst about ourselves right up front. Right now. And then decide if we ever want to see each other again."

Our server approached. We ordered a miniature loaf of bread with assorted spreads made from nuts and roasted red peppers and hummus.

After the server left, I said, "Okay, we're going to be totally honest?"

"Brutally," said Leela.

"All right. I'm game. But I may have switch to whiskey."

"You don't like mint juleps?"

"They're okay. A little sweet for me. But I wanted to be festive."

Leela smiled, "Okay. You order girly drinks to ingratiate yourself with women. Noted. And since you started with an easy one, so will I." She smiled. "I'm a pain in the ass to go out to eat with. Big-time food issues."

"Do you send your meal back to the kitchen sometimes?"

She nodded. "Often."

"But what we just ordered is okay?"

"Probably not. We'll see. Now your turn."

"All right. Here's one: I'm obnoxiously picky about women. Not for me so much, but they have to meet a high bar to be around my kids. So I dump a lot of perfectly nice people."

Leela shook her head. "That's not a bad thing about you. That's a good thing. You love and respect your children. Total humble brag. Try again."

"Wow. Science is hard. Give me a second. . . . Okay, here's one—since we're being brutally honest—and hope this isn't another humble brag—I am emotionally fucked up."

Leela tilted her head, stared at me, gave away nothing, and said, "Can you be more specific?"

"Something's wrong with me. I don't feel . . ." I stopped, looked away, then back at Leela. ". . . I don't feel things I should."

"Like you're a sociopath?"

"Probably."

"You're not a sociopath. Sociopaths don't think they're sociopaths. What kind of things don't you feel that you think you should?"

I stirred my julep with its tiny red straw and said, "I don't have much empathy for people."

"None whatsoever?"

"I do for kids. And for animals. My dog died last year—I was a wreck. Barely left the house for a week. And I have empathy for my parents and sisters and their kids. But really, not for anyone else. I hear about people's problems. I hear someone's parent dies, it kind of bounces off me. I know they must be in pain, but it's knowledge. Nothing more. I don't feel for them."

"Interesting."

"You know what's *not* interesting is that we're just talking about me," I said. "What about you?"

"We'll get there. May I make a hasty judgment?"

"Yes, please. I've based my entire existence on hasty judgments."

"When you were young, probably somewhere between two and seven years of age, you learned it was okay to express your emotions about animals and children and family. But you learned it was not okay to express your emotions about unrelated grownups."

I said, "That's it? After the long wait to get in to see you? After paying your exorbitant fees?"

Leela laughed and said, "No, that's not it. I would like to add that when you're uncomfortable expressing emotion, you replace that emotion with humor."

I felt the truth of what she'd just said in my chest and said, "I don't know if that's an insult or a compliment."

Leela smiled and said, "Neither. What it is, is my professional opinion." She raised her dark eyebrows with a sense of play. She looked more East Indian than Caucasian, though I knew she was half of each. I had been on so many first dates in the last few years. To each I had brought anticipation and, worse, hope. But with Leela, I'd had no time to pack my bags with either. My mother told me to go out front and there she was. I was blindsided. Knocked to the turf without knowing what hit me. I did not want to get up.

Leela said, "Okay, my turn. I'm the breadwinner in my family. I work full-time and have my kids six days a week. I have no time for you."

"Your ex doesn't work?"

"He's a failed musician who thinks he's too precious to get a real job. He's also too irresponsible to get the kids to school and activities on time, so they're with me Sunday through Friday. Oh, and I'm on the hook for paying my kids' college tuition. That leaves me with no time or money to invest in us." She drained the last of her drink, then said, "Your turn."

"No, no, no. Not so fast. Your defect isn't a defect. It's a situational obstacle. I want to know where you're broken."

"I don't think I am."

"What a rip-off this experiment is."

"Really?" said Leela. "I'm having a good time."

"All right. Then you'll love this. Not only do I struggle with empathy, but I have an inferiority complex. My sisters have meaningful, society-benefitting careers and solid marriages. My mother taught middle school. There is no more selfless job than that, except my father's, who, as a physician, ran a free clinic. My ex-wife is a high-powered attorney who represents sexual assault victims in civil litigation. Everyone's making the world a better place except for me, who's filling it with crap costume jewelry."

Leela said, "I'm impressed with your honesty. I'll give you that."

"Don't start liking me. I see myself as an underachiever like your ex. The only way we'd work out is if you have a tendency to repeat destructive behaviors. Then I'm perfect for you."

"Well," said Leela, "I have some tendency to repeat destructive behaviors. I'm not saying you have a chance with me, but my weakness for losers does make it possible." She smiled a smile that just about sucked the flame out of our hurricane lamp.

I said, "Why would I think I have a chance with you?"

"Well," said Leela, "you're holding my hand."

It was true. Our hands were touching, right on top of the table in plain sight. I knew it, but had ignored that I knew it. I said, "Since our first date is in the name of science, do you have a hypothesis for why that is?" I did not move my hand.

Leela shrugged. "We're on vacation. It's something to do." She did not let go of my hand. "I will confess my parents started talking you up months ago, so I had time to Google you and learn you're not subhuman."

"Stop. You're embarrassing me."

"Then I came up with this experiment of showing our worst sides first. I think it's pretty good."

I said, "It is pretty good. Except you haven't shown me your worst side. Just coaxed mine out of me."

Our tiny loaf of bread arrived and we ordered a second mint julep for Leela and a bourbon for me. Leela waited for the server to leave, then said, "Okay. Here's something. I hate my job. Not the teaching part but I only teach one day a week. I hate my patients. I'm sick of hearing about people's problems. And worse, I bring the work home with me. I'm a dark cloud walking through the door. I can be miserable to be around. And I self-medicate with alcohol."

I let that hang for a while, then said, "Will you marry me?"

Leela laughed for the third time that night. My phone buzzed. A text from my mother.

Leaving tomorrow bright and early at 6 a.m.! Set your alarm for 5:30 so we can talk before I go. Hope you're having fun with Leela! xoxo

Leela said, "Tinder?"

I showed her the text.

Leela said, "It's getting late. Maybe we should pick this up again tomorrow."

Tomorrow? I had no idea what kind of test she'd just given me, but apparently I'd passed. I said, "Are you asking me for a second date?"

She said, "I don't ask. I tell. Another terrible thing about me. Bossy. Put it on the list."

Our second drinks came. We talked more about our kids and parents and I had the oddest feeling, one I hadn't experienced since I'd started dating after the divorce. I wanted my kids to meet Leela. Thank God Emily and Hank were a ten-hour plane ride away so I wasn't tempted to introduce them to this woman I'd just met. As I'd told Leela, I had a higher bar for my kids than I did for myself. Maybe it's just a father's inflated opinion of his own kids, the same way my father thought I could have played college basketball when I am pretty sure no college coach shared his optimism, but I would not introduce Emily and Hank to someone who wasn't worthy of their company. Somehow, after barely knowing Leela Bellerose, I thought she was.

I know, I know. It's a crazy thought to have after meeting a person once. But the fact is, I did have the thought and it meant something. I just didn't know what.

We walked home under the Spanish moss. I kissed Leela goodnight a block away from the houses, out of parental view. A quick but soft kiss. An invitation, offered and accepted, for tomorrow.

5

At 5:45 A.M. I struggled to keep both eyes open as my mother bounded around the kitchen in a red Adidas track suit. She opened a lower cupboard and pulled out the biggest plastic pill box I'd ever seen. It was more of a pill suitcase or a 3D advent calendar with dozens of tiny flip lids indicating not only days but times of day, each labeled and color coded. "Here are Dad's pills," she said, "all loaded and ready to go. He takes them four times a day. And here's a separate small container for when you're on the boat this afternoon."

"That's a lot of pills."

"Well," said my mother, pointing at various compartments, "cholesterol, blood pressure, an anti-depressant, an anti-anxiety, a blood thinner . . ." She stopped. "Joey, are you sure you're up for this?"

"Mom. I'm sure. I know how to follow directions."

She nodded but the worry didn't leave her face. "This is so generous of you. I do need a break."

"You really do. So stop worrying and go have fun. I came down here to help you and to spend some time with Dad. You leaving for a few days is a perfect way to do both."

She smiled and nodded. "That does make me feel better. Thank you. Just please remember to keep the doors dead-bolted from the inside."

"I will. I promise."

"I'm sorry. I'm just being thorough. When Dad wakes up, he'll have forgotten about the fishing so he'll be happy to hear about it. His friends don't take him anymore. It's just too much bother with his memory problems and the pills. I think what they're really worried about is him wandering away at the fish camp or falling off the boat. It'll be so good for him to get out on the water. He'll never forget how to fish—he's been doing that since he could talk."

She walked across the kitchen and said, "I'm putting this note on the refrigerator if he needs any reassuring. Oh, and Ted and Kajal have altered tonight's dinner plans—they've invited just Dad. They're so sweet with him. So if you'd like to go out with Leela, you're free to do so." I didn't respond. My mother sighed with exasperation at my silence and said, "Well . . . how was last night?"

"Good." The entirety of my answer.

"Good? What are you, fifteen? That's all you have to say?"

"I like her."

"Hey, that's something."

"But it's kind of ridiculous you and Kajal are playing matchmaker with us."

"I don't think it's ridiculous at all."

"Leela and I live in different time zones."

My mother shrugged. "You never know."

"Oh, yes. We know. We have kids in different states. And exes. Neither of us is free to move. In the one in a million chance we'd want a relationship, we couldn't have one."

She dismissed my objection by sipping her coffee, then said, "How long is the flight from Chicago to Boston? An hour? That's nothing. And get this: Meredith Gainsley is seventy-one and she met her husband on a blind date last year. Now it's hot and heavy. Believe me. She tells me *everything*."

"Do me a favor," I said, "and keep it to yourself."

"Ha ha, mister. Just remember, you're never too old to fall in love. And you can internet date all you want, but the internet doesn't know you as well as your parents do."

"Sadly, that's not true. But you might have gotten lucky on this one. Leela is smart and attractive and I look forward to seeing her again."

"Oh?" said my mother. "You two talked about that?"

"You'll get a full report when you get back from Florida."

"I'd better. Another thing. It'd be nice if you and Dad visited Uncle David. Maybe before fishing today. He'd love to see you. I hope you got his genes. He's ninety-one and sharp as ever. Still practices law and walks three miles every day."

"Maybe the key to his longevity is he never married."

My mother ignored my comment, went to the coffee machine, poured us each a cup, and looked out the window over the sink. The sky had lightened to a soft gray. The palm trees looked black against the sky. Birds sang to announce the coming day.

She said, "It happened again last night."

I didn't have to ask what happened.

She said, "Dad was talking to Trip Patterson. Let me know if he does that when I'm gone."

"I will."

"Dad seemed awfully upset. I tried to ask him about it, but he got angry and told me to mind my own business. He never talked to me like that before he got sick. So if he does that with you, know that it's not personal. It's his disease."

A pair of headlights swung into the driveway. My mother picked up her suitcase and repeated her instructions as if I really were fifteen and she was leaving me home alone for the first time. Then she stepped out the back door with more bounce in her step than I'd seen in a year. I removed the key from my pocket and locked the back door.

Uncle David was my father's uncle, the only surviving sibling of five. At ninety-one, he still practiced law a few blocks away in what once was an old house on Carteret Street. The sign out front said "Green and Green," though one of the Greens, my great uncle Charles, had passed away ten years ago. Virginia Rampell greeted us. She was my great-uncle's paralegal.

"Look at this!" said Virginia. "Joey Green. Welcome to Beaufort, darling. It's just so nice to see you."

"You too, Virginia. You look great."

"Oh, shush."

I wasn't being polite. She did look great, which I found disconcerting. For as much as Beaufort had changed since I was a child, most things hadn't: the old drawbridge, Hunting Island State Park, whole blocks of buildings downtown, the house on Craven Street, the foliage, and, strangely, Virginia.

She had aged in the last thirty years, but she had never stopped being beautiful. Virginia wore her long, silver hair piled atop her head. She wore no makeup and had lips so naturally full you might mistake her for a concert tuba player. Her green eyes contrasted with her pink jacket and matching skirt. Virginia had never married and had no children, and since I was old enough to understand such things, I'd wondered about the breadth and depth of her relationship with my great-uncle, who was thirty years her senior, which also might explain his vitality at ninety-one.

Uncle David stepped out of his office and into the reception area. I shook his hand. He was not of the hugging generation. He stood about five feet six, dressed in a navy blue suit, white shirt, and yellow tie. He'd been wearing suits so long I imagined he could always find something in his closet that had come back in style. His hair was white and, like his body, had thinned. He wore round, rimless glasses and always kept a cigar in his vicinity, rarely lit, functioning more as an affectation or pacifier.

"Y'all coming down to the office, this sure will be my favorite meeting of the day," said Uncle David. "Please, sit down. Virginia, what can we offer these good people?"

"Cokes, water, coffee, tea, hot or iced, anything they want." She spoke in a higher octave than most women, softened with age, conveying a comforting intelligence. "If we don't have it, I'll take a walk and get it."

"Any chocolate gators?" said my father, referring to a specialty of the candy shop down the street.

"I am ashamed to admit we are fresh out, Mr. Marshall, but I'll go get some. Now, do you want your chocolate gator in dark, milk, or white?"

My father smiled his infectious smile. "That sounds like an invitation to accompany you to the candy store."

I said, "No, no, Dad. We're here to visit Uncle David."

"That's right, Marshall. And it'll only cost y'all five hundred an hour."

He was kidding about the money but not about the message. Virginia picked up on it and said, "Let's go, Dr. Green. I need a strong, handsome man at my side to walk through this neighborhood."

She was joking, the neighborhood being one of the most upscale and picturesque in the area. If you've ever seen the movie *The Big Chill*, it's not like that neighborhood—it *is* that neighborhood. But like Virginia, I got the message from my great-uncle and let it happen. Virginia walked my father out of the office and shut the door behind them.

My great-uncle led me into his office, which felt like another page in *Southern Living* magazine. A painting of the Beaufort waterfront hung behind his desk chair, and a musket, framed and mounted behind glass, hung on the opposite wall.

Uncle David said, "Very kind of you to visit your daddy during this time. And I understand your mother is in Florida playing pickleball."

"You've been watching ESPN."

He smiled. His teeth looked healthy and real, but I had no idea if they were. "Well, good for her. You're a good son."

"I'm always happy to visit Beaufort."

Uncle David reached for his cigar, put it in his mouth, and said, "How's your daddy doing? I haven't seen him in over a month."

"He doesn't leave the house as much as he used to. His short-term memory is pretty much shot. But his long-term memory seems sharper than ever. He's hallucinating some, which is hard to see."

"Well, sure it is. That's unfortunate, Joey. Just unfortunate. He's a good man, your daddy. Better than you know."

"Yesterday he had an imaginary conversation with someone named Trip Patterson. Do you know who that is?"

Uncle David removed the unlit cigar from his mouth and set it in the clean ashtray. "Boy drowned when he was in high school. Tragic."

I nodded. "My father and Trip were friends?"

Uncle David looked at me through his spotless lenses. "I believe they were, though they grew up in different sorts of families."

"What does that mean?"

"The Pattersons were working-class white folk. What y'all sometimes refer to as white trash. As you know, that is not how your daddy was raised."

I said, "Was that unusual? For someone like my father and Trip to be friends?"

"Not so unusual. Beaufort was a small town. Tiny compared to what it is now. Back then, white folks and black folks wouldn't socialize outside the workplace, be it industrial or domestic. Seemed to me we all got along fine, but after work everyone went home to their own. But two white boys, even from different religions and socioeconomic backgrounds, all sorts of reasons they might be friends, the biggest of which is your daddy and Trip Patterson knew each other when they were little boys. My brother, Julian, your grandfather, didn't want the professional life of a lawyer or doctor. The man had retail in his blood, so he began his adult life working his way up from the bottom, living in a working-class neighborhood on Pigeon Point until he made enough to buy the house on Craven Street. Moved when your daddy was about ten years old. I think that's why Marshall is so comfortable with all sorts of people. He remembers where he came from. Never looks down on people who are less fortunate. Less educated. It's also why he stayed friends with Trip Patterson even though they ran in different circles after your daddy left Pigeon Point."

"My mother asked my father about Trip, and he blew up at her."

"That doesn't sound like the Marshall I know."

"Yeah. Me either. The other thing that sets him off is Hammond Island and the Hammonds in general."

Uncle David shook his head and smiled. "That's just local head-butting. Let me tell you something. I represent the Hammonds on their real estate deals. They're good people. You can bank on that, otherwise I wouldn't work for 'em. Why would I associate with anyone disreputable? Especially at ninety-one years of age? The answer is simple. I wouldn't. I don't need that headache. The Hammonds are good people, Joey. Despite the local chitter-chatter. That family has done a lot for this town. Sure, we've had growth. Plenty. And some of it painful. But you know what they call a town that doesn't grow? Unincorporated. Or a ghost town. Or Hicksville, USA. And Beaufort isn't any of those things. Second-oldest city in South Carolina behind Charleston. We have a rich history. And thanks to our growth, plenty of people are here to enjoy it."

He picked up the cigar and put it in his mouth. He was in full lawyer mode, representing his favorite client: Beaufort, South Carolina. There was nothing my uncle David loved more than talking up his hometown. I suppose that's true everywhere. People who stay where they were born want everyone to love the place as much as they do.

Uncle David moved on to his second-favorite client and said, "The Hammonds are generous people, Joey. Gave me that musket on the wall for my ninetieth birthday. That musket is valued at over $30,000. It's an 1863 Confederate Fayetteville rifle, carried into battle multiple times. The Hammonds are great collectors of antiquities. Civil War artifacts and art from all over the world. Some of it they've donated to the museum down the street. The Hammonds are good people, Joey. Good people indeed."

There was a knock on the door. My great-uncle told whoever it was to come in, and the door opened. The woman who entered looked like she'd just fallen out of a Burberry catalog. She was about fifty but had the money to appear forty. A lab-made blonde with hair so highlighted it was almost white. A painted face, a black tank over a black-and-white checked skirt with black-and-white high heels. A gym body, lean and strong. Long fingernails lacquered black. Platinum earrings. She looked like the kind of woman who, if blasted with a firehose for a solid minute, would crawl away with different skin. A different face. Different hair. Different fingernails.

Uncle David stood and said, "Gail. Nice to see you." I stood. "This is my great nephew Joey Green from Chicago. Marshall and Carol's boy. Joey, this is Gail Hammond. The Hammonds live right behind the office in the Old Point."

"We stop by almost every day to make sure our lawyer's not sleeping on the job." Gail Hammond laughed. She spoke in a heavy southern accent, as if she were a politician reminding her constituents where she'd come from. "Nice to meet you, Joey. And we are so sorry to interrupt. We will come back another time, and you enjoy your visit here in Beaufort."

I said, "Please stay. I have to get going anyway. We're due at the marina soon."

An older gentleman walked in and stood next to her. Somewhere in his seventies, I guessed. He stood tall and thin and wore a suit of pale yellow over a heavily starched white shirt and cream-colored tie. Tortoiseshell glasses with perfectly round lenses tinted orange. Silver hair combed straight back, highlighting his Roman nose. He smelled as if he'd bathed in Lagerfeld cologne, a scent favored by my college roommate and one that will forever be burned into my nostrils. He carried a wooden cane, dark and polished. And I mean carried. He did not lean on it, which made me think the cane was more of an ostentation than a medical necessity.

My great-uncle David said, "Thomas, this is a nice surprise.

Joey, this is Thomas Hammond, Gail's husband. Thomas, this is Marshall's boy, Joey."

We exchanged nice-to-meet-yous and I shook hands with the subject of my father's ire. Thomas Hammond. Sons of bitches, all of them, according to Marshall Green.

Hammond threw me a warm smile and said, "Why are you just visiting, son? Why not move down permanently and leave those Yankee winters behind like your daddy has?"

"You will have to excuse my husband," said Gail. "He is a born salesman. He cannot help himself."

Hammond turned to his wife, who was his junior by a quarter of a century. "A man should use the talent bestowed upon him by the good Lord. Lest he seem ungrateful."

I said, "You don't have to sell me on Beaufort. I love it down here."

"Well, then. Perhaps you oughta consider Hammond Island. We have five basic floorplans which you can customize to your liking. Everything from traditional to modern. We're building a country club right on the island with a PGA-caliber golf course and Olympic-size swimming pool. Membership comes with the purchase of a home. As does a golf cart, which will be the only method of travel once on the island. All electric and quiet, to harmonize with nature. We're building a solar farm to supply most of the island's power. And did I mention each floorplan contains a main-floor bedroom so you can age into your home without worrying about stairs?"

Gail said, "Joey is much too young to think about main-floor living."

"Sweetheart, how am I supposed to keep you in spa treatments and Jaguar automobiles if you keep undercutting me?" Thomas Hammond laughed, but I couldn't see what his eyes were saying behind those orange-tinted lenses. Orange-tinted lenses. The only other person I was aware of who'd worn orange-tinted lenses was John Lennon. It seemed a safe bet that was all Thomas Hammond and John Lennon had in common.

I figured Thomas Hammond wouldn't lay off the sales pitch until I left, and the last thing I wanted was for my father to return to find him in Uncle David's office. A chocolate gator can soothe away a great deal, but I doubted it would temper Marshall Green's anger toward the Hammonds. I said, "Uncle David, I'm sorry. I really do have to get going. Very nice to meet both of you. I hope our paths cross again."

Uncle David smiled toward Thomas and Gail Hammond. "Not bad manners for a northern boy, huh? Joey, I'll catch up with you in a day or two."

We said our goodbyes and I left, the scent of Thomas Hammond's cologne on my hand and in my nose. The Hammonds' Jaguar sat out front. A convertible in butter yellow with baseball-mitt-brown leather seats. It reeked of old money but managed to look gaudy next to my great-uncle David's 1972 Mercedes SL in racing green. As my father would say, Green car for David Green. Smart.

6

I walked toward the candy store and intercepted my father and Virginia on their way back, my father working his way through a dark chocolate gator, smears of candy in the corners of his mouth.

"Joey," said Virginia, "why aren't you at the office?"

"Uncle David had some clients stop in. I'll catch up with him later." I did not mention the clients were named Hammond. No reason to upset my father when he was mid–chocolate gator. I thanked Virginia, then took possession of my father and started the slow walk home.

My dad said, "Remember that time, Joey, when you got those gerbils? What were their names?"

"Starsky and Hutch."

"Right. Damndest things. Running on their wheel all night long. Making a racket."

"Eating all our toilet paper tubes."

"That's right. They did. Then one of them disappeared."

"Hutch. He got on top of the water bottle and pushed the lid off."

"You cried. Oh how you cried. We tried everything to catch that rodent. I bought live traps at the hardware store. Baited them

with seeds and peanut butter. But no sign of him. We thought he
was gone for good like your hamster. Six months later, we're eating breakfast, and there he was just standing in the middle of the
kitchen floor. Then he scurried into the tiny crack between the dishwasher and cabinet."

"I remember. You let me stay home from school that day. And
you went into work late so you could help me catch him."

"We made a little harness for the other gerbil. Used the cap-
tive one to lure out the escapee. And it worked. I don't think your
mother and sisters appreciated our ingenuity. That was quite an
accomplishment."

I put an arm around my father. "Maybe the greatest achieve-
ment in the history of father and son teams."

"No doubt about that, Joey. No doubt at all."

We fished near islands and sandbars, casting toward reds and sea
trout tailing in the tall grass. Our guide's name—I shit you not—
was Bubba. He stood six feet four inches and weighed three hundred pounds. Pink cheeks over a red/gray beard and a watermelon
size head. Bubba was in his mid-sixties and had guided us dozens
of times since I was a kid and Bubba was in his twenties. He wore
a peach Orvis fishing shirt with the sleeves rolled down, quick-
dry pants, and a Tilly hat atop Oakley sunglasses. His shirt had
enough pockets to hold an entire tackle box, but they lay flat and
empty on his big body except for his front right breast pocket that
held a tin of Skoal. Bubba tongued at a wad of tobacco packed in
his cheek and each time he tied on a new lure or piece of bait, he
spit on it and said, "That'll get 'em riled up."

We stopped for lunch on a deserted sandbar with a quiet lagoon. I jumped out of the boat and helped my father do the same.
He squeezed my arm until we'd climbed out of the water and onto
the beach. Bubba was right behind us, pulling the boat's anchor
with one hand and a floating cooler with the other.

He'd made us a lunch of pulled pork sliders drenched in slaw, potato chips, dill pickles, and for dessert, Goo Goo Clusters. He'd packed Cokes, Budweisers, and bottles of water. My father and I each drank a Bud. He washed down his pills with his first few sips.

He winked at me and said, "Don't tell your mother."

"Don't worry. I won't."

"Boy, the fish we've caught together, huh Joe? Bubba, you should join us on one of our fishing trips up in Wisconsin. Muskies. Nothing like 'em. They say you make a thousand casts just to get a follow. And when those monsters see the boat, they do not back off. You put your rod tip in the water and make a figure eight with your lure before lifting it out of the water. Half the time that's when they hit. Pow! And boy, do they run! Man! Muskies! Nothing like 'em!"

"Nothing like 'em, Dad." I smiled toward my father.

A friend once told me women have face-to-face relationships and men have shoulder-to-shoulder relationships. Men do things like watch football and go fishing. My relationship with my father was, in most ways, just that. We spent time together. We did not interact in a deep way. I had neither my father's altruism, his extroversion, nor his love of people, and it left us little to talk about other than baseball and fishing. And now, with his short-term memory fading, we had even less to talk about.

My father stood and said, "That hit the spot. Thanks, Bubba. You never disappoint."

"My pleasure, Mr. Marshall."

"I'm going to take a leak. Don't you fellas forget about me and leave." He laughed and wandered up the sand toward a clump of grasses.

Bubba waited for him to get fifty feet away and said, "How's he doing?"

I shook my head and said, "He's on the off-ramp."

"Oh man, Joey. I'm so sorry to hear that. Marshall Green is one of my favorite people. Ever. Very kind to me when I was a boy. I was a happy man when he moved back here."

"So was he. Hey, Bubba, you remember a boy from Pigeon Point named Trip Patterson?" I finished the last of my Bud, which somehow, warm and flat, tasted good with my peanut, chocolate, and caramel cluster.

Bubba gave me a long look and said, "Yes, sir. Poor Trip Patterson. God rest his soul."

"What happened?"

"They found Trip Patterson floating in Factory Creek the summer between his junior and senior years of high school." Bubba opened a second can of beer, which didn't concern me. The man was so large it would probably take four beers for him to even feel it. "Trip was night fishing on the creek and drinking pretty heavy. Tide was low, and he'd had a few too many. Passed out on the bank, then the tide came in and Trip drowned. Police found him the next morning."

I glanced over my shoulder. My father stood at the brush, his back toward us. I said, "Was my dad friends with Trip?"

"Yes, sir. I know because the Pattersons lived down the street from us. He and your daddy were pals when they were little and your daddy still lived on Pigeon Point. He'd moved away but would come back sometimes. I was just a boy then. Your daddy would drive over to pick up Trip. Whenever he'd see me playing with my friends, he'd give us sticks of gum or whatever he had."

"He's an extrovert. Makes friends wherever he goes."

"Ain't that the truth. But it was special to me and the other kids 'cause we didn't see many rich kids in our neighborhood. And your daddy, no offense, was a rich kid. At least compared to the kids in my neighborhood. The sons of doctors and lawyers and businessmen didn't make friends with the sons of shrimpers, bridge painters, and pulp millers. Except Marshall Green was friends with Trip Patterson and was kind to all of us."

I looked back toward my father, who had turned around and

spotted us, but even from a hundred feet away, I could see he'd forgotten where he was. Then something clicked and he started toward us with tiny steps.

Bubba pinched a wad of tobacco from his tin, tucked it in his mouth, and said, "That's why I remember your daddy so well. And the truth is, we never met a Jewish fella before. Somehow we all knew your daddy was Jewish, and we were cocksure Jews had horns on their heads. I remember Whitey Clarke asked your daddy if it was true. Bunch of kids were standing in the Pattersons' front yard. And Marshall, he just smiled and got down on his knees and said we should all touch his head to feel for horns. And we did just that. Of course there weren't any."

"What's this, boys?" said my father. "No shore lunch? I expected to smell fish in the pan."

He had forgotten we'd just eaten.

Bubba said, "Not today, Mr. Marshall. But let's get back on the water and let those speckled trout know who's boss."

We fished a couple more hours, then Bubba opened up the engine and we headed toward the marina. My father and I sat on opposite ends of the stern, him wearing his new life vest, his face tilted toward the sun with eyes shut. I had researched Lewy Body Dementia before we left the house and learned something my mother had not told me: the disease would kill him. Not today or tomorrow. The article said he'd probably live five more years. My sisters used to joke that he'd outlive us all. At seventy, he had the body of a fifty-year-old. The energy of a forty-year-old. Looking back on his sudden and unexpected retirement, I wondered if he somehow knew. If he'd experienced symptoms that his medical training wouldn't let him ignore. Even if he hadn't had a conscious thought about those symptoms, he had the education and experience to know what they meant.

We all know we're going to die, that our time is limited. But life distracts us with tasks big and small. Careers and weedy gardens. With conversation. With books and movies and TV shows. With the theater and music. With planning vacations and family get-togethers. Dinner with friends. Shopping. Sports. Day-dreams.

My father had lost most of those distractions. He couldn't hold anything in his head long enough to anesthetize himself with the simple diversion of thinking ahead. His past was his only safe haven. He could linger there to relive what he'd already lived. His present offered nothing but giant steps toward the end.

7

I returned from fishing to find three texts on my phone. My kids sent a picture from Hawaii—each had a monkey on their arm. Another was from the office saying a shipment of bangles was held up in customs. The last was from Leela. It read:

Contradiction I must confess. I'm a staunch feminist but enjoy the man taking the lead during sex.

I texted: *So should I hold the bedroom door open for you or not?*

Leela replied with a chin-scratching emoji.

By 4 P.M., my father and I had napped and showered and dressed and had a couple hours to kill before we'd walk next door to Kajal and Ted's. We sat in the kitchen eating Ruby's praline cookies. I thought of going outside to the garage to look for his pistol, but that could wait until my mother returned.

My father chewed on a bite of cookie and said, "Where's your mother? She'd better get ready for dinner."

"Mom's in Florida at a pickleball tournament."

"You're kidding."

"Nope. Went with Judy Campbell."

He shook his head and took another bite of cookie and said, "Did I know that?"

When you have your first child, you go from not being a parent to being a parent with one snip of the umbilical cord. No responsibility to the biggest responsibility of your life. I felt like I became my father's parent just that fast. I said, "Yeah, Dad. You knew Mom went to Florida, but no big deal."

He held out his arms, palms up, and said, "I'm getting worse, aren't I? They're going to put me in a home."

"No, Dad. *They* are *we,* and we won't let that happen. Besides, you remember what's important. Mom and all of us. Your grandkids. Your parents and growing up here. That's what counts."

He shook his head, not in denial but in defeat.

I said, "Hey, you want to watch some TV before we go to Ted and Kajal's?"

"Why are we going there?"

"You're having dinner with them. I'm going out for dinner with their daughter, Leela."

He looked at me with raised eyebrows. "Is she single?"

"Yep."

He nodded and smiled.

We went into the den and turned on SportsCenter. My father watched but didn't understand. He knew the team names, but most of the athletes were unfamiliar to him, as if he'd been plucked out of the past and dropped into the future.

"This is nice, Joey," he said, "you and me watching SportsCenter. Let's hope your mother doesn't come in and ask to watch PBS."

I didn't remind him that she was in Florida. I said, "You know, we can do whatever you want while I'm here. I can drive you around to visit friends."

He nodded. "Maybe Dick Connors."

"Sure. Do you keep up with your old friends?"

He stared blankly at the screen. "I don't know." He shrugged. "I really don't."

"Bubba said you were very nice to him when he was little."

He laughed. "Bubba was never little. That's why they call him Bubba." The same beer commercial we'd watched yesterday came on. My father laughed and said, "Clever ad. Just great."

"Bubba said he'd see you on his block when you visited Trip

Patterson." My father said nothing. "He also said Trip died when you two were in high school."

He nodded. "Tragic. Eh, a real waste."

"How did he die?"

"Drowned."

"Bubba said he was fishing a creek—"

"God damn it, Joey!" He yelled as loud as his old, tired voice could yell. "Why are you bringing up Trip Patterson?! It was terrible! Just terrible! That's all there is to say!"

My father's voice reverberated off the plaster walls. He hadn't yelled at me like that in thirty years, since back when the pressures of paying for three kids in college while he worked seventy-hour weeks for donations could ignite him like gunpowder.

I said, "Sorry, I won't bring it up again." But I wasn't sorry. My father was like a block of wood. Tap all around and it made the same sound. But Trip Patterson was a hollow spot. A cavity. Something in that cavity mattered. I knew it. No. I *felt* it.

Then the oddest thing happened—I cried. Cried during a commercial for Ford pickup trucks.

My father watched the television and kicked back in his recliner. Neither of us said another word.

Leela said, "You cried?"

"Like a tornado survivor on the evening news."

"Are you a crier?"

"Almost never, and usually at something like a YouTube video of a dog greeting a soldier it hasn't seen in a year."

Leela and I sat on the patio of a restaurant called Plums. We picked at calamari, shrimp, a big green salad, and drank Manhattans with extra cherries. She said, "So it's safe to say you're not a crier. But your memory-impaired father yelling at you for five seconds made you cry?" Leela popped a cherry into her mouth. "That might be worth talking about more." Tourists and locals walked the waterfront. Leela wore a black skirt and a gauze top of faded indigo. Her dark eyes looked like melted chocolate. She said, "What do you think about that?"

I leaned in and kissed her. Leela did not object and kissed me back. Then she said, "You may think you're invulnerable. That your lack of empathy will protect you. But one day something will jar loose the scar tissue. It will fall away and leave you exposed and it will hurt like hell."

"I just kissed you in public on our second date and that's your response?"

She smiled. "Yes."

I said, "Are you this warm and fuzzy with all your clients?"

"You're not my client. You're my date. My second date."

"Your second date in the name of science."

Leela removed her hand from mine, reached up, and cupped my face. I wanted to bottle that moment, our eyes so focused on each other that it seemed we were the only two people on the patio. She said, "If I write a book about this dating technique we're developing, will that bother you?"

"Will I get credit?"

"Only as Subject A."

I said, "Huh."

"What?"

"You might be curing me."

"What do you mean?"

"When you called me Subject A, I felt a wisp of empathy."

"For who?"

"For me."

Leela smiled. "I don't think you know what empathy means. Maybe you can tell me more about this feeling, Subject A."

Of Leela's many attractive facets, it was her playful intelligence that ensnared me without hope of escape. I could never tire of it. I said, "Now you're just being cruel."

Leela shook her head. "Please. Tell me more."

I shrugged. "I don't know more."

She finished her Manhattan, caught the attention of a passing server, and ordered two more. Leela said, "Do you like to take care of people?"

I thought of Emily and Hank and said, "Yes."

"And animals?"

"Definitely."

"Are the people you like to take care of in need of taking care of?"

"I never really thought about it."

"Are you attracted to single mothers?"

I kissed her again and said, "I'm attracted to one single mother."

She laughed. "No, are you attracted to single mothers in general?"

"That's a weird and personal question."

"It's for the sake of science, so please answer it."

I fished a cherry out of my glass, ate it, and said, "Whether or not a woman has children does not affect my attraction to her."

"Really?" said Leela. "What have been your most significant relationships since you started dating?"

I'd had two short relationships since getting divorced, each about three months long, and one that lasted a year. All three of the women were divorced with kids and had deadbeat exes. I said, "How did you know I like to take care of people?"

"Just a guess. And you know what else? You've hardly joked in the last few minutes. You're feeling your way through this conversation. Not avoiding it. And another thing: you think you're so different from your father. You think he's disappointed in you because you don't serve the greater good like he did. And yet, we just established that you, the non-empath, like to take care of people just like he took care of people."

My eyes stung. Damn it. First my father yelling at me and then Leela telling me I was more like him than I'd realized. I wondered what had weakened my protective shell, if I missed my kids, or if it was seeing my father in his deteriorated state. Emotion was trying to escape like steam from a covered pot. I didn't know if it was sadness or relief—I just knew it was about to blow. I took a couple of deep breaths and said, "This is kind of heavy. I'm supposed to be on vacation."

"Vacation," said Leela, "is a time for reflection."

"Well, then I'm glad you're my mirror."

She blinked and swallowed and blinked again. "That might be the nicest thing anyone has ever said to me."

A server brought our second round of Manhattans. I watched a flock of gulls silhouetted against the fire-pink sky follow a shrimp boat across the water, white billowy thunderheads gathering in the distance. Leela took my hand and kissed it. Then her phone rang on the table. She glanced at the caller ID and said, "Damn."

8

Ted Bellerose was tall with thick gray hair and horn-rimmed glasses, translucent yellow framing gray eyes. Kajal was short and dark like Leela with hair pulled back promoting deep amber eyes. She spoke with a hint of an East Indian accent, and wore red lipstick from another era that wicked up and into the smoking lines around her mouth. Both attractive and well-dressed septuagenarians of New England money, they belonged to the class of waxed cotton canvas, loafers, and ties embossed with nautical insignia.

Leela's parents met mine when the Belleroses bought the house next door. Kajal and Ted had friends who wintered on Hilton Head and Fripp Island, but they opted to live in antebellum Beaufort because its historical preservation reminded them of Beacon Hill, not the architecture but the antiquity.

Their house, like my parents', like the inn on Bay Street, was full of intricate spindles, furniture with curved wooden legs, and heavy trim painted white to contrast with colorful walls. The electric lamps looked like they'd been modified from those that once held candles. The ceilings were high and the windows tall. Antique rugs lay over heart pine floors. It was as if every family in the neighborhood used the same interior decorator.

My father had fallen asleep on their couch. I checked on him and found him on his back, his stocking feet elevated on one armrest, eyes shut and arms folded over his chest. The couch sat under a pair of swords mounted in a shadow box on the wall. I wanted to read the plaque but didn't want to risk waking him, so I left the swords and my father undisturbed and joined Leela in the kitchen with her parents. She'd pulled her hair back like her mother's, poured four Pimm's Cups, and presented them on a silver tray that she set on the kitchen island of white marble.

Leela handed me one as I said, "He's sleeping under the swords."

Ted said, "They're the one thing we brought down from Boston. They belonged to a cavalryman in the Union Army. Rare in a war where the sword was fast becoming obsolete to the bayonet-tipped musket." He adjusted his glasses in the manner of a great pontificator and continued. "Even more rare because the soldier carried two swords. It was somewhat common to carry two guns—you can find matching sets more easily in the marketplace—but matching swords are almost impossible to find. That's what makes them valuable."

"He doesn't care about their value," said Kajal. "He wants to inform our guests he's a Yankee through and through."

"It's not my fault," said Ted, "that the war ended over a hundred and fifty years ago and people still need reminding who won. Cheers."

The four of us clinked and Kajal dropped her smoky voice into a faux whisper.

"It was the strangest thing," she said. "We were having a nice chat when Marshall looked at the other end of the couch and started up a conversation with someone who wasn't there."

Ted shook his head. "It's very sad to see something like that. Marshall went in and out of it. Talked to whomever he saw. Then talked to us. Then back to whomever. Then he shut his eyes and talked some more before falling asleep."

I said, "It's happened a few times before. Hallucinations are a symptom of Lewy Body Dementia. I'm sorry you had to deal with that."

"Oh, no need to apologize," said Kajal. "Marshall is welcome anytime. Your parents have been so good to us, showing us how the locals live. We wouldn't have interrupted your evening except Marshall seemed pretty upset."

"Did he say who he was talking to?"

Leela walked over and stood next to me. I wanted to put my arm around her but the boy in me thought *not in front of her parents.*

Ted said, "Yes. He mentioned the name Delphi a few times. He told Delphi she needed to leave Beaufort. He said something about going to Savannah but it probably wasn't far enough away— she should go to Atlanta. Maybe even Tennessee. He acted like she was arguing with him, like she didn't want to go. Then he yelled at her and said, 'You have to go! You have no choice!'"

Leela's phone rang. It was her kids calling to say goodnight. She excused herself and went into the other room to talk to them.

"It's just so unfair," said Ted. "Marshall devoted his life to medicine. He gave proper care to people who couldn't afford it. Now he needs care, and what can medicine do for him?"

Kajal said, "It's so nice what you did, Joey. Sending your mother to Florida. We sure are glad you're here. I know Leela shares our sentiments."

I didn't know how to respond. First Kajal complimented me to soften me up, then she turned the conversation toward Leela. It was her way of fishing for my opinion about her daughter. I settled on a non-revelatory answer. "It's been nice for me to have someone to talk to."

"We were thinking," said Kajal, "that we could spend tomorrow with Marshall and you two could take a day trip to Savannah. It's such a beautiful city. So much history."

I was about to tell them I didn't feel right convincing my mother I was happy to watch my father then dumping him on babysitters when we heard, "Carol? Carol, where are you?!"

I left the kitchen and found my father standing in the Belleroses' living room looking at a shelf of family portraits, trying to piece together where he was. I said, "Hey, Dad."

He turned around. "Joey. Where's your mother?"

"In Florida. She'll be back in a couple days. We're visiting Ted and Kajal. You fell asleep. I didn't want to wake you."

He looked at me with an expression somewhere between fear and capitulation. He sighed, nodded, and said, "Take me home, Joey."

We said goodnight to the Belleroses, my father turning on his extroverted charm until we were out the front door. The sun had set. Street lamps cast shadows on the old sidewalks. An approaching storm was in the air. My father walked with tiny steps, stooped forward. I kept my eyes on the ground looking for uneven pavement, staying close in case he stumbled.

He took a few slow steps, then said, "Let's go for a walk. I like to walk at night."

I said, "Feels like it's going to rain." I did not want to go for a walk. Not at half a mile an hour. But I was in Beaufort to spend time with my father, and if he wanted to walk, then we'd walk. I said, "But we probably have time for a short one."

"That a boy."

A bat fluttered in front of the street light. My father jerked like a prizefighter ducking a punch. "Christ," he said. Then he laughed. "Damn bats."

"That was a pretty quick reaction, champ."

"I walk slow. But I can be quick if I want to."

"All right. Just give me some warning so I don't fall behind."

We took a few more steps, then he said, "Joey. Do you have the pistol?"

The air hung dead still and humid. It made no sense to me, my obsession with my father's old gun. Every time I thought of it I could feel my heart race. I tried to steady my voice and said, "No, Dad. Why would I have the pistol?"

"It's not safe to walk around at night. Not anymore. Not like it used to be."

"Do you carry the pistol sometimes?"

He sighed. "I don't know. I can't remember."

"Does Mom know about the pistol?" He shrugged. "Did you ever take it anywhere other than out on the water?"

"I don't think so."

"Do you remember the last time you saw it?"

"No. Do I still have it?"

"I don't know." A melancholy washed over me. I had hoped my father had forgotten about the gun. But like everything else in his distant past, he remembered it. I said, "I'll take a look in the morning. Until then we'll be fine. We're not going far."

"That's right. We'll stay close. Hey," he said, "feels like it might rain," repeating what I'd said a few minutes ago.

We walked around the block. It took half an hour. We weren't quite back to the house yet when the drops began to fall. We cut through the backyard and climbed the steps to the back porch. My father patted his pockets and said, "Oh, no."

"I have the key, Dad."

"I can't find mine. Must be in the house."

"It must be."

I unlocked the back door and we entered the kitchen as the phone rang. It was my mother calling from Florida. She sounded like her old self. She and Judy won the first two rounds of their pickleball tournament and she was headed to bed early because tomorrow they had a tough match against a couple of dynamos from St. Petersburg. My father sported a big smile while talking to her. Told her he and I were having a great time. I held up my phone as a cheat sheet to show him pictures of the fish we'd caught, of him and me on the boat, of him and Bubba, and he used the visual reminders to fabricate stories of our day on the water.

As if he could remember.

My father was in bed by ten. I called Emily and Hank, who'd just returned from whale watching off the coast of Maui. They texted pictures of a deep blue ocean that purportedly included breaching whales that I couldn't see. "You have to zoom in, Dad." I zoomed in and saw the tiniest spray and tried to sound excited. That is what you do for your children. I missed them terribly but tried not to sound too sad about it. Another thing you do for your children when they're vacationing in paradise. They said they had to get to the pool to meet some friends. That I understood well. After we hung up, I texted Leela.

Drinks on the porch to watch the storm blow in?

I checked in on my father to make sure he was asleep, exited the front door, and locked it behind me. Then I walked next door and climbed the steps to the Belleroses' front porch. The door opened and Leela stood behind the screen.

She said, "Is it okay if we sit in the dark? It'll be more romantic to watch the storm that way."

"We've advanced to romance, have we?"

The porch light turned off, and Leela stepped outside. "Romance and delinquency." She held up a silver flask that flashed in the light from street lamps. "Join me on the porch swing?"

I did, and Leela handed me the flask. I unscrewed it and took a sip. "This tastes expensive."

"I raided my parents' liquor cabinet. My father is a small-batch bourbon aficionado. One good thing about being an only child is he doesn't care if I help myself to the good stuff."

"What's that have to do with being an only child?"

"Because when you don't have siblings, your parents become your siblings. They age you into adulthood faster than you would if you had other kids in the house. You play with your parents. You fight with them. You bond with them as if they're your only family because they are. And they don't mind if you help yourself to their liquor because there's only one of you and enough to go around."

I took another sip of the good stuff and said, "Do you wish you had siblings?" I gave the flask to Leela.

"Not really." She took a swig. "I see so many people in my practice who defined themselves in contrast to their brothers and sisters, just to carve out their own identity. If their older sister was a straight-A student, they screwed around in school. If their older brother was a fuck-up, they became an overachiever. So I'm kind of glad I became who I am without having to fight for my identity."

"Hmm . . . I have two older sisters. The means I'm doubly fucked up."

Leela kissed me, then said, "I doubt it. Only because you're the boy. That alone gave you your own identity."

I kissed her, and a gust of wind filled the air with the scent of rain and dust and blooming flowers. Lightning lit up the sky. A crack of thunder rolled in a few seconds later.

Leela said, "Maybe we should take this inside."

"I thought you wanted to watch the storm from here."

"I've changed my mind."

"We won't bother your parents?"

"Are you kidding? Next time my parents see you they're going to offer you a dowry. Plus, they won't know. I sleep in the guest suite above the garage."

Leela and I made love on a wrought iron bed in a suite fit for royalty. Antique furniture, hardwood floors, eyebrow windows, and patinated brass hardware. The walls were white but painted yellow-orange by a dozen candles that flickered as the wind pushed from the outside and thunder boomed. Rain plinked off the steel roof. The setting was obnoxiously intimate. The storm seemed to hover overhead at peak intensity as if its sole purpose was us. It finished when we did, and we rolled onto our backs and watched the ceiling fan's slow rotation.

Leela said, "I have a confession."

"Ah. The experiment continues." I rolled onto my side and looked at her.

She shook her head and smiled. "No. My confession is I've lost control of our experiment. I've failed as a scientist."

I placed my palm on her cheek. "You don't sleep with all your subjects?"

"Don't you even. You are the first. And I'm sure the last. What I'm saying is, the experiment has gone haywire."

"Aren't some of the greatest scientific discoveries the result of experiments gone wrong?"

She took my hand and squeezed it. "Yes. But the thing is, we've stopped telling each other terrible things about ourselves."

"You just told me you're an abject failure."

She laughed. "You know what I mean."

"Well, maybe we're not so horrible. Maybe we just ran out of things to confess."

Leela said nothing for half a minute, then looked at me. "How old is he?"

"My father?"

"Yes."

"Seventy-five."

"That's not that old. Not anymore."

"No, it's not."

"I have clients our age. One week they're complaining about their spouse not taking out the garbage, the next week they tell me their mother or father died. I see my parents aging. Each time I visit they're a little slower. A little weaker. A little smaller."

"They're showing us the road ahead."

"Yeah . . . and it's messing with me."

"And our experiment?"

She nodded, turned away, and curled her back into me. "Seeing them age is messing with everything."

We fell asleep tucked under the eaves listening to distant thunder and rain dripping from trees to roof. I woke just after midnight, kissed Leela goodnight, and left. The storm had passed. The air felt cool. I unlocked my parents' front door and felt guilt punch me in the stomach for leaving my father unattended. I walked upstairs. His door was ajar. I bounced my phone's flashlight through the crack and onto the ceiling.

He slept, snoring softly. I backed away, felt a rush of relief, brushed my teeth, threw my clothes on the floor, and fell asleep.

The sirens woke me at 5:05 A.M.

9

The emergency vehicles came one after the other, their high-pitched wail slowing to a growl just outside the house. I tried to fall back to sleep, but another wave came ten minutes later. I could hear voices outside the house. I got out of bed and went to my father's room. He slept under his covers, rolled onto his side, his back facing me. I returned to my room, threw on my jeans and T-shirt, went downstairs, and peered out the glass in the front door. It was still dark. Neighbors gathered on the sidewalk, lit by street lamps and porch lights. Some people wore robes and slippers, coffee cups steaming at their chins. I pulled the keys from my jeans pocket, unlocked the front door, stepped outside, and locked the door behind me. The incident, whatever it was, had happened about a block east near the history museum. Emergency vehicles gathered, their lights flashing among squawks of unintelligible chatter on radios and walkie-talkies.

"Woke you up, too?"

I looked down and saw Ted and Kajal standing on the sidewalk.

Ted said, "Damndest thing."

"What happened?"

Kajal said, "A man was found shot to death. Margaret Perkins discovered him a little while ago when she was walking Goliath."

I must have had an odd expression on my face because she added, "Her toy poodle."

Ted said, "I didn't hear any gunshots. Maybe because of the storm."

I had an urge to run back upstairs and check on my father even though I'd just seen him. But instead I said, "Who is it?"

Ted looked up at me and said, "Thomas Hammond. Ever hear of him?"

I had not only heard of Thomas Hammond, I had met him yesterday in my great-uncle David's office. I pictured his round glasses with orange lenses, yellow suit, white shirt, cream tie, and cane made of dark, polished wood. He was a salesman, and tried to sell me on Hammond Island. What was his wife's name? The woman twenty-five years younger with the heavy southern accent and black fingernails? Gail. I wondered how Gail was.

I said, "Yes. I've heard of him. The Hammonds are old Beaufort."

"What a shame," said Kajal. "A terrible shame."

I did not see Leela. The garage and the guest quarters over it were behind the Belleroses' house. Maybe she couldn't hear the commotion from back there or maybe she was in the shower or maybe a woman who lived in the heart of Boston slept through sirens as if they were crickets. The crowd parted for a white van with CORONER painted on the side in blue. I told Ted and Kajal I'd see them later, then went back in the house and heard noises from the kitchen. I found my father eating cereal at the table, a freshly picked orange next to the bowl, complete with stem and a few leaves.

I said, "Good morning. You're up."

He said, "Good news. I haven't forgotten how to make coffee. Should be ready in a minute. Hey, what's all the commotion about outside?"

I opened his pill suitcase and took out his morning allotment. "Thomas Hammond is dead."

"What?" He looked pleasantly surprised, as if I had just delivered unexpected and wonderful news.

I felt a shiver. "He was shot and killed just down the street."

"The last of the Beaufort Hammonds. No sense crying over that." He said it matter-of-factly and spooned more cereal into his mouth. The great altruist Marshall Green had a dark side. Wherever his short-term memory had gone, his manners had gone with it—he made no attempt to show respect for the dead. Not if the deceased's name was Hammond.

The more time I spent around my father, the more I felt the young and old are alike. Uncensored. Unabashed. Truthful to their core. Like when I was four and my grandmother added her strawberry to my basket and I dumped the whole lot in the dirt. I essentially said, "Fuck that, old woman. Get your own basket." They laughed because I was four. But it's not so funny when the outspoken one is seventy-five.

My father said, "Hey, Joey. Want to taste something great? Nothing better than a ripe orange fresh off the tree."

"I'll have a section. Thanks."

He began to peel when I realized he couldn't have just picked the orange. Unless . . . I went to the back door. The deadbolt was not locked. The back porch light was on. I turned to my father and said, "You just picked that?"

"I think I did. You can go get another if you want your own."

I turned the handle and pulled. The door opened. I must not have locked it when we returned home after our walk around the block last night. Maybe Leela was on my mind. Maybe I rushed to answer the phone. Maybe I just wasn't paying attention. I said, "Yeah, I'm going to go get another one."

He said, "Squeeze it first. You don't want one that's too hard."

I stepped outside. My God. Thomas Hammond was shot down the street. I'd left the back door unlocked. I'd left my father without supervision or short-term memory. And last night, his gun was on his mind. He'd brought it up when we walked around the block. He hated the Hammonds. Couldn't even hide his delight when hearing Thomas was dead. But I knew my father. Just the thought of him killing Thomas Hammond was ridiculous. Idiotic. Impossible. And yet, I could not shake the idea. Something about it . . .

I ran down the back steps into the yard and headed straight for the garage service door. It too was unlocked. I flipped on the light. The old tackle box was shut, its hasp closed. I opened it and rummaged through the bottom section. The gun wasn't there. I was about to shut the lid when I noticed two of the fold-out levels were stuck together, like an extra-thick step in a staircase. I pulled them apart and there it was, the canvas sack I'd looked for yesterday. I was sure I'd searched the tackle box thoroughly. And yet. There the gun was, right where I had looked for it.

I removed the pistol. There was no mistaking it. I knew almost nothing about guns and had no idea how old it was but it seemed old when I was a kid. The most unique thing about it was its ivory handle featuring a carved eagle's head. I felt the revolver's weight.

How could I have missed seeing the gun the day before? It's possible I overlooked two levels of compartments stuck together in all the clutter, that I'd fallen victim to the emotional whammy of seeing my hyper-orderly father's decline into chaos. And if you asked my ex-wife if I was capable of finding a jar of olives in the refrigerator, she would tell you I was not, even if that jar of olives was the only thing in the refrigerator.

My father had let me shoot the pistol dozens of times while out on the sandbars and islands. Taught me how to load and aim it. How to clean it and keep it safe. A sick feeling rose from my gut. I looked under the workbench, found the cleaning kit, and removed a white patch and swabbed the gun's muzzle. The patch came away smeared with propellant residue.

The gun hadn't been cleaned since it was last fired. Given the state of my father's workbench, I wasn't surprised. But still. I released the cylinder and swung it open—a shell filled each of the chambers. But one of the shells had a dent in its primer. I tilted the cylinder into my palm. Out fell six shells, one of them empty.

The sick feeling in my gut spread throughout my entire body. Had I missed the gun the first time I looked for it? Or had my father or someone else returned it to the tackle box since yesterday?

I put the five live shells and one empty in the front pocket of my jeans, double-checked the gun to make sure there were no more rounds in it, then shut the cylinder, returned it to its burlap sack, and looked for a place to hide it. The garage had a makeshift ladder along one wall, rungs made of two-by-fours nailed into the bare studs. I climbed toward the rafters, carrying the pistol by the cinched sack, popped my head up through the joists, and set the gun on a board that ran across the rafters. There it would be safe from my father.

When I returned to the house, he was not in the kitchen. His bowl of cereal was empty and remained on the table. His orange was gone. I checked every room in the house. No Marshall Green. My mother had warned me a thousand times. Keep him locked in the house, otherwise he'll wander off. I didn't know whose safety I feared for more. My father's or my own when my mother found out I hadn't locked the back door.

He left me a trail of orange peel starting in the backyard leading east. With every light in the neighborhood on, it wasn't hard to follow. I found him standing in his robe along the yellow cordon of police tape with the most ravenous rubberneckers and tripods of police floodlights, half of his peeled orange in his hand. My father couldn't see anything—the coroner had erected a white tent around Thomas Hammond's body. As his fellow onlookers expressed concern and curiosity, my father smiled and ate his orange as if it were popcorn at a popcorn-worthy movie.

"Hey, Dad."

"Joey! Come have a look."

"I think we should head back to the house."

"I want to see who comes out of the white tent."

"No one's coming out soon. Let's go."

He said, "I wonder who's in there."

A woman said, "It's Thomas Hammond. Someone shot him. Shot him dead."

My father could not help himself. He smiled. Smiled and chuckled. Reverent faces turned our way. Faces trying so hard to show respect they tamped down outrage and incredulity. Scorn and disapproval. My father didn't seem to notice. His smile only grew as he said, "Well, all right. That's just all right by me."

A police officer enforcing the yellow tape glanced our way. He was tall with an athletic build under a crew cut and close-shaved jaw. His gray eyes seemed to photograph my father. Quick glances like a shutter opening and snapping shut. If it had been another time of day—later morning or afternoon or evening—my father's mental decay would have presented itself in more contrast to those around him. But with half the onlookers wearing robes over pajamas, their hair shaped by their pillow, Marshall Green fit right in.

I put an arm around him and forced him away. He resisted for a second, then acquiesced. Perhaps he'd forgotten why he wanted to stay.

When we returned to the house, Leela and her parents were out front speaking to a police officer. She had light brown skin and black hair pulled tight and fastened behind her head. She wore street clothes and the only thing that identified her as a police officer was a badge that hung from a lanyard around her neck. I pretended I didn't see them and steered my father toward the concrete steps that led up to the house.

Then I heard Leela say, "Oh, good. Here he is. Joey."

I started up the stairs, but my father's pace held me back.

"Joey!"

There would be no escape.

10

I turned and smiled. "Good morning."

"Hey," said Leela. "Come here a sec."

Ted and Kajal made a fuss over my father and invited him into their house for just-baked scones. He went without complaint, leaving me alone with Leela and the police officer, who checked her notes and said, "Are you Joey Green?"

"Yes, ma'am." I don't know where the "ma'am" came from. Spend two days in the South and you start talking like Rhett Butler.

The officer said, "Mr. Green. I'm Detective Chantal Cooper with Beaufort PD. I'm interviewing people in the neighborhood about what they may have seen or heard last night. And I understand you were with Ms. Bellerose. From when to when would you say that was?"

Detective Chantal Cooper had just received that timeframe from Leela, so I had to match it. "Oh," I said, "I wasn't paying attention to the clock, but I probably went over there sometime around 9:30, give or take. We sat on the porch for a while, then spent some time inside when the storm blew in."

"When you say inside, you mean where exactly?"

"In the guest space over the garage, where Leela is staying while she visits her parents."

Detective Cooper made a note. "And what time did you leave?"

"A little after midnight, I think. Probably somewhere around 12:15 or maybe 12:30. Ish. Again, I wasn't really paying attention to the time."

"Do you live in this home, sir?"

"No. I'm visiting from Chicago. This house belongs to my parents."

"And were they home all night?"

I told Detective Chantal Cooper about my mother's trip to Florida and that I'm watching my father because of his Lewy Body Dementia.

Detective Cooper looked up from her notepad and said, "So you left a man with dementia alone in the house for approximately three hours?"

"He's not a child. He's not an invalid. He has short-term memory issues and gets confused sometimes. I checked on him right before I left and he was sound asleep. And I checked on him when I got back to the house. He was right where I'd last seen him, snoring away." I used the momentum of the truth to lie. "And he was locked inside with a keyed deadbolt while I was gone."

"You lock your father in the house?"

"We keep both doors, front and back, locked at all times. He does not have access to a key."

"And when you say we . . ."

"My mother and I. She insists on it."

Leela said, "Officer, I'm a clinical psychologist, and locking a memory-impaired individual in their house is a common practice to help protect the individual in case they would step outside and then forget where they are."

"Thank you for that, Ms. Bellerose," said Detective Chantal Cooper. I could not tell if she was being sarcastic.

"Mr. Green, do you or either of your parents own a firearm?" The question came out flat and weightless, as if it were just one on a form of a hundred questions, like when you visit the doctor for a checkup. I supposed she was just getting the obvious concerns out of the way. Maybe she'd get lucky and save herself a lot of work.

I had lied about the back door being locked all night, but I did so knowing my lie was impossible to prove. The answer to the gun question was different, a field of trap doors. I had to stick to the truth, or snapshots of the truth. Snapshots that didn't tell the whole story because snapshots never do. I said, "My father would sometimes take a gun out on the boat when we went fishing. But that was years and years ago. We went fishing yesterday. He didn't have a gun."

Detective Cooper said, "Do you know what kind of gun it is?"

"A pistol."

"Can you be more specific?"

I wanted to make contact with Leela to ask for her silent advice, but she couldn't know what I'd be asking about so I kept my eyes on Detective Cooper. As far as I knew, only three people knew that gun existed. Me, my father, and Bubba. I didn't want to ask either to lie about it. I wasn't even sure my father could lie about it. He was incapable of remembering a simple directive like that. I said, "It was a revolver. Old with an ivory handle that had an eagle head carved on it. It's the only gun I've ever been around, so I don't know much about them."

"Do you know where it is?"

"I looked for it yesterday when I was putting the fishing stuff together. I didn't see it anywhere."

Detective Cooper stopped writing and looked up at me. "So a firearm just disappeared?"

"I asked my father about it. He has no idea where it is."

"And your mother?"

Something skittered across the sidewalk. I looked down and caught the tail of a bright green chameleon leaving the gray-white concrete and entering the thick lawn, where it disappeared into a Crayola sampler of greens. I wished I had that ability to do the same. To hide in plain sight. But the only color I could turn was red and I hoped to hell I wasn't doing that in front of Detective Cooper. I never was much of a liar. Or at least I wasn't any good at it. I had developed some skills, a small repertoire of half-truths I employed when telling the buyer at Target why her gross of sparkly unicorn pendants was late, but that was the depth of my arsenal. I said, "My mother doesn't know about the gun. The thing just always existed since I was a kid. It must have belonged to my grandfather. The only time I ever saw it was when we went fishing. My father said it was for protection in case someone tried to steal our boat out on the water. But he swore me to secrecy because my mother is no fan of guns."

"Do you know what caliber the pistol is?"

I knew but I lied. I had six shells, one spent, in my jeans pocket. "No idea." I didn't realize Leela had moved closer to me until I felt her shoulder brush against mine. I reached for her hand and found it.

Detective Chantal Cooper looked down at our clasped hands. "Mr. Green, when is the last time you saw the gun?"

I had to lie again because I could not say half an hour ago just before I hid it in the garage rafters. So I tried my damndest to time travel back to yesterday when I could honestly say, "Two years ago. I was down here visiting, and my dad and I went fishing. Just the two of us. It was in his tackle box."

"And it wasn't in his tackle box yesterday?"

"No. I looked for it." True and true.

"Does your father always keep the gun with his fishing equipment?"

"Yes. If it ever found its way into the house, my mother would have discovered it and all hell would have broken loose."

Detective Cooper smiled for the first time. "I bet it would have. Have you checked your garage this morning for any sign of a break-in overnight?"

I shook my head. "No. I haven't looked for any signs of a break-in." True and true again.

"All right. Well, please take a look." She handed me her card. "Let me know if you discover anything unusual or if the pistol shows up."

"I will."

"Thank you. One more thing: did you see or hear any gunshots last night?"

"No. Just the storm."

"It was a hell-raiser. That's for sure. All right, Mr. Green and Ms. Bellerose. You two have a nice day. I'll follow up if I have any other questions."

"Have a nice day, Officer."

She turned then stopped, froze for a full second, then looked back at me. "Oh, I almost forgot. Did you or your parents know Thomas Hammond?"

A fog of dread enveloped me. My father grew up in Beaufort. Thousands of people knew that. To lie about it would draw more attention than telling the truth.

I said, "I'm sure my dad knew Thomas Hammond. He grew up here and they're about the same age."

"Thank you. And your father's at the Belleroses' now?"

"Yes."

Leela said, "Do the police think someone in the neighborhood shot Thomas Hammond?"

"Darling," said Detective Chantal Cooper, "the police don't think anything. I don't even know what time Mr. Hammond was killed. We're just starting our investigation and my assignment is to ask questions in this neighborhood. Could be worse. I suspect folks around here drink damn good coffee. I'm going to need a hell of a lot. Probably work a double and then some."

Detective Cooper turned her body toward the Bellerose home and climbed the steps to the front porch.

11

"Excuse me, Officer." Leela ran toward Detective Cooper. Actually ran.

Detective Cooper stopped and turned around.

Leela said, "Marshall Green has Lewy Body Dementia. He has virtually no short-term memory. He won't be able to follow you from one question to the other. If you talk to him, I suggest you do it in the presence of a mental health professional."

Detective Cooper smiled. "Well, it's my lucky day. You're a mental health professional. Let's go."

Leela said, "I'm afraid I can't provide services here. I'm not licensed in the state of South Carolina."

Detective Chantal Cooper shook her head and smiled. "You're going to fuck me up if I go in and talk to Dr. Green, aren't you?"

"It's not personal. I took an oath."

"Yeah," said Detective Cooper, "so did I." She looked Leela up and down, then said, "All right. I'll talk to my C.O. We'll get a social worker or shrink or whatever we have to get."

Leela said, "Thank you. It's in your best interest, too."

"It's in my best interest to talk to everyone in this neighborhood. Which reminds me, Mr. Green, when is your mother due back?"

I said, "Tomorrow night, I think. Depends how far she goes in her pickleball tournament."

"Old ladies hitting the road to play pickleball. It's quite a life some people live." Detective Chantal Cooper smiled, then walked toward a new group of onlookers.

Leela said, "Well, this isn't exactly my idea of the perfect morning after."

"Yeah. Mine either. I should get my dad home."

Leela tilted her head, a gesture I learned was her prelude to a question. "Why? He's fine with my parents. Probably thrilled. Let's take a walk and find some coffee."

"I really should get him back home."

Leela's smile evaporated. "Oh. Okay. I get it." She shrugged. "We tried."

"Leela. You're misreading the situation. Misreading me."

"It's okay. You don't have to explain. We're on vacation."

"Come over for a second."

"Excuse me?"

I stepped toward her. "Please. Come over to my parents' house. So we can talk."

"Why can't we talk here?" She folded her arms, her eyes shiny, her mouth small.

Neighbors congregated around us like gnats. Detective Chantal Cooper talked to a clump of them twenty feet away. Leela had not raised her voice, but I felt eyes on us. Curious eyes. We were strangers to them, two visitors from the north. I said, "I'm not asking you over to talk about us. I don't need privacy to tell you I am quite taken by you and our experiment or whatever it is. For the sake of clarity I will say it another way. I am smitten with you. I am dreading one week from now when regular life will intervene like a fucking wrecking ball."

Leela's eyes grew large and filled with tears and questions.

I stepped toward her and pulled her tight. She did not fight me as I whispered in her ear. "I need to discuss a private matter that has nothing to do with us." Leela nodded against my chest.

We sat in the kitchen drinking a fresh pot of coffee, eating oranges just picked off the tree. I told Leela what my father had said about Hammond Island and the Hammond family on our drive from the airport. About his uncharacteristic hatred of the Hammonds. About his applauding while standing at the police tape outside the white tent that sheltered Thomas Hammond's body. About how he drew the attention of a steel-eyed cop who was working crowd control.

Leela said, "And you think the police will suspect your father of shooting Thomas Hammond?"

"I know it sounds crazy. My father seems ancient and he's crazy slow. But he loathes the Hammonds and has little inhibition about voicing his feelings. Couple that with him not being able to verify his whereabouts, and, well, I just have this sick feeling. Even if he didn't actually shoot Thomas Hammond—"

"Of course he didn't shoot Thomas Hammond."

"But he could be a suspect. That could destroy him. And my mother."

"Joey." She reached out and took my hand. "I have some experience working with the courts and correctional institutions. Am I right to assume your father has no criminal record?"

"None that I know of."

"Your father is sweet and barely functioning. No one is going to accuse him of shooting Thomas Hammond. Are you worried about his missing pistol?"

I considered telling Leela that the pistol wasn't missing. I considered it for a second, then discounted the notion because telling her would make her complicit in my cover-up. My God, is that what it was? A cover-up? With one simple climb of a ladder I went from mild-mannered slinger of tween costume jewelry to a criminal accomplice. And yet, I didn't want to lie to Leela. I didn't want to start a relationship that way.

Leela must have seen the broken cogs clanking behind my eyes because she said, "You are worried about the missing pistol."

I returned to the present and said, "Yes. As my father used to say about everything from hammers to spatulas, 'Well, the damn thing didn't walk away on its own.'"

She smiled. "Maybe when he was in the early stages of dementia, before he was diagnosed and he still lived his regular life, he took the gun fishing and accidentally dropped it in the water or left it on a sandbar or someplace like that."

"Maybe." I lied to a clinical psychologist. I lied to a woman I'd made love to last night. I lied, and she knew it. I saw she knew it.

She said, "Tell me."

I shook my head.

"Ah. Okay," said Leela. "I understand. You're not going to tell me you know where the gun is. That you looked for it and found it. Or you weren't looking for it and found it. I appreciate your not telling me. We can both swear to that and be honest about it."

I said nothing.

Leela squeezed my hand and said, "The chances of your dad having anything to do with this is almost zero. He's lovely. He's dedicated his life to helping people. Everyone likes him. Him misplacing an old gun isn't going to change that."

She was right. I knew what people thought of my father. He was the selfless humanitarian. I tried to see the situation from an outsider's perspective. From a logical perspective. But I couldn't shake my sense of dread. I said, "I know. But just the possibility he had something to do with Thomas Hammond's death . . ." I squeezed her hand.

Leela stood up out of her chair while holding onto my hand, then sat on my lap. She wrapped her arms around me and held me tight. I was overcome by the dichotomy between the anxiety I felt about my father and the bliss I felt from her embrace. It was almost too much to carry at one time.

I managed to say, "Thank you."

"Come on," she said. "Let's go get him."

When Leela said that, I thought I loved her. We went to Leela's parents' house, then I walked my father home through a thinning crowd, his belly full of two breakfasts. He asked what all the commotion was about, and I told him I didn't know. The last thing I wanted was him celebrating Thomas Hammond's murder out on the street. A minute after we entered the house, my cell rang.

My mother had read the news on Nextdoor. She said, "Does your father know?"

"He did. Now he doesn't."

"I think that's for the best."

I said, "You're up early. Did you get enough rest for your big match?"

"Plenty. If we win today, we have the finals tomorrow. I'll be home tomorrow night either way."

"No rush. Take an extra day or two if you want."

"The neighborhood must be all out on the street."

I didn't want to talk about the shooting. I feared she'd sense my concern over my father's possible involvement. Mothers can do that. Even if their son is forty-six years old. I said, "The neighborhood is definitely abuzz. So was the match close yesterday?"

"Yes. It went to fifteen–thirteen in the third game. Are the police asking if people saw or heard anything?"

My mother had a strong network of informants. I had to confirm what I'm sure she already knew. "Yes. An officer made her way through the crowd, talking to everyone."

"Did she talk to your father?"

I told her about Leela's interceding on his behalf. My mother was glad to hear it. I said there was nothing to worry about, and she should focus on pickleball. When I hung up, I found my father asleep in his recliner. I checked both doors to make sure they were locked, then started up the stairs with the hope of getting more sleep.

The back door opened.

I had just locked it. My heart jumped, then I heard, "You just have a seat and we'll be out of here in no time."

I reversed course on the stairs and made my way to the kitchen to find Ruby emptying the dishwasher, her husband, Lawrence, sitting at the kitchen table eating a praline cookie. The tin was either bottomless or Ruby had baked another batch.

Ruby said, "There's my boy! I thought maybe you were out on the water."

"Ruby, please stop doing that. It's not your job."

"I just wanted to drop off another tin of cookies and I'm sure you have your hands full with Mr. Marshall, so I thought I'd help out a little."

I gave her a hug and shook Lawrence's hand. "I am capable of unloading a dishwasher. Good to see you, Lawrence."

"And you, Joey," said Lawrence in a baritone that must have made him the most intimidating English teacher at Beaufort High School.

Ruby said, "Did you hear about the murder?"

"Sweetheart," said Lawrence. "We don't know if it's a murder."

"You think Thomas Hammond shot himself in the middle of the night while out for a walk?"

I said, "I heard about it. The whole neighborhood was on the street a little while ago. The sirens woke us up." I placed my hands on Ruby's shoulders and steered her away from the open dishwasher and took over the job of unloading.

Ruby reluctantly sat at the kitchen table and said, "We saw the Belleroses out front a minute ago. And if you don't mind me saying so, I think that Leela is sweet on you."

"Yeah?"

"She gets all twinkly when your name comes up. Not only that, she's the one bringing up your name. Pretty and smart lady, if you ask me. You might want to scoop her up while she's available."

I said, "Ruby, don't tell me you're part of the matchmaking conspiracy."

Lawrence laughed. "When it comes to matchmaking, my wife treats this town like one of her quilts. No tolerance for loose threads dangling all alone."

Ruby said, "I just want everyone to be as happy as we are, baby."

"No one can be as happy as we are. They're fools for even trying. You just like sticking your nose where it doesn't belong."

Ruby smiled at me. "He's right. I do." Ruby and Lawrence laughed hard. A shared celebration. Sparks still flew. After fifty-plus years of marriage. I envied them. And pitied my mother. She and my father had their past, but no present in which to anchor it.

Lawrence said, "Oh, before I forget . . ." He reached into his pants pocket. "Marshall lent this to me a couple weeks ago." He removed a small pair of pliers. "It removes the barbs from fishing hooks. Makes the release part of catch-and-release a lot easier. For the angler. And the fish. I'll just put it out in the tackle box where I found it."

I told Lawrence that wasn't necessary. I'd take it out later. He handed me the barb smasher, and I slipped it into my pocket, his words *where I found it* bouncing around in my head when I heard:

"Delphi?"

All three of us turned toward the hall to see my father standing at the kitchen entrance, looking at Ruby.

"Delphi, what are you doing back in Beaufort? I told you to never come back here."

Ruby and Lawrence swung their eyes toward me. I saw questions and pain and said, "Dad. This is Ruby. And Lawrence. They dropped by to say hello."

My father looked at both of them, then turned toward me. "What?"

"Ruby and Lawrence are here." I kept my tone light, once again responding as if he were a small child, as if I were saying, "Yes, thunder is loud." I showed no fear, no concern to magnify his own.

He manufactured a smile. Always the charmer, my dad. "Aw, hell. What did I say?"

"I don't remember. Want a cookie? Ruby smuggled in a fresh batch."

He nodded and smiled. "Don't tell your mother." He took a cookie and shoved it into his mouth. I didn't know how I was going to explain my father gaining ten pounds over the three days my mother was gone. Then he grabbed the newspaper off the kitchen table and said, "I'll be back in a jiffy." No embarrassment that he was off to use the bathroom. He walked out of the kitchen, into the hall, and started his slow climb up the creaking stairs.

I said, "Sorry about that."

"Oh, don't be sorry," said Ruby. "Poor man is not well."

I nodded and watched their faces. The concern was still there. "He gets confused. And hallucinates. Last night, he had a conversation with Delphi over at the Belleroses'. Do you know who she is? Or was?" Ruby and Lawrence looked at each other. I checked the hall to make sure my father hadn't somehow snuck down the stairs to eavesdrop. When I turned back toward them, I saw sorrow on their faces. Deep sorrow. I said, "Forget it. Let's drop it. It's none of my business."

Ruby placed a hand on Lawrence's back. "It's okay, baby."

Lawrence turned to me and said, "Delphi was my sister. She died a long time ago. Some fisherman found her in a gill net under the drawbridge."

I felt acid rise into my throat. "That's horrible, Lawrence. I'm so sorry. I had no idea."

Ruby said, "Delphi was my best friend. That's how I got to know Lawrence so well. You know, she worked here sometimes when your grandparents had parties. They treated her like family. Sweet, that girl. And beautiful. Like a model. The only thing she did wrong was fall in love with a white boy. That's why she got killed. I'm sure of it."

I said, "You mean she was murdered?"

Lawrence said, "The police never arrested anyone. But there were rumors."

Ruby said, "Rumors my ass. It was Roy Hammond." Ruby had a malice in her eyes I'd never seen.

I said, "The Hammond brother who disappeared way back when?"

"In 1975," said Lawrence. "Went out on the water by himself one day. Neither he nor his boat returned. Lot of rumors about that, too. People think he's still alive all these years later. He'd be about eighty now."

"Sounds like your sister fell in love with the wrong guy."

"You mean Roy Hammond? No, Joey. My sister despised Roy Hammond. But that didn't stop him. He hounded her night and day despite her having a beau."

Lawrence dropped his eyes. Ruby wiped a tear from hers, looked into the hall then back at me. "It was Mr. Marshall, Joey. Delphi and Mr. Marshall were engaged to be married."

I walked over to the sink, looked out the back window, and felt a rush of clarity. It suddenly made sense. My father's altruism. His insistence on moving back to Beaufort. Why Ruby had remained so close with my parents long after she'd stopped working for the family. The extraordinary bond between Ruby and Lawrence. My father and Ruby and Lawrence were all, through each other, keeping Delphi alive. And my father's disproportionate hate of the Hammonds, that also fell into place.

I stared at the garage and felt the most intense desire to dispose of the pistol. Thomas Hammond's death needed to be the period at the end of a dark sentence. No one else should suffer. Not my father. Not my mother. Not Ruby and Lawrence. I could put an end to all of it.

The doorbell rang. Detective Chantal Cooper said she'd return to interview my father. I considered not answering the door when the bell rang again. Better I got to it before my father. I walked to the front door and opened it, my excuse prepared for why Detective Cooper couldn't talk to my father. But it wasn't the police standing on the front porch.

12

"Joey. May I come in?"

"Of course."

Uncle David stepped into the house. He wore a white linen suit with a baby blue pocket square and matching tie. "Am I interrupting anything?"

Twenty minutes later, Uncle David and I sat in the living room. Ruby and Lawrence had left, and my father remained upstairs, probably having forgotten Ruby and Lawrence were ever there. Probably having forgotten I was, too.

Uncle David took a cigar from the breast pocket of his white suit coat and stuck it in his mouth. The cigar had never been lit. "Joey, I've come to ask a favor."

I said, "Whatever I can do." My response felt automatic, a courtesy, though in truth Uncle David asking me for a favor felt monumental, a shift in hierarchy in a place where hierarchy seemed paramount.

"I'm sure you're aware Thomas Hammond was shot and killed late last night or early this morning."

"Yes. The whole neighborhood was out on the street at five A.M."

"The Beaufort Police Department is investigating. Thomas Hammond, as you know, was an important person in Beaufort from an important family with a long history. Everything I told you yesterday was true. The Hammonds have been a great asset to Beaufort, helping it grow by creating a healthy business climate, both in real estate development and by providing seed money to attract business to the area." He stuck the cigar in his mouth and drew on it, as if he could suck the nicotine out of the tobacco.

"But despite my admiration for the Hammonds," he said, "Thomas and Gail fired me yesterday. This happened after you left. They were very kind with their words, but the reason was not so kind. They said, in essence, they needed more vibrant legal representation than one old man sitting in an office by himself. They wanted new blood and new ideas. As if my age somehow prohibits me from keeping up with the law and current manner in which it's practiced, despite the fact that I've been keeping up with the law since I was twenty-four years old."

"Doesn't seem fair."

"It wasn't fair. It was business. And a poor decision. I did an excellent job for the Hammonds representing their interests. Their accountants can attest to that. And Gail can attest to the fact that I accepted my dismissal with grace. What else would I do? Beaufort is a small town. It doesn't pay to fracture relationships, even when you've been treated unfairly, because sooner or later, the opportunity to work together again will come your way."

I wanted to remind my great-uncle he was ninety-one years old and maybe future business shouldn't be his biggest concern. Instead, he should live out his life in comfort and style—he'd earned that.

"The favor I need from you, Joey, is to tell the police what I said about the Hammonds yesterday."

I started to say *of course* but stopped myself. That lesson I'd learned decades ago about not trusting family made me feel like I was about to stick my finger in a light socket.

Uncle David said, "Is there a problem?"

I said, "What story are you going to tell the police?"

"I'm not going to tell them a story, at all. I'm going to tell them the truth."

"And that is?"

"Joey. You were there, son. You know the truth."

"Yes. I do. I told you my father griped about Hammond Island and the Hammonds in general and that's why you defended them. But if you tell that to the police, and I tell that to the police, they'll want to talk to my father. And you and I both know he's in no condition to be questioned."

My great-uncle David rolled the cigar around in his mouth, then said, "Perhaps I could just say you asked me about the construction on Hammond Island."

I said, "How about I just said it looked like there's a lot of construction in town. And you told me about the development on Hammond Island and how wonderful the Hammonds are."

"That would work just fine." Uncle David took the cigar from his teeth, the mouth-end dark and wet. He looked at it as if he had expected it to morph into something else. "I'd be delighted to tell that to the police. And I'm sure this will all be over soon. The police want to get the murderer behind bars so the rumor mill doesn't scare away all the visitors."

"I don't know."

"You don't know what, son?"

"Can I trust you?"

"What are you getting at, Joey? I'm your great-uncle. You're talking to me like I'm a stranger off the street. Like it's beneath you to give me the time of day." His face reddened, and spittle flew from his mouth. "I would never sell out your father. He is a fine person. Always has been. Even when he was a boy." He shoved the cigar back into his mouth and wedged it between his molars. "Don't tell me you're worried Marshall had something to do with Thomas Hammond's death."

"Of course not." I heard myself say the words, but that dreadful feeling clawed at me. I let silence fill the room as Uncle David found his composure. When he'd settled back down, I said, "Did you know Delphi?"

He hesitated, then said, "Who are you talking about?"

"Lawrence Hill's sister. Delphi. She was murdered when my dad was in high school. They found her in a gill net under the drawbridge."

"Oh, sure. That Delphi. I remember her and that tragic day. She was a friend of the family. Worked in this very house sometimes. God rest that poor girl's soul. What does she have to do with this conversation?"

"I have no idea. But my father has imagined seeing her twice in the last couple days. I wonder why she's come up after all these years. I thought maybe you'd know something about it."

Uncle David said, "There's nothing wrong with Marshall's long-term memory. I suggest you ask him."

I wanted to ask my great-uncle about the pistol. Where had it come from? Did it belong to my grandfather before my father? But I did not trust David Green. He was a survivor and survivors are good at saving their own skin. It was possible he didn't even know the pistol existed, so it made no sense to tell him about it. I had watched enough detective shows and read enough crime stories to think that sooner or later the police would have a ballistics report. They would know what caliber bullet killed Thomas Hammond. And if it turned out that bullet could have been fired from a .32 caliber revolver, well, Uncle David didn't need to know my father owned one.

I said, "I will tell the police you spoke highly of the Hammonds after I mentioned all the new construction in town."

"Well, I sure am glad to hear that, Joey. Because they will question me before the day is out. I'm sure when they ask Gail what individuals might have had a grudge against Thomas Hammond, my name will be on the list. It will be a long list, mind you, but my name will be toward the top because he fired me yesterday."

My great-uncle tipped himself forward in the winged armchair and launched himself up and onto his feet. "What you need to understand, Joey, is my reputation is all I have. Or should I say, my reputation is the only valuable thing I have. My money, my property, isn't worth much to a man my age. But my word. My standing in the legal community. That's the real gold. I've had to endure some cruel talk over the years. Never got married. Never had children. You can imagine what folks have said about me. All rumors and innuendo. But I have overcome it all through hard work and adhering to an upright moral code, no small feat in the legal profession. I don't need any kind of scandal at this point in my career. Plenty of great men have been toppled in the end. The beloved football coach who was found to look the other way when a sexual predator worked on his staff. The respected politician who was exposed as a taker of bribes. The multi-millionaire businessman who sold IP secrets to the Russians. That's a fast way to the grave, Joey. I did nothing wrong, but if I get tied up in a murder investigation, that'll be my end."

I walked Uncle David through the living room, though it felt more like him walking me as if he owned the place. I had to remind myself he'd been visiting this house for almost seventy years.

He said, "We'll be sure to have dinner together when your mother returns." He opened the door and stepped outside.

After Uncle David left, I went upstairs and found my father asleep in his bed, curled up on his side wearing a plaid shirt tucked into khaki pants, red suspenders stretched over his shoulders and across his back, his body rising and falling with each breath. It was like watching a child sleep, only it was my father, a man who had given me and my sisters and my mother so much. And that was in addition to the medical care he had given to thousands of people over the years. All free of charge. He had sacrificed so much for us and for them, and some reward he'd received: Lewy Body Dementia.

In that moment, standing over him, I did not care if my father had shot and killed Thomas Hammond. If Thomas Hammond had anything to do with Delphi's murder, even passively, if he covered for his brother or simply didn't speak up, if he in any way allowed that crime to go unpunished, then he got what he deserved. My only desire was to protect my father and, indirectly, my mother. I would do whatever it took to ensure Marshall Green lived the rest of his life with the same dignity he worked so hard to give others.

I went downstairs and found Bubba's phone number on the list my mother had stuck to the fridge. He answered on the first ring.

13

I booked Bubba for a half day to take out three anglers: my father, Leela, and me. We met at the marina at one o'clock and motored down the Beaufort River, rigged and ready to go, lines taut, rods bent. My father rode in the passenger seat next to Bubba, his head turtle-like poking out from his life jacket. The clouds hung fat and white like scenery in a grade school play. They were not a threat to our perfect afternoon.

Bubba kept his eyes on boat traffic. My father faced forward and seemed immobile in his flotation cocoon. Leela tilted her face toward the sun, her eyes hidden behind a pair of aviator sunglasses. I slipped one hand into my fishing vest and removed the old pistol in its burlap sack. I'd retrieved it from the garage rafters earlier that day and wiped it clean of fingerprints before returning it to its burlap sack along with whatever ammunition I'd found and a handful of fishing weights I'd affixed to the gun with wire. I looked behind us, saw no boats, double-checked to make sure my shipmates had their eyes elsewhere, then dropped the sack into the water, the sound drowned out by the roaring boat engine and wind rushing past our ears. Bubba didn't know. My father didn't know. Leela didn't know.

But I knew. I looked back to make sure nothing floated and nothing did. A steel gun in a burlap sack with lead weights would go straight to the bottom. I didn't know how deep the river was but I knew one thing—it started inland and made its way to the sea. Driftwood, dead fish, kelp, and floating refuse may ride the tide and wash up on shore, but a lead-weighted gun would not.

The hull seemed to rise in the water, as if I'd unloaded a metric ton from the boat. I felt as if I'd woken from a nightmare. I raised my left hand to my mouth and tasted the salt water, the stuff from which we're made. With my right hand, I reached for Leela and touched her upper arm. She looked at me with a smile, her eyes hidden behind dark green lenses.

What a strange and wonderful sensation it was to free-fall for Leela Bellerose. A Bostonian psychologist and divorcée who I didn't know existed a few days ago. We shared over ninety years of life experience between us, and it felt the sole purpose of that experience was to prepare us to meet each other. I had said to myself a hundred times, *This is vacation. This is not real life.* And yet, the only way we could have found each other was by stepping out of real life. The land of palmettos and shrimp boats gifted us our only opportunity. To discount it as "vacation" felt ungrateful.

I squeezed Leela's hand, checked to make sure Bubba's eyes were on the water and my father hadn't swiveled around in his swivel chair, and drew Leela's hand toward me and kissed it. She lowered her sunglasses just enough to peek over the gold rims and melt me with her amber eyes.

Twenty minutes later we fished the creeks in and around Port Royal, casting shrimp toward the grass. Bubba referred to Leela as Miss Leela. He did not swear in her presence, nor did he spit on the bait and lures before handing her the rod, which he'd fit with an anti-backlash reel to make her day (and his) more pleasant. Leela had not fished in decades but she cast well for a relapsed angler and caught the first fish of the day, a big red with a telltale blue dot near its tail fin and another on its back. My father held the fish, one hand supporting its underside and the other holding its tail, while Leela put her arm around him and I took the picture.

Then Bubba took the fish from my father. "See what I'm doing here," said Bubba, "even with barbless hooks, sometimes the bait gets taken too deep to extract the hook without harming the fish. So I cut the line and leave the hook in." He waited for Leela's expression of concern, then said, "The fish's digestive acids will dissolve the hook in a few days and she'll be back to normal. Plus she gets to keep the shrimp for her troubles to give her the strength she needs to court some fine young fella so they can fall in love and make babies."

Bubba released the fish into the water. We'd been returning fish for so long that catch-and-release felt natural, but for Leela's benefit, Bubba went into his speech about overfishing, changing pH levels, rising sea temperatures, and its resulting devastation on the food chain and migratory patterns.

"I've been fishing these waters for sixty years," said Bubba, "and what I've seen in my lifetime would break the most heartless man's heart. You might think I worked in the telecommunications industry and saw the change from rotary dial phones to pushbutton phones and fax machines and all that being wiped out by cell phones and computers and the internet with email and texts. But I don't work in the telecommunications industry. I work in the sea. The earth. With God's creatures. And it's changing faster than technology."

Bubba reached into the live well and retrieved a new shrimp and harnessed it up for Leela's rig. "All this havoc on the earth, the ice sheets melting into the sea, the polar bear going extinct, the monster hurricanes and fires and floods, I don't see it as Man destroying the planet. No, I see it as Man making the earth sick. Just like a person gets sick. The immune system kicks in to fight the foreign invader. Temperature rises, violent expulsions, anything necessary. The body will inflict more damage on itself than the disease does if that's what it takes to get rid of the disease. That's what the earth is doing now. And got to be honest, I'm rooting for the earth. There's some people on it who are making living here impossible for the rest of us. I say bring on a biblical flood. But no

Noah and the ark this time. Wipe us all out. Give some new creature a chance in our place."

"Fish on!" said my father, his rod tip bent and vibrating toward
the water.

The line cut through the surface darting left then right, the red
drum's metallic flank reflecting the spring sun with flashes of gold
and silver. My father's physical and mental deterioration yielded to
muscle memory. He knew how to fight and land a fish, which gave
him a few minutes of his former self. Strong. Competent. Intel-
ligent. Joyful.

I put my phone's camera on movie mode and captured most of
it. When my father reached into Bubba's rubber fishing net and
removed his catch, I said, "Show me what you got, Dad."

He turned toward me, held the fish out, and sprouted the most
genuine smile. A child's smile. I said, "How do you feel?"

"Fantastic."

Bubba helped him release the fish, and I emailed the movie to
my sisters in case I dropped my phone into the deep.

"Joey and Miss Leela," said Bubba, "you picked a good week to
visit Beaufort. We used to reel 'em in like this all the time. Soon
as the water warmed. Now, we're lucky to get four or five good
weeks a season. Mr. Marshall, you want shrimp, mackerel, or a
rubber worm?"

"You pick."

"Shrimp seem to be working so we won't mess with success."
Bubba grabbed another shrimp out of the live well and said, "Tell
you one thing, Thomas Hammond meeting his maker is not
gonna hurt the fishing. Nice enough fellow when you talked to
him. I know he tried to be less harmful to the environment than
other developers. But to me that all seemed like more of a sales
pitch than sound environmental policy. From where I'm sitting,
Thomas Hammond's motto must have been *Think Globally, Destroy Locally.*"

My father said, "Thomas Hammond died?"

Bubba and Leela looked at me, and I said, "Yeah, Dad. He's dead."

My father smiled his smile again. Pure and genuine without the encumbrance of guilt or propriety, so magnetic it could have pulled his gun from the bottom of the sea.

Bubba said, "Thomas Hammond will not be missed, will he, Mr. Marshall?"

"No, Bubba, he will not be missed one bit."

14

We dumped our gear in the garage, then started the slow climb up the back steps of the house. My father saw it first, a business card wedged into the screen door near the handle. He pulled it out and read, "*Detective Chantal Cooper. Please call me.* What do you think this is about, Joey?"

"You might be wanted for eating too many Goo Goo Clusters."

"What?"

He had forgotten about Bubba's Goo Goo Clusters as well as Thomas Hammond's murder. I took the card. "I'll give Detective Cooper a call while we're getting ready for dinner."

We showered and dressed. My father kicked back in his recliner for a nap, and I stepped into the backyard, locking the door behind me. Detective Cooper answered her phone directly.

"Thank you for calling, Mr. Green. I'm just following up to see if you've found your father's firearm."

"No. I'm sorry. I haven't. I've looked everywhere."

"Hold on," she said, "just checking my notes here . . . Okay, did you have a chance to ask your mother?"

"I think I told you this morning that my mother doesn't know about the gun."

"That's right. Is it possible she came across it and disposed of it?"

"I suppose it's possible. I'll ask her. I just need to do it in a way that doesn't end a fifty-one-year marriage."

"Sounds like she does not approve of firearms."

"She does not."

"Well, please keep my card and contact me as soon as you talk to her."

"Will do. And do you mind if I ask a question?"

"Go right ahead, Mr. Green."

"There must be more guns than people in South Carolina. Are you tracking all of them?"

"No, Mr. Green. That would take more years than I have on this earth. But our forensics team has determined that the bullet that killed Thomas Hammond was a .32 caliber round. That narrows our search significantly."

My heart felt like it dropped into my stomach. My father's old pistol took a .32 caliber round. Of that I was sure—I had loaded the bullets into the burlap sack with the gun before I'd dropped it into the Beaufort River. And I'd burned the ammo box, as well.

Detective Cooper said, "The .32 is not common anymore, but it was popular for older guns, which limits our search considerably. Sadly, not as much as you'd think. The older guns get, the more valuable they become. You mentioned your father's pistol was old. I know he has memory-impairment issues, but you said it was his short-term memory that's primarily affected. Do you think he'd know the model and manufacturing year of his missing pistol?"

I didn't know what I was going to do but I said, "I'll ask him."

"Thank you, Mr. Green. I'd appreciate that. And I've talked to a psychologist who sometimes works with Beaufort PD. She is available tomorrow to participate in a routine interview with your father. Will you both be home at ten A.M.?"

Tomorrow? This was moving too fast, but the last thing I wanted was to appear evasive. I said, "Yes. We should be home then."

"Then we will see you tomorrow. Thank you, Mr. Green."

I pocketed my phone and returned to the house, where I scoured the pantry and found a decent bottle of Shiraz and another of Chardonnay, the latter of which I put in the freezer. My father still slept in his recliner. I stepped out front onto the porch, again locking the door behind me. The neighborhood appeared to have settled back to normal other than the police tape surrounding a white tent a block to the east with a couple of uniformed officers enforcing the barrier.

The relief I'd felt after dropping the gun into the water was gone, replaced by a wave of dread after hanging up with Detective Chantal Cooper. I knew nothing about how police operated, but I would've been a fool to think they hadn't focused on my father. The logical explanation was his past with the Hammonds. There was bad blood and the police knew about it. Maybe Gail Hammond told them. Maybe my uncle David had. It could have been one of a thousand people who had grown up with my father and the Hammond brothers.

I regretted dumping the gun in the Beaufort River. By doing so, I eliminated the chance for the police to prove the bullet that killed Thomas Hammond did not come from my father's gun. Maybe forensic technology had advanced enough to determine the last time a gun had been fired or at least if it had been fired recently. I didn't know, and I couldn't Google it. Computer searches, I knew, were traceable. The truth was, when it came to guns and police investigations, I knew nothing other than what I'd read in detective books and had seen on TV. And for all I know, that information served fiction more than the truth.

I would know more tomorrow after 10 A.M.

I heard a knock on the door behind me. My father waved from inside, smiling. He tried the doorknob but it was locked. I unlocked it and went inside.

"Joey!" he said and gave me a hug. He stepped back, saw the question on my face and said, "How long have you been in Beaufort?"

"A few days."

He shook his head. "It's a terrible thing. Not remembering. Hope it's not hereditary."

"It's not, Dad. Not what you have. It's just bad luck."

He looked at his hands and said, "We were out in the sun today."

"With Bubba."

"Man," he smiled, "I bet we caught fish."

"We sure did. I'll show you pictures. Hey, Dad. Remember your old pistol?" He turned away from me and walked back toward the kitchen. I followed him. "Where did you get that gun?"

He opened the refrigerator, pulled out a can of Coke, and popped the top. "I don't remember."

I retrieved his pill suitcase and flipped open the tiny lids. "You've had that gun since I was a little kid. You remember everything from back then. You don't remember where it came from?"

"Nope." He sipped the Coke. But it was more than a sip. It was a cover. A lie. He avoided eye contact and his voice faltered as if he had more to say but not the breath with which to say it. He did remember how he'd acquired the gun. He just didn't want to tell me.

Ted and Kajal Bellerose had been busy while Leela and I were on the boat. They bought fresh shrimp at the marina, peeled and deveined them, and made shrimp scampi that filled the air with garlic and butter. Kajal made pasta from scratch, a salad of greens cut from their garden, and a loaf of sourdough from her own starter. They dug out the good china and crystal and candles and I half wondered if they were going to propose to me on Leela's behalf or vice versa.

Leela made gimlets—my father's favorite, though I was pretty sure I'd never told her that—and between a couple rounds of those before dinner and the two bottles of wine I'd brought, the evening was greased for conversation.

My father was in a fine mood at dinner and regaled the Belleroses with one of his stories. "Joey was just a little fella. We were down visiting from Chicago, staying with my parents in the same house we live in now. We'd just driven into town and word had spread throughout the family. It took no time before my aunts and uncles and friends of the family filled the living room. Ruby was still working for the family then and stayed late to help my mother feed everyone. But Joey and his sisters were having none of it. They'd been cooped up in that car for two days straight. Greta was six then and Bess was eight so she was old enough to watch her younger siblings out in the world, at least that's what we believed at the time. So I gave them each a dollar, which wasn't nothing back in 1975, and sent them into town to get some ice cream or candy or whatever their dollar would buy.

"They couldn't have been gone more than half an hour when they marched into the house with the biggest smiles you'd ever seen and their little hands held behind their backs. Do you remember this, Joey?"

"Not even a little bit. What did we buy? The suspense is killing me." I winked at Leela and she returned it with a smile that knocked the air out of me.

"Well," said my father, "we had no idea how the purchasing power of one dollar could generate so much excitement. Your little faces were bursting with pride. Bess, being the oldest, was in charge. She led the count. One. Two. Three. Together you held out your hands, and what do you think we saw?"

I glanced around the table. My father, even with his mind a dull fraction of its former brilliance, had captured his audience. We each sat forward, focused on Marshall Green, our perfect meal forgotten.

My father set down his knife and fork and said, "Goldfish!" His infectious laugh caught fire. "Our three children went to the five-and-dime and bought goldfish. Each one in its own sealed plastic bag. I said, 'How the heck are we going to get those fish back to Chicago?' And Greta said, 'In a pickle jar. With a lid so their water doesn't spill.' Must have been twenty people in the living room, and every one of 'em in stitches. Those sweet children just couldn't understand why." His laugh faded, replaced by something melancholy and distant. "Thinking you can buy goldfish on a trip a thousand miles from home, that's innocence. That's something you're gifted until it's taken away." He shook his head and drifted away from us.

Kajal, Ted, Leela, and I looked at each other, then Kajal said, "What happened?"

My father returned from wherever he had gone. "Huh?"

"What happened to the goldfish?"

"Oh," said my father, "my mother pulled out three Mason jars—big ones—and Bess, Greta, and Joey each had a goldfish for the entirety of our visit. Apparently, eight-year-old Bess negotiated at the five-and-dime so their three dollars bought not only three goldfish but also a can of fish flakes."

I said, "Did we take them back to Chicago?"

"No, Joey. We did not. Your mother and I felt certain those fish wouldn't survive the trip in sealed jars with all the jostling and temperature changes. So the day we headed back to Chicago, Neil Lipsitz took those fish for us. You remember Neil, he worked at the shoe store downtown. They had a talking myna bird that would always ask for Joe. Joe was Neil's father and owned the shoe store. That bird lived to be twenty-some years old. And each of you kids would get a new pair of Stride Rites every summer to last you through the next school year." My father loved to backfill his stories with tangential bits of unnecessary information. "Anyway, Neil dropped by the house as we were loading into the station wagon. Let me tell you, there were some tearful goodbyes as he took those fish and drove away."

Leela said, "And Neil gave them to his children?"

"Oh, no," said my father. "Neil didn't have children. Not yet anyway. What Neil did have was access to a freshwater pond that was stocked with brim and bass. Some doctor who practiced in Savannah owned it. Man by the name of Artie Kohlbrenner, kept a house in Beaufort on a plot of land with that pond. He'd give friends permission to fish there."

Ted said, "And Neil let the fish go in that pond?"

"No, sir. Neil used those fish as bait."

"What?" I heard an embarrassing amount of incredulity and outrage in my voice. "You gave away our pets as bait?"

"Sure. Just slip the hook into the meat of their tail. Doesn't hurt 'em a bit. They can swim just fine and are lively as can be. And let me tell you, that'll get the attention of a hungry bass, those gold flashes lighting up their territory. Goldfish are a hell of a bait but illegal in a lot of states. Not South Carolina, though, not that it mattered, since Neil fished a private pond on private property."

Leela said, "Well, that was an unexpected ending to an otherwise adorable story."

Kajal said, "Remind me to never ask you to take my Ritchie fishing with you."

My father looked confused.

I said, "Ritchie's the dog who's sleeping under the table." I glanced down to see a Cavapoo, copper with a white chest, not more than ten pounds.

My father had met Ritchie a hundred times but had forgotten. He glanced under the table and smiled. I imagine he would have said something like he'd never use Ritchie for bait, but he may have forgotten that's what we were talking about. Instead he said, "This scampi is delicious. Just delicious."

The remainder of our dinner conversation bounced from topic to topic, but by the time Kajal appeared with her homemade key lime pie, Ted was talking about when they'd head back north for the half of the year they spent in Boston.

"We're going to wait until May first this year," he said, "too many spring blizzards now. Last April, we were snowed in for three days, ironically because the world's getting hotter. Did you see someone caught a houndfish off the coast of Massachusetts? That's a Caribbean fish. Next thing you know they'll be catching bonefish and barracuda. All the lobsters will move to Nova Scotia. Joey, you'll have to visit us while you can still get a decent New England lobster roll. You should come during summer. When the water gets cold, the lobsters toughen up. In summer they're tender and sweet."

I wondered if Ted had planned on using climate change as a segue into inviting me to Boston or if he'd wrangled the opportunity in the moment. It was such a bold move—Leela must have told her parents how we'd sparked to each other—she must have talked to her parents the way daughters often do and sons often don't. My sisters have shared volumes of information with my parents. About their work. Their children. Their marriages. And by doing so have made me look like I'm withholding, which I am not. It simply never occurs to me to say things like, "Hey, guess what? I slept with the neighbors' daughter last night."

They say boys are more difficult to raise than girls from birth through grade school because girls are more focused and patient and boys are more wild. But as teenagers, girls grow more complicated and difficult and boys more stoic. That is a generalization. A stereotype. But having been a boy who fit the stereotype, I believe stoicism is a mischaracterization of our behavior. We are not more stoic than girls. We are more ashamed. Of our boy-thoughts and risky deeds, mostly revolving around or inspired by sex or at least the idea of sex. That seemingly unattainable nirvana ignited by blossoming bodies and invisible pheromones. That shame sends us underground. Quiets us. Our vortex of shame is so powerful all our thoughts and deeds get sucked into it, so we share nothing.

But Leela must have told them, if not everything, then something. Or why else would Ted Bellerose invite me to Boston right in front of her. And why would Kajal, her mother, say, "I suggest us old people wind down with a living room chat and you young people go out for a nightcap."

15

Leela and I returned to the inn on Bay Street where it began with Leela's proposed experiment of revealing the worst about ourselves. That was two nights ago. Now, I had new confessions to make, like aiding and abetting and destruction of evidence. I don't know if that's what I did, but I'd heard those terms before and dropping a pistol into the Beaufort River seemed a likely fit.

We sat at the same little bistro table as we did our first visit. We'd consumed plenty of gimlets and wine already, so we ordered club sodas. We made it about five minutes into the conversation when I reached across the little table for Leela's hand and said, "So are we going to talk about your father inviting me to Boston?"

Leela tried to smile but couldn't manage it. "That conversation scares me to death."

"Can you tell me more about that, Doctor?"

"Not here," said Leela.

I said, "We should have gone for a walk."

"We will in a few minutes."

"Now I'm worried."

She squeezed my hand and said, "Don't be."

"Joey?" I turned and saw Virginia from Uncle David's office, her gray hair down on her shoulders. She was with another attractive woman about her age, but less natural looking than Virginia. Blond hair framing a too-taut face with inflated lips over bleached white teeth.

I stood and gave Virginia a quick hug and introduced her to Leela.

"This is my sister, Christine," said Virginia. "It's our big night out on the town."

Leela invited them to join us. Virginia and Christine made noise about not wanting to intrude, which we pooh-poohed until Christine finally sat down and Virginia headed off to the ladies' room.

"Thank you," said Christine. "This is a nice surprise. I've met your father, Joey. Very sweet man. Beaufort is happy to have him back. And now it's nice to meet the both of you. I wasn't quite sure how tonight would go. I just knew I needed to get Virginia out of her condo. She's tied in knots over Thomas Hammond's death."

I wanted to say join the club but instead said, "I'm sorry to hear that. Did Virginia and Thomas Hammond know each other personally?"

"Yes," said Christine, "but not in the modern era. They were actually engaged to be married back when Thomas worked for his father and Virginia had just graduated high school. Ask anyone who lived in Beaufort forty-some years ago, my sister was the most beautiful woman in town. Some people think she still is. And Thomas became the most eligible bachelor—this was just after his older brother disappeared and Thomas became first in line for the family business."

I said, "The brother who disappeared. Was that Roy Hammond?"

The server returned with our club sodas. Christine ordered a glass of rosé for herself and a Sauvignon Blanc for Virginia.

"Yes, it was Roy Hammond who disappeared. Back in 1975, I believe. He was quite the playboy. Rumor was he had girlfriends in Charleston, Atlanta, Savannah, Myrtle Beach, everywhere. Used to run his boat up and down the coast as if he were a sailor with a woman in every port. Not a very nice man. The kind of guy women would say gave them the creeps. Am I talking too much?"

I said, "No, please continue. I'm interested."

"Well," said Christine, "Roy Hammond would prey on young, vulnerable women. Dangle the promise of marrying a Hammond then abuse the poor girl until he tired of her and moved on to the next one. And Roy Hammond was the same in business. My husband, he's a bit older than I am, he was in Roy's class at the Citadel. He said Roy was one of those win-at-all-costs types who was only interested in the short-term transaction regardless of the long-term costs. Chewed people up and spit 'em out. But Thomas Hammond was not like that. I knew him socially and found him to be, yes, a bit boastful and always wearing his salesman's hat, but he was kind and the people who did business with him genuinely liked him."

Leela said, "But he and Virginia never married?"

Christine shook her head. "Virginia has never told me the whole story. Still, to this day. Can you imagine that? I'm her sister. But all she says is it didn't work out. I'm sure there's quite a story there, but I cannot get enough wine in her to find out the truth. Lord knows I have tried."

Virginia returned from the restroom, sat down, and launched a slew of questions toward Leela, telling Leela she'd known me for thirty years, ever since she went to work for my uncle David. "The good news," said Virginia, "is that some of these Greens live a long time. If things work out with you two and you get married next year, you could celebrate your fiftieth anniversary one day."

I will admit I'd had the same thought but said, "Wow, Virginia. No pressure. We've only known each other forty-eight hours."

"I'm sorry, Joey. I can't help myself. I am a romantic through and through."

Leela said, "Are you married, Virginia?"

Virginia answered with a smile. "No. Never have been. Just wasn't in the cards for me."

"Wasn't in the cards for me, either," said Leela, "but I got married anyway." She laughed at her joke, which is what made it a joke and not tragic.

"We all suffer in our own way," said Christine. "I am married to a man whose snores are so loud they're cracking the plaster in my ceiling. I keep telling him he's got to sleep with one of those machines that pushes the air into his nose but he refuses. Says it'll turn him into Darth Vader. I say I'll take Darth Vader as my lawfully wedded husband if he lets me sleep at night." The server returned with the wine. Christine raised her glass and said, "To the indignities we all suffer. Those gaps between who we are and how we live. May we endure them, and may they not define us."

Leela's eyes grew even more big and beautiful. "Hear, hear, Christine. That is the wisest thing I've heard in . . . well, maybe ever. I'm going to steal that. Maybe even put it on a T-shirt."

The three women laughed. I would have joined them but I had the odd sensation they'd forgotten I was there. I was the invisible man seated at a table of women with their wine and I wanted to stay invisible as long as possible. It was voyeurism, pure and simple.

Virginia said, "My sister here always asks why I never married, then proceeds to tell me about her husband snoring or wearing his golf shoes in the house and I feel just fine with my life. But I will admit I struggled for a long time with not being married. Especially living here in Beaufort. This is a small town in the South with no shortage of quote-unquote family values and those who have an in-your-face attitude about it, especially since I am a woman of a certain age. I have been gossiped about. And that's behind my back. To my face people have just come out and asked why a girl like me isn't married." Virginia sipped her wine. "It made me feel less-than for decades. Then when I turned fifty, something magical happened. I thought, I'm fifty. That's something. Every day I get from this point forward is a bonus. And anyone who questions how I live my life, well, pardon my French, but fuck 'em."

Leela initiated another round of clinked glasses and said, "Oh, that gives me hope. Five more years until I can say, 'fuck 'em.'"

I didn't raise my glass. They really had forgotten I was there.

"It is a glorious freedom," said Christine. "One day age will be our oppressor, but until that happens age is our liberator. My Charles is eighty-two years old. Eighteen years my senior. And he is as free as a bird. We could be out for dinner at a fine establishment and he could whisper in my ear, 'Darling, see that beautiful woman over there. I would like to take her home to our bed.' And I would say, 'Charles, honey. If you can make that happen you have my support. You're eighty-two years old. God bless you.'"

Virginia smiled. "Oh, Christine. You are full of it. Charles would never say that."

Christine said, "No, he probably wouldn't. But he talks dirty to me, which he never did before he turned seventy. Now it's nonstop. The things I hear on a daily basis, my Charles emboldened by age and a prescription of little blue pills. You know, my niece is pregnant with her first child and the baby is wanting to come early, so the doctor put her on vaginal rest. When I heard that I thought, how do I get put on vaginal rest?"

The conversation continued for a bit, then Leela asked the server to bring two more glasses of wine and the check. A few minutes later, she and I said goodnight to the sisters and stepped out into the salt air, where Leela said, "It's time to conduct phase two of our experiment."

I said, "Did I know there was a phase two?"

"No. It's privileged information until you graduate from phase one, which you have. Congratulations."

We returned to Ted and Kajal's and walked in on my father telling the Klan story. I'd heard it a few dozen times. At least. Sometimes from my father. Sometimes from one of my relatives. It varied with each telling, but the gist of it involved a KKK member inviting my grandfather to a meeting in the 1930s. My grandfather explained he was Jewish and therefore ineligible to be a Klan member. The Klan member responded in a friendly tone. "That don't matter. It's not like you're one of those New York Jews."

Ted and Kajal weren't sure if they were expected to laugh at this, so each managed a chuckle combined with Kajal's "Oh my" and Ted's shake of the head with pursed lips.

The Klan member's response is the part that makes me suspect the story is true because one of my most vivid childhood memories of Beaufort is sitting on the big porch with my father and Uncle David in 1984. They were arguing about the upcoming election and my father was aghast Uncle David had announced he'd be voting to reelect Strom Thurmond. My father responded by saying no self-respecting Jew would vote for a segregationist.

Uncle David said, "You forget where you come from, Marshall. We're not like those New York Jews."

It was the most anti-Semitic thing I'd ever heard in person. And it was from my own family.

We said goodnight to Ted and Kajal, then walked my father back to the house, and he went straight to bed. I made hot tea that we took into the living room and set it on the antique table in front of the couch. It was dead quiet in that old house.

I said, "I would have guessed phase two of our experiment would be in the physical sciences, but that was last night."

"Phase one was about our faults. Phase two is about our wants."

I said, "Okay. You go first. I had to go first in phase one."

"I'm the scientist. I decide." She tried to smile but couldn't hold it. "Tell the truth. What do you want? A wife? A fuckbuddy? A relationship? An open relationship? A polyamorous relationship? A friendship? A vacation fling?"

I kissed her. She kissed me back. Then I pulled away from her and said, "I want marriage or a marriage-like relationship. I don't care if the government is involved. Or any kind of religious institution. But I do want a long-term commitment and exclusivity. Oh, and just so I don't sound too old-fashioned, the person I'm committed to for the long term must also be a fuckbuddy. And my best friend. You want to write all this down? I can find you a pen."

Leela smiled. "I think I can remember it."

"Some scientist you are. Now you tell me what you want."

"I want to get married. Or at least have a fake wedding for my parents. It would mean a lot to them." She leaned into me and rested her head on my shoulder. "Actually, I'm okay getting married for me, too. When I first got divorced, I thought I never needed to get married again. But you know, it's not really about the institution of marriage, it's about family. And family I want. Family I need."

We talked a little more, then I walked Leela to her guest house over the garage, making sure I locked both doors of my parents' house. She invited me up, and we made love under the eaves. There was an extraordinary amount of eye contact, as if we were continuing our conversation from earlier. But naked. I lay with her after and she said, "I wish you could sleep over."

"Come sleep at my place."

"Your father will know."

"Maybe. But he'll forget."

16

Leela went home before the sun rose, and Detective Chantal Cooper knocked on the door at precisely 10 A.M. She had a briefcase tucked under one arm and two colleagues at her side. One was the tall, young, severe-looking officer I'd seen policing the perimeter of the crime scene when my father had wandered over to the yellow tape. Chantal Cooper introduced him as Officer Jack Doyle.

Officer Doyle said, "Mr. Green, this is the department psychologist, Selena Cruz."

Selena Cruz looked twenty-five years old. She stood ramrod straight and shook my hand with a firm grip and said it was nice to meet me and she looked forward to meeting my father. She wore her dark, shiny hair in a bob blunted straight above her shoulders. Her bangs angled from hovering over her right eyebrow then slanting down to nearly cover her left eye. It was the haircut of someone who worked with police but wanted to show she wasn't police.

I had considered coaching my father for the interview, but he wouldn't have remembered a word of our conversation. I considered insisting a lawyer be present, but that seemed like the demand of a guilty person. My biggest hope was that my father would come off as too incompetent to murder someone. Actually, it was more than a hope. It was my intention. I asked Officers

Cooper and Doyle and Selena Cruz to wait in the foyer and went upstairs to get him.

"There are some people here, Dad."

"Who?"

"Come downstairs. I'll introduce you."

My father could still walk up and down the stairs, but you could time him with an hourglass. That was my exhibit A. The police and their psychologist waited in the foyer so they had the best view in the house for watching someone descend the old wooden staircase. Creak, creak, creak. For two solid minutes.

He got three-fourths of the way down the stairs and said, "Joey, what are the police doing here?"

I said, "They just want to ask you a few questions. Remember, I told you upstairs?"

His expression said he did not remember. And he shouldn't have remembered because I didn't mention the police. I wanted to ensure they saw him at his worst. When he finally reached the foyer, I introduced everyone, then we started the long journey to the dining room table.

Thirty seconds after we sat down, I said, "Oh, I almost forgot." I got up and went into the kitchen and returned with a glass of water and my father's pill suitcase. He wasn't due for his next round of meds until noon, but I figured it wouldn't hurt if he took them a couple hours early. I counted out fourteen pills in front of the police and Selena Cruz, the department psychologist.

I said, "Sorry, we have to do this four times a day and I don't want to get off schedule." I began handing the pills to my father one at a time and he swallowed each with a sip of water.

Detective Chantal Cooper said, "Thank you for your time today, Dr. Green. We only have a few questions."

"What kind of questions?" said my father between pills.

Detective Cooper said, "Do you remember where you were two nights ago between the hours of eleven P.M. and four A.M.?"

"No," said my father. "I was probably asleep, but I don't know. I really don't."

Detective Cooper looked at Selena Cruz, and Ms. Cruz looked at my father with her one visible eye and said, "Dr. Green, do you remember what you had for breakfast this morning?"

"No," said my father. "Maybe Rice Chex. I like Rice Chex. But I don't know."

"Dr. Green. Do you know what day it is?"

"No."

"Do you know why we're here?"

"No."

"Who's the president of the United States?" He shrugged. "Do you know that Thomas Hammond was shot and killed two nights ago?"

"I did not know that but I'm not sorry to hear it."

Detective Cooper looked at Officer Doyle and I tried to look ho-hum about what my father had just said. I knew he'd say something negative about the Hammonds and I had rehearsed looking nonchalant when it happened. I had no idea if I pulled it off.

Officer Doyle said, "Why do you say that, Dr. Green?"

"Because the Hammond family are not good people. They were all about Jim Crow. They got people riled up on hate and, when everyone was distracted, they stole public land. They donated a small percentage of it to schools and hospitals to make themselves look charitable. They're the worst kind of people."

Detective Cooper said, "Did you know any of the Hammonds personally?"

"Sure did. Roy Hammond was a few years ahead of me, and Thomas Hammond was my year."

"And you disliked both of them."

"I hated Roy Hammond. That boy was pure evil. Thomas I didn't hate, but I didn't like him either. He might have turned out different if he was born into a different family. But he wasn't. He has no backbone. He's the just-following-orders type. After the rest of 'em died off, I'd hoped Thomas might be a better person. But he just keeps being a Hammond. Like he doesn't know better."

Selena Cruz said, "You switched to talking about Thomas Hammond in the present tense. Do you know he's dead?"

My father hesitated then shook his head. "I'm sorry. Did you just tell me that?"

"Yes. A minute ago."

"I can't remember anything. My God, this is no way to live."

"Dr. Green," said Selena Cruz, "we understand you've been diagnosed with Lewy Body Dementia."

My father shrugged. "I don't know."

I said, "Excuse me. A few hundred people live in this neighborhood. Are you questioning all of them like this?"

Detective Cooper said, "This is my block. I interviewed everyone on it yesterday. Everyone except your parents. Your mother was gone the night Thomas Hammond was killed. I've checked her alibi. But we haven't spoken to your father. We're just doing our jobs, Mr. Green. And no, we don't question everyone like this, but you told me your father's gun is missing."

"My old pistol?" said my father. "You can't find it, Joey?"

"No, Dad. I've looked everywhere."

"I keep it in my tackle box."

"I know. That's the first place I looked. But it's not there."

He appeared confused. And so ashamed. He took a sip of water, pushed another pill into his mouth, and said nothing.

Detective Cooper said, "Dr. Green, does anyone other than your wife or Joey have a key to the house or garage?"

I dreaded that question and wished Bess and Greta were there to play our childhood game Divert Dad.

"Sure," said my father. "Ruby and Lawrence Hill. They've had a key for decades." He said it without a care in the world. "Ruby doesn't work here anymore. She opened a bakery downtown."

"I've been there too many times," said Detective Cooper, patting her stomach. "Why does she still have a key if she doesn't work here?"

"Ruby keeps an eye on the place when we visit our grandkids. Sneaks us day-old treats, too." My father laughed.

I cringed and hoped I didn't show it. Lawrence had told me he could return my father's barb smasher to the tackle box where he found it. That meant he'd been in the garage. Lawrence suspected Roy Hammond of murdering his sister, Delphi. If the police were looking for a quick arrest in the Thomas Hammond murder, a person of color with motive and opportunity might be an easy target. I felt no relief in that possibility. Ruby and Lawrence were like family.

Officer Doyle said, "Dr. Green, can you tell us what kind of gun your old pistol is?"

"It's a revolver."

"Do you know the brand?"

"No. I just know it's old with an ivory handle with an eagle carved on it."

"Where did you buy it?"

"I didn't buy it." He paused, looked at me, then looked away. "My father gave it to me. I don't know where he got it."

My father had told me last night he didn't know where the gun came from. I thought he was lying then and I thought he was lying again to the police when he said his father had given it to him. His father was long dead. There was no one around to verify his story.

Officer Doyle said, "Can you describe the gun in more detail?"

"Sure," said my father. "It's a revolver. Thirty-two caliber. Chrome except for the handle is made of ivory."

"Do you remember the last time you saw it?"

He shook his head. "No."

"Are you missing anything else? Is it possible you've had a break-in?"

My father looked small and fearful. Weak and old. "I don't know," he said. "I really don't." He held up his hands in a kind of surrender. His memory loss terrified him. I knew that, but I wasn't sure the police knew that. They could easily have interpreted his expression as a man who is beleaguered with guilt.

Officers Cooper and Doyle exchanged eye contact, then both

looked to Selena Cruz. It was like they were talking to one another in a foreign language. Then Detective Cooper put her briefcase on the table and opened it. She reached inside and removed a gallon-size Ziplock bag.

The bag contained my father's gun.

17

Impossible.

I'd dropped the gun in the middle of the Beaufort River less than twenty-four hours ago. Steel doesn't float and I'd wired lead fishing weights to the pistol for insurance. My mind flipped through the possibilities. Police divers searched the river bottom. A shrimp boat pulled in its net and there it was. A recreational fisherman trolled the deep and snagged it. The river's current pushed the gun out to sea where the tide went out but didn't take the gun with it, leaving it high and dry on the beach like a piece of driftwood.

All of those scenarios seemed absolutely impossible.

Officer Doyle looked at me and said, "Mr. Green, are you okay?"

I hesitated to answer, then said, "Yeah. Just surprised. I've looked everywhere for that."

Detective Cooper looked at my father and said, "Dr. Green, is this your gun?"

"Hey," he said, a big smile on his face as if he'd been reunited with an old friend. "My gun. Why is it in that bag?"

I said, "Where did you find it?"

"We can't say at the moment," said Detective Cooper. "This gun is part of an active investigation. What we can tell you is it's a .32 caliber Winchester manufactured between 1902 and 1905. The handle seems to be a custom job. These came from the factory with pearl handles. We're waiting for forensics to determine whether or not this is the gun that killed Thomas Hammond."

I said, "This is . . . unbelievable. And frankly, unethical." I leaned toward Selena Cruz. "What is your purpose at this interview? Shouldn't you function as an advocate for my father? Or are you just a decoration to distract from an otherwise abusive and possibly illegal interview?"

Selena Cruz did not answer.

My father said, "What's going on, Joey? Why are the police here?"

"That's a good question, Dad. Why are you here, Detective Cooper? And how long have you had my father's gun? Weeks? Months? Why don't you just level with us like we're doing with you?" No one responded to my little speech, so I continued. "I'm not from Beaufort but I've been coming here my entire life. I know this is a big tourist town. A horse-drawn cart passes this house on the hour and it's full of sightseers. Every boat going up and down the Intracoastal Waterway stops here. There has to be a ton of pressure on you to make an arrest for the Thomas Hammond murder. But this is ridiculous. And please, don't insult us by saying you're just completing a routine questioning of everyone in the neighborhood. Do you take a gun in a bag to everyone in the neighborhood? Did you find fingerprints on that gun, or didn't your little Beaufort PD Detective Toolbox come with a fingerprint kit?"

I regretted saying that last thing but I felt I had to stay on the offensive. I was met with another silence. They let it sit for a minute, then Officer Doyle said, "Mr. Green, we'd appreciate your cooperation in this investigation. Of course, if you refuse to cooperate, we're happy to report that to our commanding officer."

I had no clue how in the hell my father's gun wasn't in the Beaufort River. I had no power. I had no authority. I had no idea what was happening. I had nothing. Except a deep love for my father and mother and a fear their lives could be destroyed after decades of decency and hard work.

I softened my voice and said, "I don't give a fuck what you report to your commanding officer. My father worked seventy-hour weeks for forty-five years taking care of the underprivileged. Treating heart disease and diabetes. Delivering babies. Setting broken bones. Healing rashes and bronchitis. Diagnosing cancer and hypertension and whatever else ailed his patients whether they could pay or not. I'm sorry one of your elite citizens was killed on the city streets that you're supposed to protect, but you're not going to pin the deed on a man who met you ten minutes ago and can't remember who you are or why you're here."

Detective Chantal Cooper removed a card from her pocket and handed it to me. "In case you've misplaced the card I left earlier. Please call me if you have any ideas about how this gun could have come into someone else's possession." She lifted the Ziplock bag containing the gun from the table and returned it to her briefcase. "Thank you for your time. Both of you. And I hope you enjoy the rest of your day."

"And please," said Officer Doyle, handing me his card, "let us know if you plan on leaving town."

The officers and Selena Cruz stood. My father watched them, confused, and said, "Goodbye. Thanks for visiting."

They thanked him again and showed themselves out. My father remained seated. I waited until I heard the door shut and said, "Can I get you anything, Dad? Coffee? Maybe some juice?"

"Why were the police here, Joey?"

"You know you have a hard time remembering things, right?"

"I do. Yes."

"Thomas Hammond was killed a couple nights ago. Just down the street from here. They're interviewing everyone in the neighborhood to find out if they saw or heard anything."

"Did I see or hear anything?"

"I don't think so."

"I can't remember if I did or not."

"I know, Dad. Listen. I need to ask you a question. Not about something recent but about something a long time ago. You're good at remembering a long time ago."

"I am." He smiled.

"And I'm sorry if this question upsets you. I'm not trying to put you on the spot here. I'm just trying to have a conversation. And it'll be a lot harder to have this conversation when Mom comes back from her pickleball tournament."

"She's out of town, huh?"

"Yeah. Florida. The championship game is today. She'll be back tonight. So is it okay if I ask you a question?"

"Sure." He didn't look nervous or upset. I supposed anything recent, even anxiety of what was happening or dread of what could happen, was hard for him to hold on to. I was almost certain he'd forgotten the police had just been there. Forgotten that they had his old pistol. And forgotten even that it had disappeared.

I said, "Would you please tell me where you got that old pistol you keep in your tackle box?"

He looked like he was going to yell at me again, then something in him quit. He slumped in his chair. "I think . . . I think a friend gave it to me." He did not look at me but rather stared at the old dining room table. A table he'd known for seventy-five years.

"Dad, it's just me. Joey. Your son. You can tell me the truth."

He shook his head and kept his eyes on the table.

"You need to let me help you. I know that's hard. You've always been the one who's helped me. But it's time to let that go. Please tell me where you got that old revolver so I can tell the police."

My father did not move.

"Dad? Do you hear me?"

"Joey." He sounded scared. "Joey!"

"I'm right here, Dad."

"I feel sick. Woozy. The room is moving. Call 9–1–1. I'm having a sorogh . . ." He gripped the sides of the table as if he were on a boat being tossed in a storm.

I called 9–1–1.

18

9–1–1 dispatched the mobile stroke unit, which arrived in less than ten minutes. The ambulance was equipped with specifically trained emergency medical technicians, an MRI machine, clot-busting drugs and devices, and a video link to a physician at the hospital's stroke unit. There was no room in the ambulance for me, so I followed behind with Leela. My first thought was to call my mother, but I opted to try my sisters instead. I spoke to Bess and filled her in. She hung up to call Greta and my mother.

Leela squeezed my right hand and said, "You did the right thing, Joey. With strokes, it's all about getting treatment right away. You've given him the best chance he could have."

I said, "He gave him the best chance he could have. He diagnosed himself and told me." The ambulance split the traffic. It felt too dangerous to stay close. I knew where the hospital was because I'd passed it a thousand times, but I had Leela navigate with her phone just in case something had changed since my last visit. "The police questioned him about his gun. They think it was used to kill Thomas Hammond. He said his father gave it to him. But he was lying. After they left I tried to get him to tell me the truth. Maybe that's what triggered the stroke. Or maybe it's because I gave him his meds two hours early."

"No, it wasn't his meds. This is not your fault, Joey. Strokes don't just happen out of the blue. They're a long time in the making. Like heart attacks. It would have happened sooner or later regardless." We drove in silence for a minute. The ambulance was out of sight. Then Leela said, "Why does it matter where your dad got the gun? You said he's had it as long as you can remember. How he got it way back when, what does that have to do with anything?"

"I don't know. I just know he's not telling me the truth about it. And my father always tells the truth. It's like he took some kind of oath to be good and loyal and honest. He's not perfect. He wasn't always fun to be around when the clinic stretched him thin, physically and mentally and financially, but that's because he had given all he could give. He had nothing left, and if I got in trouble at school or one of my sisters stayed out past curfew, he could really lose his temper. If anything, he's guilty of trying to hold us to the standards he set for himself."

We turned left on Ribaut Road and headed south. The paramedics had made a point of telling me they were going to the Naval Hospital, not Beaufort Memorial, even though we'd pass Beaufort Memorial on the way.

I said, "My father never lied. At least I don't know of him ever lying. Trust me when I say there's something very wrong with him not being honest about where he got that pistol."

Leela said, "I do trust you."

"Thank you."

When we walked into the emergency entrance, my father had already been rushed into the stroke unit. A nurse asked us to have a seat and said someone would be out shortly to update us on his condition. We sat in silence for a minute, and a tidal wave of shame crashed over me for having dropped the gun into the Beaufort River.

Leela saw it on my face and said, "Are you okay?"

A woman who looked too young to be a doctor but, according

to her name tag, was a doctor, approached and said, "Mr. Green?" She had dark skin and tightly cropped hair.

"Yes?"

"Can you come with me, please?"

"Is it okay if my friend joins us?"

"That is up to you."

Leela and I followed the doctor down a corridor and into a private room with a desk and a computer with a large monitor on the wall. It looked like a room where they gave loved ones the bad news.

"Our preliminary diagnosis is your father had a transient ischemic attack, which is sometimes referred to as a mini-stroke. The good news is that medical technicians got to your father within minutes and injected him with TPA, which dissolved the clot." She turned on the wall monitor. An X-ray of a head filled the screen. "This is where the clot was." She pointed to a blur in the brain that looked like every other splotch of gray and white. "We won't know for a little while yet, but it's probable your father will exhibit no symptoms of the TIA, and no lasting damage was inflicted."

I said, "So what's the bad news?"

"The bad news is that when a patient suffers one transient ischemic attack, they are likely to have more."

Leela squeezed my hand.

"We can try to prevent it by prescribing a blood thinner and keeping your father as calm as possible. Increased heart rate can contribute to a reoccurrence."

Leela said, "How's he doing right now?"

"He's doing well. Quite the talker, your father. We'd like to keep him overnight for observation, but he should be able to go home tomorrow."

The doctor added that they had a few more tests to run, then would admit him into a room for the night. She said he was in good spirits, telling one story about how he'd known the architect of the Naval Hospital, which had been built not long after my father was born. The doctor suggested we go eat lunch and return to see him in a couple hours.

Leela and I drove over the bridge to Lady's Island. The water was gray-blue, and the edges of the marsh shined wet and reflected the midday sun as the tide receded. The dark mud and sand reminded me of my childhood trips to Beaufort. Greta and Bess and I would explore the wet earth for hermit crabs, pick them up by their shells, and watch them disappear inside. Then we'd set them down and look for another.

Beaufort held so much wonderment for me. The ocean, the palms, green grass during winter, the blades thick and coarse, unlike the fine and soft blades of grass in the Midwest. The place felt otherworldly. Chameleons, pelicans, sharks, dolphins, shrimp. These were mythical creatures to a boy from Chicago, and yet I had seen them alive in their natural habitat.

We drove the main strip on Lady's Island, found a pizza place, and sat outside. I ordered a beer. Leela ordered wine. It was in the time between when our drinks had come and our pizza was still twenty minutes away when Leela took my hands into hers on top of the table.

She said, "I know I said yesterday that I appreciated you not telling me what happened to your father's gun, but I've changed my mind."

"Leela, I—"

"Please, Joey. Please, please, please. Let me help you."

I sighed. "And I was worried we weren't going to have anything to talk about at lunch."

"Do not joke right now. Face this one head on." She smiled, and I felt helpless.

I told Leela everything. How I'd first looked for the pistol and didn't see it. How I woke to sirens and returned from the street of onlookers to find my father in the kitchen with a fresh-picked orange because I'd forgotten to lock the back door when returning from her parents' house the night before. How I searched the garage a second time and found the pistol where I thought I'd originally looked for it. How, in a panic to protect my father, I took the gun fishing the second time with Bubba, and with Leela sitting across the stern from me, I reached over the gunwale and dropped the weighted revolver into the Beaufort River.

19

Just as I finished telling Leela I tossed the gun overboard, the server arrived with our pizza and set it on a giant can of stewed tomatoes. Leela ordered a second glass of wine. I asked for water. I had to keep my head clear. Especially with Leela staring at me, giving nothing away. She did not blink. The server left. I spatulaed a slice of pizza onto a plate and handed it to her.

I did the same for myself, and she said, "Okay. I understand why you didn't want to tell me."

"Let's forget I did."

"We can do that. No one else will know." She extended her right hand. I shook it. She said, "But you and I can talk about it." She nibbled at her slice, then said, "I think the gun was stolen from your garage, used in the crime, and then returned. That's why you couldn't find it the first time you looked for it but did find it the second time."

"Or the expanding trays were just stuck together, and I overlooked it."

"Either way . . ." said Leela, "you dropped it into the river. Maybe the current carried it into a fishing boat's net. The crew found it and turned it in to the police."

I said, "Maybe . . ."

"I've worked with a lot of people, Joey. I couldn't tell you which ones were capable of shooting someone, but your dad, come on. Old retired guys don't go around shooting people unless they're suffering from mental illness or white supremacy, and your father suffers from neither. His impairment is short-term memory loss—he hasn't forgotten who he is. He hasn't forgotten his moral code."

"He also hasn't forgotten his grudge against the Hammonds."

"Your dad doesn't seem like a vengeful man and he's not stupid. He wouldn't risk ruining the rest of his and your mother's life over one moment of satisfaction."

"But he hallucinates. He talks to people who aren't there. Dead people from his past. He's quick to lose his temper. And with how much he hates the Hammonds, what if he thought Thomas Hammond was Roy Hammond? It is possible—he thought Ruby was Delphi."

"Your father would have had to think that while he just happened to be walking around late at night with a pistol during a thunderstorm because you just happened to leave the back door unlocked."

"He does wake up in the middle of the night all the time because the medication has him on an abnormal sleep schedule."

"His shoes and clothes would have been wet if he'd gone out in a thunderstorm."

"He could have slipped out after the storm was over. And by the time I'd realized I'd left the back door unlocked, his shoes and the back entranceway would have dried."

"You sound like a prosecuting attorney."

"I . . ." I took another bite of pizza and shook my head and felt a rush of sadness.

"What is it?"

"I don't know. I really don't. My gut tells me he could have done it. And that is a terrible feeling."

Leela helped herself to another slice of pizza and said, "Joey, I've been involved in a number of criminal cases as an expert witness. I've seen trials. I'm pretty sure if the police had any hard evidence like fingerprints or a witness, they would have arrested your father."

"I know for a fact they're waiting on a ballistics report. It's not like my dad's going to run."

"Your dad is not a killer, Joey. Maybe if he was forced into a self-defense situation. But memory impairment doesn't change a person's personality. It changes their memory."

My phone rang. It was my mother. I answered it and heard:

"Joey, you are talking to the champion of the women's seventy-plus division of the Northeast Florida Pickleball Tournament. Judy and I ran the table."

"Hey, congratulations. That's great, Mom."

My mother heard in my voice what she hadn't heard from either of my sisters—she apparently hadn't talked to them yet. There was a pause, then she said, "What's wrong?"

I told her about the police, the bagged gun, my father's stroke. The joy drained out of her voice. She returned to her pre-trip state of worry and burden, which she compounded with guilt for having left. I did my best to assure her everything was fine. Paramedics dissolved the clot within minutes of the stroke. The overnight stay in the hospital was for observation, not treatment. She seemed to take little consolation in that, and said she'd be home in three hours and ended the call.

Leela said, "I think you should call the police."

"Tell them what?"

"Tell them your father had a stroke right after they left. They don't need to know any more than that. Tell them thanks a lot. It might buy us some time."

"*Us?* You're embracing your role as co-conspirator." I'd meant it as playful banter, but it didn't come out that way.

Leela said, "I trust you, Joey."

"You trust if things go bad, I won't mention your name?"

She nodded. I pulled her hand across the table and kissed it, then dug Detective Chantal Cooper's card out of my pocket and made the call, ratcheting up my voice with indignation and sorrow and sarcasm when I ended the call with, ". . . so if you need to question him any more, you can find him in the stroke unit of the Naval Hospital." I hung up without waiting for her reply.

We had another hour or so to kill before returning to the hospital. I asked Leela if she was okay swinging by my uncle David's to see if he was home so I could tell him about my father. I could have called him, but I wanted to show Leela more of Beaufort.

He lived only a few minutes' drive in a small development that looked like it had been built as a guard-gated community only they never got around to installing a gate or hiring a guard. The neighborhood had one entrance off Sam's Point Road and backed up against Factory Creek. The homes had been built in the last twenty-five years, but were all styled to look as if they'd been built a hundred years ago. Clapboard or brick siding, steep eaves, big shutters, all on high pillars to stand above the storm surge that would one day come.

More than the architecture, the neighborhood felt from another time because of its antique-style street lights and old, craggy oaks. The garages and driveways were hidden behind the homes as if they were stables, only accessible through an alley. I circled through the neighborhood and pointed out his house.

"That's it."

"The huge brick one?" said Leela.

"Yep."

"I thought you said he lives alone."

"He does. I suppose when you never support a family, you can afford a giant house even if you don't need one. Before we stop, let's get into the alley. You can see his view of the water from there. And his dock."

"Does he have a boat?"

"I'm not sure. He used to. A big sailboat. He'd take us out when we'd visit. I was always jib man. Uncle David was a stern captain, barking orders, saying I'd better not drop the winch crank into the water because it cost more than my life was worth."

"Sounds like a lovely man."

"He's not bad, actually. Just never had any kids so he never learned how to talk to them. Before we stop, let's circle around through the alley. You can see his view of the water from there. And his dock." As we came around the bend toward his place, his garage door opened. I expected him to back out of the driveway, but the taillights I saw did not belong to his old Mercedes. They belonged to a Jaguar in butter yellow. I stopped the car and put it in reverse.

Leela said, "What are you doing?"

"That car belongs to the Hammonds." I stopped where I could make out the car through the leaves of a young tree. "Or I guess it belongs to just Gail Hammond now. What's she doing over here?"

"Dealing with the aftermath of her husband's death?"

"Maybe. But the Hammonds fired Uncle David. At least according to him they did. And he's a stickler for appearances. Always worried about his reputation. If meeting with Gail Hammond was business, he'd do it at the office."

"Or not. His home is more private," said Leela. "Especially the back alley. Her husband was murdered. This might be the most discreet place to meet with your lawyer. Or ex-lawyer. Or whatever he is."

Uncle David exited the garage and walked onto his driveway. Gail Hammond rolled down her window. We could hear nothing of their conversation. They talked for half a minute, then David reached in and patted Gail Hammond's shoulder. After that, he walked back into his garage, and the door closed behind him.

I said, "There's no way they're sleeping together. He's ninety-one."

"You'd be surprised what a ninety-one-year-old man can do."

"Is this phase three? Revealing our sexual past?"

Leela laughed. "My knowledge on old man sex is strictly clinical."

"You have a weird job."

Gail Hammond backed into the alley and pulled forward. I waited a few seconds, then followed.

Leela said, "We're not going to visit Uncle David?"

"I'd rather see where Gail Hammond is going."

She headed back toward the neighborhood's only exit, then turned north. A few minutes later, she turned left toward the water and a few minutes after that, parked her car in front of a row of townhomes that looked like they'd been built in the 1980s and not updated since other than freshly painted front doors, each a different color as if there were a filing system for the types of people who lived behind them. Gail exited her Jaguar wearing a black dress with black shoes, a black purse over one shoulder, her unnaturally blond hair combed back and held in place by some unseen force.

Leela said, "She's dressed head to toe in Chanel." I gave her a curious look and she said, "I have a client who wears nothing but and it's her favorite topic of conversation. Gail Hammond is walking around in twenty thousand dollars right now."

I said, "Maybe that's how the rich mourn."

Gail Hammond approached a townhouse with a red door and rang the bell.

Leela said, "Think she's visiting a lover?"

"Could be. Or the trigger man."

"Could be one and the same."

I said, "You must watch a lot of Scandinavian crime dramas on Netflix."

"I do."

"Me too."

Gail Hammond rung the doorbell a second time.

Leela said, "Maybe we can figure out how to sync up Netflix and get on the phone so we can watch Scandinavian crime dramas together from our respective homes."

"They did that in *When Harry Met Sally*, only it was regular TV not Netflix so they didn't have to sync the pictures."

Leela grabbed my hand. "Do you like *When Harry Met Sally*?"

"I love that movie. But be warned, it is the only romantic comedy I love."

"Not *Say Anything*?"

"Okay, those are the only two romantic comedies I love."

"What about *The Sure Thing*?"

"Okay, those are the only three—"

The townhouse door opened. Gail Hammond walked inside. A woman stuck her head out, panned the street for a second, and went back inside, shutting the door behind her.

Leela said, "Is that the woman we met last night? Virginia?"

"It is."

"And she works for your uncle David?"

"She does."

Leela said, "Virginia makes way more sense for a lover than Uncle David."

20

Leela and I returned to the hospital but stopped short of entering my father's room when we heard him say, "This was Halloween of '77." He still carried photographs in his wallet and might have been the only living person who did. "Bess is the Statue of Liberty—she's ten here. Greta is Princess Leia—she's eight. And little Joey is Luke Skywalker. And this is Joey holding up his first speckled trout. He owns a big fashion jewelry company now. He's really done well for himself. And talk about nice kids—best grandchildren a guy could ask for."

A woman said, "You're a lucky man, Dr. Green, having kids and grandkids like that. I'm going to change out your IV now. Is that okay with you?"

"Sure, if you put a shot of bourbon in there."

"Never heard that one before, Dr. Green. But I'll see what I can find in the doctors' lockers."

I led Leela into the room. My father looked over and said, "Joey! This is a nice surprise."

He looked at Leela, and I saw the confusion on his face. I said, "Dad, this is Leela, Ted and Kajal's daughter. She's visiting from Boston."

"Nice to meet you, Leela."

"Nice to meet you, Dr. Green."

My father smiled at me. "I like her."

"Me too. Hey, Mom should be here in about an hour."

"Does she know why I'm in the hospital?"

"She does, Dad. You had a transient ischemic attack."

"A stroke?"

"A tiny one. But the EMTs showed up right away."

He shook his head. "Aw, Joey. Once a patient has a stroke . . . Hell, I saw it hundreds of times."

"They've made a lot of progress since you retired, Dad. There are new anticoagulants and treatments."

He shook his head. "Eh."

The nurse said, "He's right, Dr. Green. More and more people are walking out of this hospital every day. Damn drugs are getting so good, they're going to put me out of business."

The nurse laughed, but my father did not. It must be hard for a doctor to get old and sick. They know too much about what's happening. When my sisters and I were kids, our father would tell us about his patients. About the perils of not taking care of yourself. Diabetes with its injections and amputations and blindness. Heart disease dropping people in the middle of a Sunday walk. Morbid obesity causing people's organs to flat out quit. And he'd tell us about the irony of taking care of yourself and getting sick anyway. The long-distance runner who died of lung cancer having never smoked a cigarette in her life. The young father of three who came in feeling run down and died four months later of colon cancer. The beautiful young college student ravaged by lupus.

He'd often end these stories with this: "Well, we all got to die of something." Maybe that's how he distanced himself from the awesome responsibility of diagnosing and treating the sick. Or simply stating the inevitability we all face. It's an easy thing to say, but being the subject of "we all got to die of something" is another matter. That's what I'd just seen on his face, and it broke my heart.

I said, "Dad, they're keeping you one night for observation. What can I get you from the house?"

He looked at me with utter blankness, as if he couldn't understand the question, or was trying to inventory his belongings and was unable to do so. He finally looked away and said, "Your mother will know what to bring."

The nurse finished changing his IV and left the room after reminding him of the call button.

With a vacant look in his eyes he said, "I made hospital rounds for forty-five years. I know how it works."

"My bad, Dr. Green. Of course you do."

The nurse left, and my father shut his eyes.

Leela and I were holding hands when my mother walked in. She noticed but didn't acknowledge it. I'm sure she wanted to celebrate her matchmaking but wouldn't gift herself even a smile. She looked better after getting sun and exercise and went straight to my father and said, "I hear you've been telling stories to the nurses."

"Have I?" said my father.

"Yes." She leaned over and kissed the top of his head.

"Are you taking me home now?"

"Not now, Marshall. Tomorrow. They want to keep an eye on you overnight. So do I. They're bringing in a rollaway so I can spend the night here with you. Joey, why don't you take a break for a few hours. I'll go home during dinner to get some things."

I let go of Leela's hand, approached my father, and said, "Dad, did you know your wife won her pickleball tournament in Florida?"

"No kidding?"

"She's still got it."

He nodded and smiled.

"Leela," said my mother, "please say hello to your parents for me. And thank them for all they've done. And . . ." Her eyes widened and her head nodded just enough to express *are you two for real?*

Leela smiled and said, "Welcome home, Carol."
I found Leela's hand, and we left the room.

On the drive home, I called my great-uncle David and told him
about my father's stroke. Uncle David said, "Well, that's just a
shame, Joey. Most of our family gets a free pass until they turn
eighty. It's not fair Marshall's had so many health challenges at
his age."

I said, "I'm with my friend Leela Bellerose. You've met Ted and
Kajal. Leela's their daughter and she's visiting from Boston. We're
just leaving the hospital and I'm showing her Beaufort. Thought
she might want to see the water from your dock. Is it okay if we
park behind the house and walk down?"

A southern gentleman would not deny my request or his opportunity to display his southern hospitality. Twenty minutes
later, Leela and I stood on the dock with Uncle David playing
tour guide. He used his unlit cigar, the mouth-end dark and wet,
to point out landmarks across the river. He explained how the tide
was coming in, and even pulled up the crab trap he'd chained to
his dock. He'd just baited it with a piece of chicken that morning,
and explained that when he caught a crab, he removed one claw
for his consumption then returned the crab to the water so it could
grow a new claw.

"Spontaneous regeneration," said Uncle David. "They've been
trying to figure it out in humans for decades. Imagine, getting
your legs blown off then getting an injection of stem cells or some
other kind of genetic kickstarter and you grow a new pair of legs.
It'll happen one day—mark my words."

He was dressed in what we'd seen him wearing earlier in the
alley with Gail Hammond. Navy slacks and a checked sport shirt
of green and white that probably had a label in the collar from
Marshall Fields before it sold its soul to Macy's or Abercrombie &
Fitch before it sold its soul to the Limited. Everything about Uncle
David was pressed and tucked-in, encapsulating the past.

A shrimp boat motored near the dock, a nucleus to encircling sea gulls. Leela walked to the end of the boards to have a closer look.

I said, "I talked to the police this morning. They didn't mention you. Just thought you should know."

"Oh, that. Joey. Turns out I spoke prematurely. The Hammonds firing me was just a bit of bluster. They never hired another firm. Gail Hammond has consulted with me on matters of insurance and property since Thomas's death. I asked her directly if she wanted me to send her files on to another lawyer, and she said that wouldn't be necessary. She would continue to retain my services."

"Congratulations. Your reputation remains impeccable."

"I wouldn't go that far, but a fella can hope. And I'd appreciate it if you kept our conversation between us. Think of it as a family matter. A family matter that we keep in the family."

Leela had seen enough of the shrimp boat and had started back toward us. I will never forget that image, watching her approach, framed by water, marsh, and sky. Everything in my field of vision looked perfect.

Uncle David said, "Do you understand what I'm saying, Joey?"

I heard he was talking but didn't catch a word he said.

"Joey? Are you with me, son?"

I returned to earth and looked at my great-uncle. He'd put on a pair of sunglasses. Translucent caramel horn rims with green lenses. I said, "Sorry. Can you say that one more time?"

"You will keep our conversation yesterday between the two of us. I'd hate to think word might get out that my employment with the Hammonds was in jeopardy."

I had a lot of questions for my elderly uncle. Like why the Hammonds had fired him before Thomas's death and why Gail had reversed the decision. And why she was at his house that morning. But all I said was, "Of course. The conversation will remain between us."

"That's a good boy, Joey. I knew I could depend on you."

"Such beautiful scenery," said Leela, the dock squeaking as she walked. "What a privilege you get to see this every day."

"Yes, ma'am," said Uncle David. "I have lived in Beaufort my entire ninety-one years. And every single time I look out on that marsh I thank God for its beauty. Do you know it's never looked the same twice? Everything's in motion. The sky. The water. The birds. The plant life. The sun, the moon, the stars. It is a painting that's ever-changing. It takes my breath away each time I look out upon it. And you, Ms. Bellerose, y'all are welcome on this dock anytime. No need to call. No need to knock on the door. Just park on the left side of the driveway and walk on out."

"That's pretty good," I said. "I never got that offer."

"You're family, Joey. That offer is your birthright." He put a hand on my shoulder. "Now, you give Marshall my best. Tell him I'll visit him at the house tomorrow. I do not visit hospitals anymore. They all try to admit me." He laughed at his joke and put his unlit cigar in the back of his teeth and looked out at the water. And I thought, do I even know this man?

21

I parked in front of Ted and Kajal's house and kissed Leela goodbye as if I'd never see her again. The sea air wafted from her hair. It was the first time I'd kissed her since telling her the truth about dropping the gun into the river, and I felt an intensity from her I hadn't imagined possible.

Life has its moments of truth. Pillars that rise from an otherwise flat landscape. You can see them. Touch them. And no matter which way you turn, you can look back and know they are still there. They do not fade from the landscape or your memory. They can't. They are too beautiful. Too horrible. Too irrefutable. Sitting in my parents' car, looking into Leela's eyes, my hands on her brown shoulders, I knew I could spend the rest of my life with Leela Bellerose. I'd met her four days ago. It's impossible to know someone after only four days and yet, my heart knew something my brain couldn't yet understand.

The gift of middle age is the life behind you. The years you've lived and what they've taught you. I was never under any delusion that Leela Bellerose was perfect. I was sure I'd discover habits of hers that annoyed me, communication challenges between us, family dynamics that made me uncomfortable. Those kinds of obstacles are unavoidable. Forty-six years had taught me that much.

She said, "Where are you right now?"

"I'm here. With you."

"You left for a few seconds."

"Ah. Probably. I was thinking about you."

"Good things?"

"The best things."

"All right, sir. That's what I wanted to hear. Extra points for you."

She smiled her warm smile, and I felt I might cry. Something happened to me on that trip. Something broke inside and out. Crushed my shell and shattered my bones. Maybe it was meeting Leela. Maybe it was seeing my father deteriorate before my eyes. Maybe it was all of it and more.

Leela said, "Are you all right?"

"Damn you, Leela Bellerose. Damn you, damn you, damn you."

She knew what I meant, and kissed me again.

I spotted a chameleon on a tree in front of the house and texted a picture of it to my kids with the caption *Any name suggestions for my new friend?* then walked into the house and found Ruby in the laundry room removing a load of clothes from the dryer and dropping them into a laundry basket. She rushed to me and wrapped me in her arms.

"I heard about Mr. Marshall. I pray he's okay."

"He is, Ruby. Thank you."

"My niece works at the hospital. She told me. It's against the rules, but I'm practically family."

"Not practically, Ruby. You are family. And it's much appreciated, but you don't need to fold clothes. I know how to do laundry."

"Oh, yes, I do. Marshall and his parents have always taken care of me and mine. I can do my old job for a few minutes to repay the favor. My mother brought your father into this world. I'm just doing my part to keep him here."

I joined Ruby at the table, plucked T-shirts from the basket, and started folding.

Ruby said, "Give me that. Men don't know how to fold T-shirts. They come out all different shapes and sizes. Might as well not even fold them at all."

"I can live with different shapes and sizes."

She shook her head and tears came. "Your father having a stroke, I just can't stop thinking about him. How when we were kids, he was so good to us. Even before he fell in love with Delphi. Does he ever talk about her?"

"No. Except when he's hallucinating. I'd never heard of her before this trip."

"I've been dying to ask that question. I can't ask your mother because if the answer is no, then I'd have to explain the whole thing. And even though Marshall and Delphi were an item long before he met your mother, learning about those two might make her uncomfortable."

I shook my head. "I'm so sorry about what happened."

Ruby took my misshapen T-shirts and began to refold them. She had stopped working for my family thirty years ago. She owned her own business. But she'd come over to help because she loved my family, so I stopped fighting her on the T-shirts. She said, "This thing that happened to Thomas Hammond, someone shooting him dead, I think that might just be karma paying back the Hammond family."

"Because you suspect Roy Hammond killed Delphi?"

"More than suspect. I'm going to tell you something, Joey, but you have to promise not to breathe a word of it to anyone else. I haven't even told Lawrence. Nor your father. No one. You promise me?"

"I promise."

"Day before Delphi was found under the bridge in that gill net, she told me Roy Hammond was going to kill her. And it wasn't some supernatural premonition—Roy told her he was going to kill her. Used those very words. Said if she wouldn't do what he wanted, she wouldn't be doing anything. We were just kids. Sixteen years old. I believed Delphi. She wouldn't make up something like that. But I didn't take her as seriously as I should have because every day's a threat to black people. And Roy Hammond was just another threat. His family was rich and powerful, and if Delphi had reported him to the police, they wouldn't have done anything about it. We had less power then than we do today. Not that we have much now. When we were out in public, we did not make eye contact with white people. Just 'yes, sir,' 'no, ma'am,' and 'thank you for your kindness.' That's how black folk stayed safe in the 1950s."

Ruby finished refolding the T-shirts, then returned to what remained in the basket. I took her hand and held it, the same hand that I once reached up for as a small boy when she walked me down to the waterfront. She said, "Delphi made me promise I wouldn't tell a soul because if Lawrence or your daddy heard about Roy Hammond's threat, they were likely to do something that would ruin their futures. Lawrence was top of his class and headed for college. That was something for a young black man in 1959. And your daddy, everyone knew he was headed to do great things. 'Cause see, if either of them heard about Roy Hammond saying he was going to kill Delphi, the only thing they could do to stop it would be kill Roy Hammond. The police wouldn't listen to either of them. A black boy and a Jewish boy. Lawrence and your daddy got along with everyone just fine back then as long as they kept in their place. That's the way it was. Stay in your place and we'll all get along just fine. A lot of folks think it's that way now."

Ruby squeezed my hand, then let it go so she could continue folding. I poured her a glass of iced tea and opened her tin of praline cookies.

She thanked me for the tea, then said, "What I should have done was put Delphi on a bus out of town." Ruby's words echoed my father's hallucination when he imagined himself talking to Delphi. I wondered if he'd known about Roy Hammond's threat. "But I didn't even consider putting her on a bus back then. Like

I said, we lived with a constant threat of violence. And Beaufort was all we knew. We never went anywhere. Never visited Savannah or Charleston. Our world was so small.

"And Delphi wouldn't have left anyway. She was so in love. At least she got to experience love. I thank the Lord for that. It's the gift Delphi gave to me and Lawrence, finding love. We fell for each other in the dark time after Delphi's murder and never let go of each other. Maybe it's our way of honoring her memory. We have our share of arguments. But we never let them damage us. Always talk it out right then and there. Like when there's a weak pillar on the pier. Got to fix it right away before the whole thing collapses into the sea."

I said, "Who else knew Delphi and my father were in love with each other?"

"Well, back in the day," said Ruby, "our family, the Wallaces, knew. And Lawrence's family, the Hills, knew. This was when I was a Wallace and hadn't yet married into the Hill family."

"How did the families find out Delphi was dating a white boy in the first place? Why did my father have to step forward and tell the Hills it was him?"

Ruby sipped her tea, looked down, and said, "That's my fault. I shouldn't have told anyone. I was shrimping, just wading a creek when the tide was halfway in and the shrimp come with it to feed. I was throwing my net and filling my bucket when that fisherman drifted up to the grass and used a pole to push himself in. He was just a boy then. Couldn't have been more than eight years old."

"There are a lot of fisherman in this town, Ruby."

"But you know this one. He and your daddy have been friends for years."

"Bubba?"

"Of course, Bubba. Who did you think I was talking about? Anyway, he used a long pole to push himself into the grass. Just disappeared boat and all. I was probably a hundred feet away or so. A minute later, he pushed himself out. Only now he had Delphi in the boat. I saw her for just a second before she ducked down. But it was her. We were best friends. You spend all your time with someone, you can recognize them from far away. Just the shape of their head or the way they hold their shoulders. It was Delphi all right."

"And Bubba was only eight?"

"I think so. He's a big boy so it was hard to tell, but I knew Delphi wasn't sneaking off for romance with a little boy. But she'd been acting like she was in love. You know, like her feet barely touched the ground. The next few weeks, I would follow her sometimes. I'd stay far enough back so if she spotted me I could just say I was out for a walk or headed to the store or something. Thing was, I didn't need to get close to know where she was going 'cause she went to the same place every time. That spot at the water. Didn't need to be a genius to figure out what was going on. That boy Bubba, he was her water taxi, taking her to meet her beau. He'd bring her back, too. Had to before the tide went out too far and their meeting spot was nothing but grass and mud."

"How'd you know Bubba was taxiing Delphi to see my father?"

"I didn't. I told Lawrence I suspected his sister was seeing a white boy. He confronted Delphi, and that family tore itself apart. They knew the town wouldn't have it. Certain people, they'd make Delphi's life impossible. Delphi wouldn't name the boy, but her parents laid down the law and forbid her from dating him. Then Marshall stepped forward to say they were in love. He promised to marry Delphi and they'd move to New York where they could live a respectable life and no one would bother them.

"Delphi and Lawrence's parents knew your father's family well. Delphi's father would take care of the yard and your grandmother would bring him iced tea and lemonade and those snickerdoodles everybody loved. Not just on hot days, but every day. And another thing, your grandparents invited black folks working at the house inside to use the restroom. That was unheard of around here in the 1950s."

"My grandparents were nice people."

"They sure were. But that's not the reason I'm telling you this.

I'm telling you this so you understand that Delphi dating just any old white boy was unacceptable. But Delphi dating your daddy was another story. Your daddy is a special man."

The doorbell rang. I excused myself, walked into the hallway leading to the foyer, and saw two figures standing on the front porch.

22

I opened the front door.

My great-uncle David said, "Joey, you remember Gail Hammond. We'd like a moment of your time if you can spare it."

Gail Hammond wore the same black outfit I'd seen her wear at Virginia's townhouse, but up close I could see she'd painted her nails a metallic pearl white, and whatever was on her lips had a translucent sheen of white as well. Her hair verged on platinum, and the makeup on her face sparkled in the late afternoon light. The diamond studs in her ears and the diamond pendant on her bronzed breastbone must have totaled five karats. She dressed as if she were in mourning, but accessorized as if she were celebrating.

I gave Gail my condolences and invited them in. When Uncle David saw that Ruby was there, he asked that she join us. "This concerns you and Lawrence as well," he said. "We've tried to contact him today but haven't had any luck."

Ruby said, "He's out at the fish camp. He'll be back late today."

I could see the question in Ruby's eyes. *What the hell does this have to do with us?* But she wouldn't talk that way to my great-uncle. She wasn't as comfortable with him as she was with my grandparents and parents. Instead she said, "How can Lawrence and I help, Mr. Green?"

Beverages were offered and declined, and the four of us sat in the living room.

Uncle David said, "I have represented the Hammonds in their real estate business for the past thirty-five years. Another firm represents their personal affairs. Nevertheless, years and years ago, Thomas Hammond gave me a letter to be opened in the event of his death. So I opened it to discover a handwritten will using proper legal language and it's notarized. The will deals with some assets that were in Thomas's name only. Assets he'd acquired before marrying Gail.

"Since Thomas's brother, Roy, passed away, Thomas was the only heir to a significant portfolio of cash, equities, and properties. Many of those he's developed with Gail, but others have remained undeveloped. The reason we're here is because, in his personal will, Thomas Hammond bequeathed a parcel of land to Marshall and Carol Green."

No, that wasn't possible. I must have misheard my great-uncle. I asked him to repeat himself. He did. I hadn't misheard. I said, "Why would he do that? I got the impression Thomas Hammond and my father were not the best of friends."

Gail said, "Thomas always spoke highly of your father." Her posture was too upright. Too formal. Gail Hammond was selling something. "But as to why Thomas would leave Marshall a plot of land, I can't answer that question. I had no idea what was in my husband's personal will. Nor did I know a personal will existed. I'm as surprised as you are, Joey."

"In addition," said Uncle David, "Thomas left a plot of land to Lawrence and Ruby Hill."

"I'm sorry," said Ruby, her face contorted with disbelief. "What did you say?"

Uncle David said, "Thomas Hammond left land to you and Lawrence."

"Why would he do that? We didn't know the man."

"I wish I could tell you, Ruby, but Thomas never shared his thinking with me."

"Or me," said Gail, her voice cold, her eyes distant.

Something wasn't right. Maybe everything wasn't right. Gail Hammond shouldn't have been there. She wasn't Santa Claus, dropping into people's homes to bestow gifts.

I said, "Hold on a minute. Let me get this straight. Thomas Hammond had a secret will in addition to his regular will?"

"That is correct," said Uncle David. "I am not the executor of the estate, but I am responsible for overseeing the transfer of some assets that belonged to Thomas Hammond only. The reason we're here now, informing you in person, is because Gail wants to purchase both plots of land."

I said, "It's not my land to sell."

"That is correct. But your father is not of sound mind to make financial decisions, and your mother is busy worrying about your father and rightfully so. That's why we're appealing to you, Joey. You and your sisters can convince your parents it's in their best interest to sell the land to Gail. Doing so will generate the cash to ensure your father has the long-term care he needs. Money won't be an issue when considering a memory care facility. Even before that day comes, your mother will be able to hire full-time help to reduce the tremendous burden on her."

Ruby said, "This is not real. I just don't believe it."

"It's very real, Ruby." Uncle David handed her a sheet of paper. And another to me. "We're offering you money that will change all y'all's lives. I hope you'll talk it over with Lawrence tonight. We'd like to close this deal in a day or two."

Ruby read the number on the piece of paper and screamed. I looked down at the sheet Uncle David had handed me. Gail Hammond had offered my parents two million dollars for the land they'd inherited from her dead husband. I looked up to see Ruby's big eyes full of questions and excitement, but I tried to act like two million dollars was no big deal. I was the victim of my experience in business—keep negotiations and transactions free of emotion. Never let the opposition inside your head.

I said, "These must be important plots of land."

Gail said, "I'm offering the assessed value plus twenty percent. You won't get that offer from anyone else because the land is virtually worthless without the adjacent properties. And those, I do own." She forced a smile. "Congratulations. Both of your families are now quite wealthy."

23

I called Leela half an hour before picking her up to tell her we were meeting Ruby and Lawrence for dinner. Leela wore a pale blue dress that draped her brown skin. I had a hard time keeping my eye on the road as I told her about my conversation with Ruby, starting with Roy Hammond's threat to Delphi and ending with the unexpected visit from Uncle David and Gail Hammond and her offer to buy the parcels of land her murdered husband had given away.

Leela said, "Do you think Thomas Hammond knew his brother killed Delphi, and he left the land to your father and the Hills as some kind of reparation?"

We had just arrived at the hospital to visit my father while my mother went home to gather some overnight things. I would tell her about the offer when she returned.

I said, "I think that's exactly why Thomas Hammond gave away those parcels of land."

"It doesn't make up for a human life, but I suppose it's something."

"Or it's motive."

"Motive?" said Leela.

"I'm worried the police will somehow think my father knew about the will. Or that Lawrence did. And that gave both of them an incentive to kill Thomas Hammond."

"Gail Hammond didn't even know about her husband's other will. How would your father or Lawrence have known about it?"

"No idea. I'm just worried how the police will perceive it."

We didn't have to wait long to find out. When we walked into my father's hospital room, Detective Chantal Cooper and Officer Doyle were there talking to my mother. She looked ashen, as if my father had died. But he hadn't. He lay on his back, sound asleep.

"Oh, Joey," said my mother. "The police think your father's gun was used to kill Thomas Hammond."

"We don't think it, ma'am," said Detective Cooper, "forensics has confirmed that the bullet that killed Thomas Hammond was fired by your father's gun."

I said, "Where's Selena Cruz? Why isn't she here?"

Officer Doyle said, "We don't need Selena Cruz to talk to your mother."

My mother walked to my father and sat on the foot of his bed. "Joey, tell them your father would never hurt anyone."

Leela went to my mother, slid a chair next to her, sat and took her hand. "Ignore them, Carol. Marshall wasn't involved and they know it."

I said, "The gun was stolen from the garage, Mom. They're just desperate to pin Thomas Hammond's murder on someone because tourist season is about to explode and they're afraid Beaufort will be known as the murder town."

Officer Doyle said, "Mr. Green, this is a serious situation. Please don't make light of it. We have a confirmed murder weapon that belonged to your father and there are three hours where he wasn't supervised."

"What?" said my mother.

She looked at me with an expression I'd learned before I could walk. An expression I tried to avoid my entire life. A mother's disappointment. A syringe full of shame injected into my heart. I fought its effect by mustering a salesman's bravado and explained that I'd left the house to continue my date with Leela, making sure both doors were locked. A lie I worried my mother could sniff out.

Her response: "Oh, Joey." That's all she had to say.

Officer Doyle said, "The hours Dr. Green was left unsupervised coincide with the victim's time of death. So don't talk about us like we're the mayor in *Jaws* who's looking for just any shark to blame. Your father isn't just any shark. He strongly disliked the Hammonds, had opportunity, and owns the gun that killed Thomas Hammond. Now, we are sensitive to his health concerns."

"Which is why you're in his hospital room just after he had a stroke." I couldn't help myself.

Leela pulled out her phone and held it up, the camera lens pointing at the police officers.

Detective Cooper saw this and said, "Ma'am, would you please put down your phone?"

Leela said, "I have a First Amendment right to video a public employee doing their job."

Officer Doyle exhaled something between frustration and contempt and said, "Like I said, we're sensitive to Dr. Green's health challenges. Physical and mental. That's why we're treading lightly here. And that's why we're going to bring Selena Cruz back to interview your father about his relationship with Thomas Hammond. You may want to have a lawyer present."

"Joey . . ." said my mother. "Make them stop, please."

"I looked at Officers Cooper and Doyle and said, "Can we take a walk?"

"I'm not a lawyer. I'm not a cop. I'm not a private detective. I'm not a reporter. But I have enough common sense to know there's a reason you haven't arrested my father yet." We sat in the hospital cafeteria with bad coffee and stale donuts. "I mean, if you had a witness or fingerprints or something at the crime scene, we wouldn't be sitting here, would we?"

Detective Cooper washed down a bite of desert-dry donut and said, "Mr. Green, we're just doing our jobs—"

"No, no. Don't rewrite history to make this sound like a routine investigation. You just told us to get a lawyer. For all I know you would have arrested my father by now if he wasn't in the hospital. Police in general haven't had the best PR lately—maybe you or your DA are just a little sensitive to the optics here."

Detective Cooper said, "What would you do if you were in our position? One of our most prominent citizens gets shot to death walking at night. No witnesses. No cars seen or heard in the area. No shouts. No sign of a struggle. Someone just walked up to him and shot him. No powder burns near the entry point so we know he didn't shoot himself and someone else walked off with the gun. We have the murder weapon. It belongs to your father. No one else in your family can account for how the gun went missing."

"Where'd you find it?"

"We can't answer that at this time."

"Why not? Maybe you pulled over a drunk driver and they had the gun. Maybe you found it in some azaleas near the crime scene. Maybe someone else found the gun months ago and turned it in and you can't explain how it was used to kill Thomas Hammond because it was in police possession. Or maybe the crime scene people made a mistake. Maybe that wasn't the gun used. Maybe it was a similar gun. Maybe you have no real evidence and you're just hoping you can bully a man with Lewy Body Dementia into a confession because he can't even understand the situation he's in much less the gravity of it."

"Mr. Green, we're not the enemy here."

"I never said you were. What I am saying is my father is dying. Dying of a terrible disease. He has no short-term memory. He's going to wake up in that hospital bed and have no idea why he's there. My mother will have to tell him, probably for the tenth time today. And I'm going to tell you why he's there for the second time today. The stress of your questioning this morning triggered his stroke. The doctor said after one stroke there will be more. So harassing him is not an option. My father dedicated his life to helping people. He's been a good husband and father. But you want to take a life well lived, honorably lived, decently lived, and destroy it. And destroy my mother in the process. All because you have a hunch. It's not even a hunch—that word implies you have some sort of skill or intuition. You have a guess. Nothing more than a guess, really, that my father shot Thomas Hammond."

Officer Doyle said, "We truly are just doing our jobs, Mr. Green. Sorry that's so hard for you to accept. We understand. He's your father. But we're not the ones who left him alone for three hours."

"He was locked in the house."

"Are you telling me if we got a warrant right now and combed that entire house we wouldn't find a key to those deadbolts stashed somewhere? Maybe in a junk drawer or a sock drawer or up on top of the door frame in case there's a fire? And can you prove you locked both the front and back doors while you were visiting your friend from Boston? Is there a security system log we can check? No, there isn't. You cannot prove the doors were locked."

Detective Cooper said, "We're not trying to destroy an innocent person's life, Mr. Green. We're trying to find out who killed Thomas Hammond. And it doesn't help matters that your father has inherited a valuable piece of property from Mr. Hammond's estate. I can see you know about that."

I couldn't hide it. I was worried they'd see the land inheritance as motive, and that's exactly what happened. I said, "I just found out. Is that why you're here? To ask my dad if he knew about it?"

"Partly, yes."

"Even though he has no memory."

"He has no short-term memory. Thomas Hammond left that piece of property to your father in a will dated in 1981. And your father seems to have no problem remembering 1981."

I said, "So what did he say when you asked him?"

"We haven't asked him. He's been asleep since we arrived."

"Oh. That's your plan. Establish that Thomas Hammond told

my father about putting him in his will in the '80s so my father could carefully plot and bide his time for the perfect moment to wander outside during a thunderstorm, shoot Thomas Hammond, and then go toss the gun in the secret place where you found it. He was a real genius to wait over forty years until he suffered from Lewy Body Dementia. A real patient murderer, my dad. Good luck with that theory. And from this point forward, you will not talk to him without a lawyer present. I'll let you know when I hire one."

I got up, leaving my coffee and petrified donut.

Detective Cooper said, "No, Mr. Green. We'll let you know when we're going to talk to him. It'll be your job to get the lawyer there."

24

The police left the hospital. I texted Bubba to see if he was available to guide me the following day, then met my mother in the room and said she should go home, get her things, and not worry about the police. She did the first two—the third was impossible. My father woke while she was gone, and I explained that he was in the hospital and why. I introduced him to Leela. Again. When I said she was Ted and Kajal's daughter, I could see him struggle to remember who they were.

My father had met Ted and Kajal four years ago, before he'd been diagnosed with Lewy Body Dementia. The disease was eating its way backward. Memory loss is like cancer. It consumes the individual, but unlike with cancer, there is no hope of stopping it. Not yet, anyway. No chemo. No radiation. No surgery. Dementia just keeps eating away until there's nothing left to eat.

I said, "You remember Ted and Kajal next door. They're from Boston. Ted has that pair of Civil War swords in the living room."

The light returned to his eyes. He said, "Nice couple. The wife is from India."

"Yes. And Leela's their daughter."

My father winked at me and said, "She's pretty," as if she weren't there.

"You're such a flatterer," said Leela.

"Just call 'em like I see 'em."

My mother returned with an overnight bag, and my father perked up. He would never forget her. You could see it in his eyes. He remembered the first time he saw her. The first time they met. Their first kiss. Their love, marriage, and raising a family together. She filled him with life the way the world could no longer do.

Leela and I were about to leave when my mother said, "Not so fast. You haven't told me what happened with you two while I was in Florida."

We were holding hands again. I raised them and said, "Nothing much happened, I guess. We just fell madly in love with each other."

Leela burst into laughter.

And my mother, my poor mother, looked terribly confused. Leela broke first and said with a heavy dose of sincerity, "We really have hit it off. You and my mother did good." Leela leaned into me and put her head on my shoulder.

My father said, "That's the way a guy should look, Joey. The way you look right now."

25

Leela and I met Ruby and Lawrence at 10 Market, a foodie restaurant a few minutes' drive away in Habersham. We spotted them standing at the bar. Ruby held a glass of white wine—Lawrence a lowball of bourbon. I expected to find them in a festive mood. Ruby had screamed when she saw the two-million-dollar figure on Gail Hammond's offer. Screamed like she'd just been called down on *The Price Is Right*. But her celebratory mood had yielded to what looked like dread.

The host led us toward a table with a view of the water and moored boats just off the property. It was a beautiful setting for an ugly topic of conversation.

Lawrence waited until we ordered drinks, then said, "Thomas Hammond has confirmed what we've suspected. His big brother killed my little sister. Ruby's best friend. The girl Marshall Green loved. The land Thomas left us—that's blood money. He's trying to buy forgiveness for his family. I'll be damned if I give it to him."

Ruby watched her husband with reverence and love.

Leela said, "What are you saying? Are you going to turn down Gail Hammond's offer?"

"Not turn down," said Lawrence. "Counter. I have a friend in the county clerk's office. He looked up the plots of land Thomas Hammond left us and your parents. Get this: they are adjacent to one another and on the bridge end of Hammond Island. Without those two parcels of land or our permission, no one can access the island via automobile. That makes the whole development contingent on Gail Hammond acquiring our parcels. I say if they want to buy us off with blood money, it's going to cost more."

I placed my napkin in my lap and said, "Do you think Thomas Hammond leaving those parcels is all blood money? I mean, it's kind of a fuck-you to Gail, isn't it? He could have just left you and my parents the money in cash or stocks."

"Yeah, I wondered about that," said Lawrence. He sipped from his lowball and put it down. "I agree, leaving us those specific parcels of land really stuck it to Gail. Or at least him doing so allows us to stick it to Gail. And that's what we plan to do. Ruby and I are countering the offer at four million. Firm. Take it or leave it. If they leave it, we're open to a lease-back of the land so they can use it. But we're not parting with it for a mere two million. I know two million is life-changing money, but not life-changing enough. Not for the life of my sister. I'll talk to your mother. The negotiation will go much better if we work as a team."

Lawrence was right, but I wasn't so sure countering at double the offer was in everyone's best interest. I kept that to myself for the moment. For Lawrence and Ruby, this wasn't about numbers—it was about Delphi.

Ruby said, "We could do a lot of good with four million dollars. Send all our grandkids to college. Help our kids buy better homes. Thomas Hammond left us a generous gift, but there's a darkness in it. A real shadow. Makes Delphi's murder feel like it was yesterday. The hurt had dulled but now it's sharp again. Razor sharp. Damn." She placed a hand on Lawrence's shoulder.

Leela said, "As a psychologist, I find Thomas leaving that land to you and the Greens fascinating. What did you two think of Thomas Hammond?"

Lawrence said, "Didn't know him, really. Met him only once at a school fundraiser. But from what I did know, I could tell he wasn't evil like his brother, Roy. Thomas wasn't a narcissistic sociopath. He wasn't a violent man. Problem is he never stood up to his family. Even after they were all dead. Just kept going along to get along. I'd say the worst thing about Thomas Hammond: he was entitled the way a lot of rich folks are. They think being rich is their birthright even though they did nothing to earn it. Thomas Hammond pretended his family's wealth dropped out of the sky. But anyone who knows the history of this area understands the Hammond family amassed their wealth on the backs of slaves and have maintained it by robbing and cheating and exploiting the people.

"Just thinking about it makes me want to counter at six million so Ruby and I could donate two million to Beaufort Public Schools. Help educate the people so the Hammonds of the world can't take advantage of them."

Leela said, "So leaving the land to you and the Greens was his only act of defiance against his family?"

"As far as I know."

"That's sad," said Leela. "If Thomas had given away some wealth when he was alive it would have been a redeeming experience for him. He must have lacked the courage to do it. It's too bad."

Ruby said, "Maybe he was afraid of Gail."

Leela said, "You think Gail intimidated Thomas like his family did? Maybe that's why he married her—the dynamic felt familiar to him."

"Not because Gail was his wife," said Ruby, "but because Gail was his family. I'm talking before they married. Gail didn't even have to change her name. Thomas Hammond and Gail Hammond are first cousins."

"What?" I said. "That can't be true. First cousins can't marry each other."

Lawrence said, "Oh, it's true. First cousins can marry in South Carolina. They can in plenty of states, including New York and California. Gail grew up in north Georgia. Her side of the family is in the bottled gas business. Filling folks' LP tanks who live out in the country. They do all right, but they don't have South Carolina Hammond money. If you haven't noticed, Gail likes the finer things in life. Travels to New York just to shop for clothes."

Leela said, "So Thomas screwing over Gail really is a departing shot at his family."

Ruby said, "You know, Thomas Hammond was engaged to Virginia a long time ago. I think he married Gail as a business consideration. They didn't marry until Gail was thirty and Thomas was fifty-five. Must have been some kind of consolidation of the family fortune. They never had kids. Thank God. Probably would have been born with three eyes and gills or something."

A team of servers brought our food, which allowed the conversation to lighten up from Delphi and the Hammonds to crab legs and broasted quail.

"I just had an idea," said Lawrence.

"Oh, good," said Ruby. "I like Lawrence's ideas."

They were still in love after almost six decades together. I glanced at Leela. Six decades with her wasn't possible. Not unless we lived to be centenarians. But four decades or five? That possibility felt like a miracle. She felt like a miracle. How strange that you didn't know someone a week ago and then days later think it unimaginable to go on without them. It was madness. The kind of madness that makes you feel alive.

"What do you think of this?" said Lawrence. "We counter Gail Hammond's offer at four million dollars firm, and she has to commission and donate a statue of Delphi to be installed at Waterfront Park." Lawrence's eyes shined for the second time that night. The first was when the server set down his order of short ribs.

Ruby said, "That's a beautiful thought, baby."

The conversation bounced around throughout dinner, but Ruby did her best to steer the topic back to Leela and me and our whirlwind romance. Neither Leela nor I denied it, and Ruby asked what we were going to do after going our separate ways next week. Leela looked at me for the answer. She had a big grin on her face.

"Uh-oh," said Lawrence. "Lady's looking at you. Pressure cooker, and I for one am grateful to have a front row seat."

I said, "I don't know. I guess we'll just give it our best shot. What else can we do?"

Leela told them the entire story. How we started our first date with a not-very-scientific experiment by telling each other the worst about ourselves, and joked how she might write a book about it for the millions of people out there trying find the right person. Or maybe even create a dating site with a long, tedious, repetitive questionnaire designed to force participants into telling the truth about their worst traits.

Lawrence smiled and said, "Your experiment doesn't have anything to do with anything. You two would have hit it off anyway."

"Maybe," said Leela, "but when you see the vulnerable side of a person on your first date instead of bravado and ego, it's pretty damn attractive."

Our server laid four dessert menus on the table. We ordered, then Ruby and Leela excused themselves to use the restroom. I had known Lawrence all my life. Socialized with him. Fished with him. I still kept in touch with his and Ruby's kids—two lived in D.C. and one lived in Atlanta. I was pretty sure Lawrence didn't have it in him to stalk and shoot a man, even a Hammond, and I was absolutely positive Lawrence would not frame my father by taking and then returning his pistol.

I said, "Have the police questioned you and Ruby?"

Lawrence nodded. "They know we have a key to your parents' house and garage."

"How did that go?"

"They asked where we were the night Thomas was shot, and we told them the truth—we were asleep in our condo all night. It's a security building with cameras on all doors. They said they'll check the footage to see if either of us left or returned to the building."

"But that doesn't prove you were in the building."

"No," said Lawrence. "But they know our cell phones were in

the building. They checked on that. Our cars, too. They both have satellite tracking so they can place them at our building at the time of the murder."

"Good. I'm sorry you and Ruby got dragged into this."

"It's ridiculous the police suspect Marshall. The man can barely walk down a flight of stairs."

I agreed, but that sick feeling rippled through me again.

Lawrence said, "It's a strange thing coming into life-changing money when you don't have that much life left." He drained the last of his bourbon, the ice clinging to the glass. "This whole business feels like when you hear about a soldier MIA, presumed dead, then decades later, the family gets the remains. They knew the soldier was dead. But getting confirmation still hurts. That's what Thomas Hammond leaving this land to us is like. God damn that Roy Hammond. I hope he got what was coming to him. Hope he just didn't run because the rumors caught up to him and now he's living life large in Europe or South America. Tell you what I really hope: I live long enough to find out that son of a bitch died a miserable death."

Lawrence wiped away a tear. And for the second time since I'd arrived in South Carolina, I felt a rush of sorrow so strong I began to cry. What had happened to my lack of empathy? I wrote it off to Lawrence feeling like family. The two of us sat there sniveling for half a minute before I said, "Okay, we got to get our shit together or people will think you took me to this nice restaurant to break up with me."

26

We left the restaurant and I still hadn't had a chance to tell my mother about the parcel of land she and my father inherited. Two million dollars would give her some peace of mind. She could hire a team of lawyers to defend my father if needed. She could post bail if he were arrested. She could put my father in the best memory care facility in the country if it came to that.

I kept telling myself the police would have arrested my father if they had any evidence. Or maybe they didn't arrest him because they weren't sure how to incarcerate someone with Lewy Body Dementia. Or maybe they just weren't worried about him going anywhere.

Leela and I returned to my parents' house. My mother was at the hospital for the night. I was in the kitchen pouring two large glasses of water when Leela called out from the foyer. "What's the story with this painting?"

"Which one?"

"The night one. *Carolina Moonset*. Is *moonset* even a word?"

"*Moonrise* is a word. Seems *moonset* should be one too." I walked into the foyer and handed her a glass of water.

She did not take her eyes off the painting. "This thing gives me the creeps."

"Yeah. It scared the crap out of me when I was a kid."

"Who painted it?"

"I don't know. There are a million artists in Beaufort. Always have been. Go into any gallery downtown and you'll see a hundred paintings of the marsh or the oaks or boats. This town has hogged a lot of paint."

"But what's the point of painting it at night?" said Leela. I kissed the back of her neck. She leaned into me but kept her eyes on the painting. "This doesn't feel like the kind of painting tourists buy. It's too morose. Usually the point of dark is to contrast it with some light like the white foam of breaking waves, or the white collar of a person in a Rembrandt painting."

"There's a light on in one of the windows of the house."

"But it's dark yellow. Almost like a shadow. There are no stars. There's barely even a moon." Leela tilted her head back, reached down with her left hand, pulled my hips into her and said, "This painting is about the darkest time. When you can't see any light. When you can't see a way out. When you're hopeless. It's fascinating."

"It's the only painting my parents have consistently hung since I was a kid. What do you think that means?"

My phone buzzed with a text from Bubba. *Full day or half day tomorrow?*

Half. Morning if it's available.

Sure is. Had a cancellation. You and Leela and Marshall?

Just Leela and me this time. Marshall had a micro stroke. He's fine, but he should rest up a bit.

So sorry to hear that. You give him my best. And I'll see you at the marina at 7:00.

"Girl back home?" said Leela.

"A little tart named Bubba."

"What? We have three more days together and you're going fishing again?" She said it with a smile on her face, a sense of play.

I kissed her and said, "I want to see you as much as possible in the next seventy-two hours."

"So you're not going fishing?"

I kissed her again. "I am."

She understood. "You want me to go fishing with you and Marshall again?"

"Just you and me. I have to ask Bubba about something that happened a long time ago, and I'd love it if you were there to help me."

She pulled back and studied me. Her eyes shined. "You mean, like we're a team?"

I considered her question and said, "Exactly like we're a team."

"I assume that means we have to get up early."

"We do."

"Then we'd better get to bed."

27

In the morning, I served coffee, poached eggs, toast, and fresh oranges from the tree out back. After breakfast, Leela went home to change for a morning on the water. My mother texted to say my father had no problems overnight and they would be home mid-morning. I said I'd be home shortly after lunch and that she shouldn't answer the door until we hired a defense attorney. I could hear the worry in her breath.

"Mom, you don't have to stress about the cost."

"Your father and I will not accept any money from you or the girls. Your money is for your children. Do you know how much college costs now?"

"Thomas Hammond left you and Dad some land in his will."

There was a pause. Then, "What? Why would he do that?"

"He left land to Ruby and Lawrence, too. Yesterday Uncle David came over with Gail Hammond, and she's offered to buy your land for two million dollars."

"Oh, that is not true."

"Call Uncle David. He'll present the offer to you. Lawrence did a little research and found out the parcels of land are crucial to the development of Hammond Island. He thinks Gail Hammond will pay more for them. A lot more."

She sounded as if I'd just told her they'd discovered life on Jupiter. "Does your father know about this?"

"No. I haven't told him yet."

"Okay. Well, it's the strangest thing I've ever heard, but it would bring some relief if it's true."

"Mom, I'm not lying to you."

"I suppose. It's just so . . . odd. I'll see you this afternoon."

I walked outside and saw it had rained overnight, leaving the streets shiny and puddled. The sky was blue with clouds amassed on the horizon for a possible attack in the late afternoon. I picked up Leela and we met Bubba at the marina. We motored north up to St. Helena Sound without saying much. I wondered if Bubba's silence was from worry about my father or if he somehow sensed the conversation coming his way.

Fishing was slow. Bubba blamed it on last night's rain and the high, blue sky. "Soon as these clouds move in, they'll start biting. I have coffee and cinnamon rolls. How about we fortify our strength before the big ones try to pull us out of the boat?"

We anchored off a sandbar where Bubba poured paper cups of steaming coffee from an industrial-looking Thermos and handed us waxed paper–wrapped cinnamon rolls each the size of a softball.

Bubba said, "From Ruby's. Had to buy 'em yesterday, but I swear they're as good the day after as they are the day they bake 'em. Hey, sorry we're getting skunked so far, but don't worry. We'll catch some fish. I have a reputation to protect."

Leela lifted her face toward the Carolina sky, her eyes hidden behind her aviator sunglasses, the green glass reflecting the gold sun. She said, "How long have you been guiding, Bubba?"

"Since before I could walk or talk. My momma worked a pulp mill in Georgia. My daddy guided fishermen. Neither could afford to take a day off or hire a babysitter. Couldn't take kids to a pulp mill, so it fell on my father. Hell, I was born in January, so I wasn't six months old when he took me and my older brother out. Not every day. Sometimes my grandmother would watch us if she could get a day off work. But a lot of days. He had this boat with a tiny two-person sleeper cabin. My brother and I would hang out in there, and when I got fussy, my father would strap me to his chest. I don't even think they had chest packs for babies back then. We're talking the 1950s. He probably made his own. I have memories of watching his hands right in front of my little face baiting hooks and taking off fish. Looking out at the water while he drove the boat."

Bubba pinched off a wad of cinnamon roll and stuck it in his mouth and followed it with a sip of coffee. He let it all melt down his throat, then said, "I swear the reason I know this water so well is because I learned it when babies can learn anything. I know every inlet and tidal creek and bay, know 'em the way I know how to talk. I don't even have to think about it. Clients all the time ask how come I don't have a GPS. How do I not get lost out here? They say every island, every sandbar, every landmark looks the same. And I say I don't need a machine to tell me what I already know. It would be like having a calculator to add two plus two. It's a waste of time just touching the buttons."

Leela said, "It's good to be an expert at something. Gives a person a sense of worth."

"Yes, ma'am," said Bubba.

I said, "When did you start guiding on your own?"

Bubba laughed, "Oh, let's just say if there were child labor laws back then, they didn't apply to me. My daddy had a problem with brown liquids. Half the days he couldn't even get out of bed before eleven A.M. Not good for a professional fisherman. My brother and I got to the point where we gave up trying to wake him and would just go out back and jump in the boat and meet the client at the marina ourselves. 'Course you can imagine, rich men from New York and Boston are down here on vacation dressed head to toe in the best garb, they see a ten-year-old and eight-year-old sitting in a boat rigged with rods and all ready to go, wearing rags or damn near nothing at all, well, let's just say a lot of 'em turned around shaking their heads and walked away.

But a few would give us a chance, and pretty soon, word spread we were just as good as our daddy if not better.

"And boy, did we get tips. Pretty soon it was Gerry and me working summers while my daddy drank 'em away. We turned every penny over to our momma. Well, almost every penny. We'd buy ourselves plenty of Moon Pies and Cokes and when we got a little older we developed a taste for beer. But we did damn well. Didn't much need my daddy anymore, but my momma kept him around anyways. Did so 'til the day he died. When I got old enough to get up the nerve to ask her why she didn't give him the boot, she said, 'Boys need a father.'"

Bubba went on to say that stopped being true when he was about six years old and told us more stories about his derelict father. That was the point, to get Bubba talking. Leela said it would go better that way instead of asking him out of the blue. Especially if he talked about how well he could navigate the water at a young age. The hope was he'd paint himself into a corner. Leela told me her clients did it to themselves all the time.

I felt the sugar and butter from the cinnamon roll. Felt it in my blood as if it were caffeine or alcohol. I listened to Bubba tell a tale of him and his brother taking a client out to the ocean to fish for cobia. They put the client over an old shipwreck and got into the biggest fish they'd ever hauled into the boat—a 130-pounder and damn near a state record. Bubba and his brother Gerry posed for a picture with the man and the fish for the *Beaufort Gazette*. He still has that clipping laminated in a scrapbook.

Bubba drained the last of his coffee and said, "Looks like those clouds are about to move in and give us a low ceiling to bring the fish toward the surface. Let's get out there see what we can do with a little cloud cover."

I said, "Hey, can I ask you something before we head back out?"

"Your dime, Mr. Joey." Bubba collected our paper plates and cups and secured them in the trash.

"Ruby was at the house yesterday and told me about the old days before her friend Delphi died."

The blood drained from Bubba's face. His smile faded, and he reached into the breast pocket of his fishing shirt, pulled out his sunglasses, and put them on his face despite the graying sky.

"Ruby told me a story, and I'm wondering if you can verify if it's true."

Bubba seemed resigned to this interrogation, almost like he welcomed it. He sat in the captain's chair and swiveled it back toward Leela and me.

"Ruby said she was shrimping a tidal creek when you drove up in the boat. You were just a kid. Maybe eight or nine. You poled your boat into the reeds, and when you poled back out, Delphi was in the boat."

Bubba dropped his head, and I knew Ruby's story was true.

"She told me that after that day, she would follow Delphi sometimes, and it was always to that same spot when the tide was high. Delphi would disappear into the reeds and you'd be there, waiting to take her to wherever she was going. No one on the water could see Delphi was in the boat because she'd duck down, maybe into that little cabin you were just telling us about. I know it was a long time ago. You were just a boy. But my father is in a bit of trouble now. The police suspect him of killing Thomas Hammond and—"

"That's bullshit," said Bubba, his first words since I'd brought up Delphi.

"My father is no fan of the Hammonds. Everyone in town knows that, including the police. They think it's motive for my father to have shot Thomas Hammond. So I'm just trying to find out more about what happened his senior year of high school so I understand the dynamic better. So I can help him or at least help his lawyers help him."

Bubba took a deep breath and let it out. Leela reached across the stern and found my hand. That was her way of telling me Bubba would talk.

Bubba opened the cooler and said, "I know it's before noon, but can I offer anyone a beer?" Leela and I declined. "Okay if I have one?"

I said, "You're the captain, Captain."

Bubba smiled. Even with his eyes hidden behind sunglasses, I could tell it was a painful smile. He popped the top on a can of Bud and said, "Ruby told you the truth." He took a sip of beer and swallowed it, then shook his head. "Damn, thought I got away with it."

28

"I was eight years old. Over half a damn century has passed." Bubba held the can to his mouth and emptied half of it. "I felt like some kind of spy. Plenty exciting for an eight-year-old boy. It was your daddy who hired me. Paid me a dollar for a round trip. And until up to a minute ago, I didn't think another living soul knew about it." He took another swig.

Leela said, "I know this isn't easy, Bubba. Old secrets don't give themselves up easily."

"No, ma'am, they do not. Secrets stay secret long enough, the lies they protect turn into truths, don't they? People believe something half a century, even if it's false, no one's around to set the record straight, or maybe not willing to set the record straight, and history gets written in stone."

Leela said, "Tell us about Delphi."

"Oh, hell. Delphi Hill is, to this day, the sweetest soul I have ever known. And a beautiful girl. I was just an eight-year-old kid and I knew she was the most beautiful girl I'd ever seen. Even with my racist piece of shit father telling me if I even looked at . . . well, I won't use his words . . . but if I ever looked at a black girl he'd whip me to the bone. . . . But I could not take my eyes off Delphi. She had golden eyes." He laughed a little laugh. "She knew I was in her powers and she was extra kind to me so my little heart wouldn't break. Imagine being eight years old and ferrying the most beautiful princess in the land to her secret beau. I loved picking her up. I hated dropping her off.

"Part of what made her so mesmerizing was that she was in love. It was infectious, man. I'm telling you, it's like she had extra love and she couldn't hold it all so some would spill out and get on me like it was a potion. I think that's why I was so extra careful boating her around. Sure, if my daddy found out I'd pay a steep price, but more than that, I wanted to do right by her. Hell, I even combed my hair in some kind of foolish attempt to look my best even though the wind would un-comb it in two seconds."

He drained the last of his beer and tossed the can with the other refuse. "Saddest two days of my life are the day my brother died and the day Delphi was found under that bridge." Bubba paused. "Can't help but think it's partially my fault things went the way they did."

I said, "Why would you say that?"

"I helped Delphi sneak off. That's what got her killed."

"Ruby thinks Roy Hammond killed her. Is that what you think?"

"I don't think it. I know it. That man was one mean bastard."

"Any ideas what happened to Roy Hammond?"

"Well . . ." said Bubba, eyeing the cooler for another beer but thinking he shouldn't.

Leela said, "It's beautiful sitting here. Have another beer."

"Thank you, ma'am." Bubba grabbed another beer and popped the top. "Rumors are a witness came forward years after Delphi's murder. Or the police found some piece of evidence that linked Roy Hammond to it. But those are just rumors. Still, could have been enough to send Roy Hammond packing. He just up and disappeared one day in his boat. It was about a thirty-five-footer. That could take him wherever he wanted to go. If he ran, my guess is he went south. Probably to the Caribbean. Maybe to Central or South America. He had plenty of money and could live like a king down there. People say if he ran, he would've come back by now.

But I don't know if that's true. No reason for him to come back. His parents died not long after he left. He and Thomas weren't close. And if killing Delphi wasn't bad enough, I think he killed Trip Patterson, too."

"What?" I couldn't believe what Bubba just said. And yet, I could believe it, and I somehow knew that it was true. "Why would Roy Hammond kill Trip Patterson?"

Bubba took a long pull off his Bud, then leaned back into his captain's chair. "A couple weeks after Delphi's body was pulled out of the water, Trip offered me five dollars to ferry him one night. I wondered why he didn't use his own boat and asked where we were going. He said he'd tell me out on the water. He lived a couple houses down from us, so about midnight we met behind the houses where we docked the boat. Didn't even start up the trolling motor. Just poled out for a few hundred yards. Then we got the electric going to push us out far enough to start the big engine without waking anyone. My daddy could identify our boat by engine noise from a mile away.

"We get out into bigger water and Trip starts giving me directions, pointing out landmarks by their lights. At a certain point he says to me, 'Kill the running lights.' So I did. Remember, I'm just a boy. This all feels like an adventure to me. Then he tells me to kill the engine and switch over to the trolling motor. Wherever we were headed, we'd arrive like we'd left our neighborhood. Quiet and undetected. Few minutes later, I realized where we were going."

A formation of pelicans flew low over the water like fighter planes trying to avoid radar. Bubba watched them until they banked around a point of seagrass and glided out of sight. "A few minutes after I switched off the electric motor, we had the poles out again and pushed our way into the grasses bordering the old Hammond estate. That way we could come at the dock from the side. There was no moon that night. The boat wasn't running lights. Wasn't much ambient city light back then. Trip told me to drop him at the dock then pole myself into the grass and wait for

his return. That's what I did and that's when I realized why he'd
paid me five dollars—I was the getaway driver.

"I waited about half an hour or so, then I hear footsteps running on the dock. It's a sound like no other. You can hear the
boards bending underfoot. So I pole out of the grass and I swear I
was at least ten feet away when Trip Patterson leapt from the dock
and into the boat and said, 'Gun it.'

"We got about a mile away and I turned on the running lights
and that's when I first saw Trip's knuckles were covered in blood.
He had blood on his shirt. And on his face, too. I was just a kid. I
didn't know anything. I asked him if someone whooped him. He
said, 'No, Bubba. Nobody whooped me. I did the whoopin'.' Then
Trip Patterson started to cry. Said Roy admitted killing Delphi.
Admitted it with a smirk on his face. That's why Trip beat him
good."

It all fit. Roy Hammond killed my father's love, so his best
friend sought revenge and pummeled Roy Hammond.

Bubba said, "I never should've ferried Trip Patterson that
night. If I hadn't, he might still be alive today. Marshall would
have his best friend, and all the Hammond evil would have died
with Delphi."

I said, "You think Roy retaliated for his beating by killing
Trip?"

"I'd bet my life on it. Roy probably followed Trip out to the
creek one night, forced alcohol down his throat, made it look like
Trip drowned."

Leela said, "So sad. And so like boys that age. One sticking up
for the other. Retaliating. Tragic."

Bubba got this confused look on his face and said, "One sticking up for the other? How do you figure?"

Then Leela looked confused. "Trip Patterson retaliated for
Marshall because Roy Hammond murdered Marshall's girlfriend."

"You think Delphi and Marshall Green were an item?"

I said, "Yes. That's what Ruby and Lawrence told me. They
said Delphi's family was upset she was dating a white boy and

demanded she stop, then my father went to the family and said he was the white boy, and Delphi's family gave in because they liked my father."

Bubba shook his head and said, "Well, Miss Leela, I guess you were partly right. But you got it backwards. Trip didn't help Marshall. Marshall helped Trip. All those times I ferried Delphi was so she could be with Trip, not Marshall."

"Are you sure?"

"Oh, I'm sure. Saw 'em kiss hello and goodbye more times than my young heart could stand. Trip didn't retaliate for Marshall. Trip retaliated for himself. And for Delphi. To this day, what I don't understand is why Trip didn't kill Roy Hammond. My guess is when it came to it, he just didn't have it in him. But I think that must have been his plan."

"Why do you say that?"

"We went back to our neighborhood the way we came in. Extra quiet, first just the electric motor then cutting that and poling our way to the dock. So it was dead quiet when I heard a loud thud. There was enough light for me to see something glint on the bottom of the boat. Trip reached down and picked it up. It was a pistol. He casually threw it into his pocket like it was a set of keys or some loose change. He'd brought it with him but didn't use it to shoot Roy Hammond."

I said, "Who else knows about Delphi and Trip Patterson?"

"Your daddy knows. Sounds like Delphi didn't tell anyone. If her own brother and best friend don't know, then who would? Roy Hammond probably knew. Maybe he saw me ferrying Delphi to Trip or maybe he just figured it out after Trip whooped him. And who knows who Roy told? Maybe Thomas. Maybe some buddies." Bubba flipped a switch on the console, and the winch retrieved the anchor. "You two are the first people I've ever told about that night. Didn't even tell my brother. After Trip died, couldn't help but blame myself. Still do."

Leela said, "If you hadn't taken Trip to Roy Hammond, he would have found another way."

"I suppose."

We fished another hour and for the first time in my forty-some years of fishing with Bubba, we got skunked. He spewed an endless stream of apologies and tried to refuse payment for the half day. After a long back and forth, we finally convinced him to accept payment and a tip after I said, "I might need you in the next few days, Bubba. Marshall might need you. You may have to cancel on some clients."

He tucked the roll of bills into the breast pocket of his fishing shirt and zipped it shut. "I'll be standing by. Anything for Mr. Marshall. Anything, anytime."

29

I dropped Leela at her parents' house and returned to find my father home from the hospital, sitting in the kitchen eating a tuna sandwich. My mother counted out pills from the pill suitcase and set them on a paper towel.

"Hey," said my father, "Joey's here." Again I couldn't tell if, in his mind, this was the first time he was seeing me in months or maybe years. "Good to see you, Joe. Come join us. Tuna sandwiches and potato chips. The lunch of kings."

My mother looked up from her pill counting and said, "Almost ready to make you a sandwich, Joe."

"I'm on it."

"I don't mind."

"I can make a sandwich, Mom, but thank you."

I knew where they kept the tuna and can opener and mayo— parents seem unable to change where they store such things. I went into the pantry. My mother followed me.

"Mom, I know where the tuna and—"

She shut the pocket door, enclosing us in the tiny space and said, "Your father has lymphoma." The words came in a whisper and a sob.

I turned toward my mother and gave her a hug. Marshall Green had been the healthiest seventy-three-year-old I've ever known.

From seventy-four to seventy-five he'd experienced a steep decline. Memory loss, hypertension, high cholesterol, a stroke, and now lymphoma. My mother explained the lymphoma wouldn't kill him—it would be something they'd manage with targeted chemo.

I said, "They're so much better with chemo now than they used to be."

"And then," said my mother, "after we got home from the hospital, that police detective, Chantal Cooper, called. She wants to schedule a meeting with Dad and said we should bring a lawyer. I told her, Joey, I told her to fuck off—that he has cancer now on top of everything else. I told her I know my husband of fifty-one years and he is not a killer."

"What did she say?"

"She said tomorrow at eleven A.M. Be at the police station. Are they going to arrest him? He can't go to jail. He's not healthy enough to—"

"I'll call Uncle David to get a recommendation."

"No," said my mother. "I'll call him. Eat lunch with your father, please?"

My mother and I emerged from the pantry. She left the kitchen, and I made a sandwich.

My father smiled. "Joey, good to see you."

"Good to see you, Dad. Mind if I join you for lunch?"

"I'd be honored. Hey, you know what we should do? We should go visit the old neighborhood. See if I still know anyone there."

He seemed excited, but when I sat to join him at the table, he looked far away, not in wistful thought, just far away. I had never seen that expression on him before—I felt it in my chest and in my throat. My eyes stung.

Mayonnaise smeared the corner of his mouth. Apparently, when people age, they lose the ability to feel when food is on their face. It's as if the nerves on that part of their body die before they do. I reached toward him with my napkin and wiped off the mayo. I didn't know which was more heartbreaking, that I wiped my father's face for him or that he didn't protest me doing so.

I took a breath and tried to sound cheerful. "Pigeon Point? The old neighborhood you lived in when you were a boy?"

"Yeah. I haven't been there since I don't know when. We'll just walk around a little."

"Great." I heard my voice shake and tried to steady it. "We can spend as much time there as you want."

My father's mind returned from wherever it had gone. He looked at me for what felt like a full minute, then said, "This time next year, Joe, I won't be here, will I?"

I did not want to lie to him. He was too smart. Too good. He did not deserve the indignation. "I honestly don't know, Dad. You've been dealt some bad cards, but medicine keeps getting better."

He said, "I had patients who knew they were going to die. I was their doctor, but I couldn't see it. I'd look at their chart, all their vitals. The numbers didn't tell me they were going to die. But they knew. I had this old crank of a man, Josiah Johnson. A walking, talking definition of curmudgeon. Complained from the moment he stepped into the clinic to the moment he left. The lights were too bright. The temperature was too warm. The other patients in the waiting area smelled bad. Every time we drew blood he accused us of trying to make him into hamburger. He was awful, one of my nurses blamed her TMJ on him.

"He had high blood pressure, diabetes, three stents in his heart. But old Josiah Johnson was a fighter. Only problem was he took that fight to everything and everyone around him, not just his disease.

"Then one day he comes in a different man. He's calm and polite and meek. Tells me a story about his grandkids while I'm listening to his heart and lungs and looking at his chart. I saw the lab messed up and didn't run one of the tests I ordered. So I gave him the news: we had to draw blood again so the lab could run the test. I braced myself for his reaction. But all he said was, 'Nah, Doc. We don't need to run the test. I'm done.' I said, 'What do you mean you're done?' And he said, 'You've been good to me, Doc. Thank you.' I didn't know what he was talking about. Next morning, his wife called to say he died in his sleep. Said before he got in bed the night before, he shaved and showered, which he never did at night. She didn't understand why he did that. But in the morning, when she called to tell me the news, she said he must have known he was going to meet his maker and wanted to look his best.

"Josiah Johnson wasn't the only one. I had dozens of patients know their time was up. They say drowning is a silent death. That the victim becomes calm and resigned—that it's a peaceful way to go. From what I've seen, I wonder if it's like that with most deaths. Life knows when it's time to step aside to let death do its thing. Dying is a magnificent gesture by the body to let the soul go."

My father found my hand and held it. I couldn't remember the last time he'd held my hand. Or if he'd ever held my hand. He said, "It's okay, Joe. I've had a great life. Won the lottery marrying your mother. Don't know what I did to deserve that woman. Never doubted she was the one from the minute I met her to right here and now. Same with you and your sisters. How does a man get so lucky? And growing up here in Beaufort. Running barefoot all summer, playing ball and fishing, what else could a boy want? I've lived a beautiful life."

I wanted to contradict him, tell him the internet said he'd live five to eight more years, but there seemed to be no sense saying something like that. Instead I let a deep sorrow wash over me combined with a gratitude for the moment. I squeezed his hand.

Pigeon Point lies between Boundary Street and Brickyard Creek. The neighborhood is full of old, small homes. Tiny red brick boxes, some bungalows. Many replaced by bigger houses—the neighborhood is a hot spot for young white-collar families.

I held my father's arm as we walked down the street. His memory missed nothing. "Dicky Britezman lived in that house. Fastest kid in the neighborhood." He pointed to a white bungalow. "Margaret O'Day lived in that gray one. Pretty Irish girl. Had the red hair and a brogue, the cross hanging from her neck. Everything."

I took out my phone, opened the voice memos app, hit record, and returned it to my shirt's breast pocket, microphone end up, and said, "I thought you were ten when you moved out of this neighborhood. What were you doing looking at girls then?"

"A ten-year-old boy knows when a girl is pretty. And I came back to visit all the time. Watched Margaret O'Day grow into quite a looker. Don't tell your mother."

We got to the end of the block. He pointed across the street. "There's the park where I played ball. Oh, God, we had fun. All day on that diamond. Mitchell Calloway threw so hard. Would have gone pro I bet if he hadn't tore up his shoulder working a shrimp boat. Oh, look, Joe. There's some kids playing. Let's go watch."

I walked my father across the street toward a sign that said Basil Green Park. We inched our way toward aluminum bleachers and he said, "One game, I was nine years old and playing with some older kids. I think the only reason they let me play is I had a catcher's mask. They let Trip Patterson play too, because he had a new bat his daddy bought him. Trip Patterson was playing first and Tommy Hiel hit a bloop single. It was the bottom of the last inning, and my team was up by a run. If Tommy Hiel made it around to score that would tie the game. And wouldn't you know it, Willie Cunningham was up to bat. Big boy. Could hit that ball a mile. Vito Spano was pitching and he was tired. Must have been a hundred in the shade that day—you know how humid it gets down here. I was sweating behind the mask, grit from the diamond getting under the pads and mixing with sweat so it was slipping around and rubbing my face raw.

"Vito was twelve. Italian kid. Had baseball in his blood like DiMaggio and Berra and Garagiola. When he was fresh, I had no business trying to catch him. That ball would pop in my mitt and if I didn't catch it square in the webbing Vito would sting my hand like a son of a bitch. But Vito wasn't fresh. He was running on fumes, and I knew big Willie Cunningham was going to smash the next pitch over the plate.

"So I called a time-out, ran out to the mound, and waved in the infielders for a meeting. Vito was mad as hell. He said, 'You little bastard. What are you doing calling a meeting?' I said three words. Can you guess what they were, Joe?"

I looked at my father. His eyes sparkled looking out at the ball field seeing himself out there sixty-six years ago. I said, "I don't know what you said, Dad. Strike him out?"

"No. Vito had nothing left, remember. Big Willie Cunningham was at the plate. Tying run on first."

"Did you say walk him?"

"Walk him is two words. I said three words."

"I have no idea."

"I told the guys to huddle up. Cunningham started yelling, 'Come on! Play ball!' And I said . . . 'Hidden ball trick.' Trip Patterson's playing first and he gets this big smile on his face. Vito thinks for half a second, then plays it cool and slips the ball to Trip, then we break and head back to our positions and Vito does something brilliant. He pretends he has one more thing to say to me and calls my name and we meet halfway between the mound and home. So everyone's looking at us and no one's paying attention to first base. The other team is hollering at us to break it up. Tommy Hiel, the runner on first, is hopping mad. He steps off the bag and says, 'We're here to play ball, not gossip like a bunch of old ladies!' And as soon as he finishes . . ." My father broke into his infectious laugh, doubling over to catch his breath. ". . . As soon as Tommy Hiel finishes yelling at me and Vito, Trip Patterson steps forward and tags him and says, 'You're out!' Then Trip holds up the ball, and we all run out to the mound and start jumping on each other."

My father laughed so hard tears ran down his face. The laughter fueled him, kept him walking toward the bleachers at the best clip I'd witnessed since arriving in Beaufort. "Then the other team starts hollering how it's not fair and we cheated. And Tommy Hiel starts crying because he knew we got him. He knew we got him and that was that. What a day, Joey. The kind you remember the rest of your life."

I said, "I'm surprised you haven't told me that one before."

"So many days, Joe. So many days it's hard to hold them all. But they seem to be coming back more often now. It helps to see the places. Smell the grass and the sea air. I don't know why we're on Pidgeon Point. I can't remember leaving Craven Street. I can tell by the position of the sun it's afternoon, but I don't remember if we ate lunch. But clear as day, I can picture Vito Spano and Britzeman and Trip Patterson hoisting me onto their shoulders because it was my idea to do the hidden ball trick."

I said, "Did the older kids let you and Trip keep playing with them?"

"Yep. They did. For the rest of that summer. Then I moved to the house on Craven Street, and I didn't see much of them after that."

"Except for Trip Patterson."

My father exhaled, and the joy and sparkle that had filled him was gone. He looked small and gray, even in the midday sun. He said, "Yes. Except for Trip Patterson. He and I remained the best of friends."

We sat in silence for a few minutes and then he said, "I took you to this park when you were little, Joey. You had that big fat red plastic bat. I wanted to pitch you a few on the same field I used to play on. I don't know if it was nostalgia or ego, but I thought it would make you a better ball player if you had a little South Carolina dirt under your feet. You had the biggest smile on your face, waiting for me to lob one over the plate. Every time you hit the ball you'd run all the way around the bases. It was a home run every time. That morning here . . . That morning was my greatest gift to you."

A pair of military jets roared overhead then banked in unison toward the Atlantic. I said, "You know what they call that, don't you, Dad?" I watched the fighter planes disappear into the clouds, expecting my father to say *The sound of freedom*, but instead I heard:

"Because later that day . . ." He began to cry. His head fell and his shoulders shook. He squeezed my hand with all his strength. "Later that day . . ."

30

My father looked at me through wet eyes. Seeing a crier cry means almost nothing. Seeing a person who never cries rips your heart out. He held on to my hand, looked away, and said, "We left this park and went to the house. Grandma had made a big lunch so we ate with Mom and the girls, then they wanted to walk down the street to visit the history museum. I'd been going to that museum for so many years I was practically an exhibit. I'd planned on going fishing and gave you a choice. The museum with your mother and sisters or fishing with me. I didn't even finish my sentence before you started hopping up and down about fishing."

A shelf of low white clouds gathered over the Atlantic Ocean east of St. Helena Island. My father stopped, looked at the aluminum bleachers behind home plate, a seemingly impossible distance to walk. He then motioned toward an ordinary park bench along the path and we headed toward that.

"I called Lawrence and asked if we could boat out to the fish camp. He said yes. We were welcome anytime. Didn't have to ask. So I geared up in the garage, then you and me drove to Uncle David's. Grandpa docked his boat there. I untied it and the two of us set out for an afternoon of fishing.

"We cast into the grass on our way to the fish camp. Caught a few. Boy, did you light up when you hooked into a fish, Joe.

You were such a little guy back then, I was so afraid you'd get pulled in I strapped you into your seat." He laughed but the laugh faded to something distant and quiet. "We got to the fish camp midafternoon. I tied up at the dock there, and when I went to get you, you'd fallen asleep strapped into your seat, the orange life preserver holding up your head like those neck pillows people wear on airplanes."

We arrived at the park bench and sat.

"You'd been going hard all day and you were wiped out. No sense waking you, so I picked you up and carried you into the little cabin to keep you out of the sun. Let you nap in there. Only problem was I couldn't just leave you and walk the sandbar, so I stayed on the boat and cast from there, working the grass on the starboard side, changing up baits and lures, catching a few speckled trout. Then I hear this motor and look up see these two fellas coming at me in a little fishing boat. Second I saw them I knew they were trouble. It happened back then. Boats stolen on the open water. So I went straight to the tackle box like I was looking for a different lure.

"When I look up I see one guy sitting in the stern, running the outboard motor, and the other guy in the bow with nothing good in his eyes. They just motored right up to the sandbar. Closer up, they looked like Florida white trash. Those boys would drive up the coast with a little fishing boat on a big trailer and drive back home with something bigger under a tarp.

"The man in the bow said, 'How y'all doing today?'"

"I said, 'This sandbar is private property.'"

"He said, 'We're just being friendly and saying hello.'"

"I reminded him they were about to trespass. Of course, all I could think about was you napping in the cabin, and they'd try to steal the boat with you still in there. Sure enough, the fella sitting in the stern gunned the engine then killed it and tilted up the prop and they glided onto the beach. Fella in the front hops out and pulls a fillet knife and tells me to get off the boat.

"I told him he should turn around, get back in his little boat, and leave. The man just grinned his ugly grin, showing me a few spaces where he used to have teeth. He took another step toward me, and I removed the old pistol from my fishing vest. You know the one. I taught you how to shoot with it."

My father had forgotten that he no longer had the gun. I didn't know why he was telling me this story now after over forty years. Maybe he didn't know either. He was in storytelling mode, the wheelhouse of a great talker, and the act had given him a sense of calm.

"I pointed that old revolver at the man, and that damn son of a bitch started walking toward me. His friend got out of the boat and did the same. Hell, Joe, I couldn't take a chance on them taking the boat with you inside. Me getting you out first and us getting stranded on that sandbar wasn't much of an option either. Now it has a little cottage on it with a generator and tank of fresh water, but back then, it had nothing. And there were no cell phones in 1975. I felt I had no choice." He looked down and shook his head. "I was a pretty good shot back then. We used to practice shooting cans. Do you remember?"

"I do. Out at the fish camp."

"That's right. I aimed about a foot to the left of his right ear and pulled the trigger. I just wanted him to hear the whiz of the bullet. He sure did and stopped. I said, 'Next time I won't aim to the side of your head.' He looked back at the boat driver, and I swiveled the pistol in that direction. It was dead quiet for half a minute other than the wind blowing and the water lapping against the sand, then the driver said, 'Another day.' The fella with the knife stared hard at me, spit, turned around, and headed back to his little fishing boat. And out they went the way they'd come in. I watched them go, keeping a bead on 'em the whole way, until they were nothing but a speck out on the water."

I said, "Thank you."

He managed a smile but it was short-lived and his eyes grew dark. "Then I heard a voice say, 'Marshall Green. What are you doing south of the Mason-Dixon Line?' I turned around and saw Roy Hammond standing in the sand."

"Was he part owner of the fish camp?"

"No, he was not. I looked around, didn't see his big boat anywhere. Just him. Now, Joe, you've heard me talk badly of the Hammonds, but you don't know the whole story. In fact, you don't know any of it."

My father proceeded to tell me what I already knew, but I didn't stop him. About Delphi and her great beauty and her falling in love with Trip Patterson, and my father telling Delphi's family it was he who Delphi loved. He told me about Roy Hammond's relentless pursuit of Delphi and her refusing him. And how Delphi was found dead in a gill net under the old drawbridge, and everyone suspected Roy Hammond of her murder but he was never arrested. Trip Patterson sought justice himself, hired Bubba to drive him to the Hammond estate, where Trip snuck up on and beat the hell out of Roy Hammond, who had admitted to killing Delphi.

"One day, shortly after Trip gave Roy Hammond that beating, he came to me with a small burlap sack. I asked him what it was, and he said it was his pistol and he wanted me to hold it for him because he was afraid he'd use it when Roy Hammond came for revenge. So I took the gun and hid it in my bedroom. About a month later, Trip died. The police said he got himself drunk while night fishing and passed out at low tide, but never for a minute did I buy that story."

"You think Roy Hammond killed Trip?"

"I sure do. So I went to my father and Uncle David and told them what I suspected. I included my uncle David because he's a lawyer and assumed he'd know how to approach the police and navigate the legal system so Roy Hammond could be charged for two murders. I was seventeen years old and a naive fool. Instead of helping me, they told me to get out of town."

"Why would they say that?"

"I suspect my father and Uncle David had different motives.

My father was worried about my safety. If Roy Hammond could kill Delphi and Trip, no reason he couldn't kill me. Uncle David was more concerned about me drawing unwanted attention to the family. Running the Green name through the mud. I swear the only thing that man has ever cared about is his career. No wife. No kids. No personal life whatsoever.

"They practically forced me to leave the state, so instead of going to the University of South Carolina in Columbia like I'd planned, I went to the University of Illinois. Undergrad and med school. Married your mother, had Bess and Greta and then you, and lived a fine life by anyone's standards."

I worried my father had sidetracked himself. I said, "Dad you were telling me about when I was little and took a nap in the boat's cabin. And the guys tried to steal the boat, but you had Trip Patterson's old gun and scared them off. Then Roy Hammond showed up."

My father nodded. "Oh, Joe. I should have told you this years ago. I'm sorry. I hope you can forgive me."

"Of course . . ."

He hesitated, and I wondered if he'd lost his train of thought again. Then he said, "Roy Hammond walked out on the dock. He had hate in his eyes. Sixteen years had passed since he'd murdered Delphi and Trip, but from the look on his face, you'd think he'd killed them yesterday. He said, 'Give me the gun, Jew.' I told him I would not give him the gun, and to turn around and get off the dock. He said it again. 'Give me that goddamn gun, Jew.' And for the second time that day, Joey, I was afraid for you. Roy Hammond literally thought he could get away with murder because that's exactly what happened. Sixteen years, Joe, and he was never investigated.

"All I could think about was you. So little. Only four years old. If Roy Hammond killed me, you would have perished out there all alone. I thought of telling him you were in the cabin, but I honestly didn't think it would make a difference. The man had no heart. No soul. And a narcissistic personality disorder.

"So I raised the pistol, aimed to the left of Roy Hammond's ear, and pulled the trigger. My aim wasn't as good as it was with the boat thieves. Roy reached up and grabbed his ear. When he pulled his hand away, it was covered in blood. He looked at it, then looked at me. He could not believe I'd just shot him.

"I couldn't believe it either. I was in some big trouble. Me, who'd always played by the rules. Been a good boy. Stayed out of trouble. Studied hard. Worked hard. Faithful husband and father. It was all gone in an instant. One mistake. Words like *attempted murder* bounced around in my head.

"Roy said something obvious like, 'You shot me.'

"I said, 'You're trespassing on private property. And you'll be just fine. Now turn around and—' And then it all happened so fast, Joe. Roy Hammond reached behind his back, pulled a gun from his belt, and raised it toward me. I don't know much about firearms, but I knew I was outgunned. I was looking down the barrel of a big semi-automatic. The kind that can hold nine or ten rounds in each clip. Roy Hammond had me and I knew it. I wasn't prepared, Joe. Physically I was. I was pointing the gun at him. An antique revolver with four more shots. But my mind had drifted off into this web of possible futures that awaited me because I'd just shot off Roy Hammond's ear. Police and lawyers and a trial and what would happen to Mom and you kids. I wasn't mentally prepared for Roy Hammond to pull a gun on me. I said a quick prayer for you, Joe, as I expected to see the flash from the muzzle."

I sat so still listening to my father's story that a chameleon crawled onto my leather shoe. Bright green out of the grass. It weighed nothing. I felt nothing. Its body chemistry went to work, and I watched it change from green to brown.

"But something distracted Roy Hammond. For a fraction of a second. And I knew, it was my only chance. I pulled the trigger, Joe. I pulled the trigger and shot Roy Hammond. A tiny hole appeared in his forehead. He looked at me as if to ask *why,* then he collapsed forward on the sand.

"I heard a tiny voice behind me say, 'Pow. Pow, pow, pow.' I

turned around and there you were, Joe. Four years old with sleep
in your eyes. You got this smile on your face. This little devilish
grin. You thought I was playing. You said, 'Got him, Dad. Now
make him wake up.'"

31

My mother invited Ted, Kajal, and Leela over for dinner to thank them for their help while she was in Florida. My father and I found them all in the kitchen when we returned from Pigeon Point, eating bacon-wrapped dates, which smelled so good they'd tempt a vegan rabbi. My mother and the Belleroses drank gin martinis and, as soon as he saw us, Ted went to work making two more.

"There you are," said my mother, "I was about to call and tell you to get your rear ends home. We have company."

I said hello to Leela's parents, then started toward her. I told myself, *Don't run to her. Walk.* There are moments in life when you feel a truth so irrefutable that every thought and emotion you've ever experienced, every joy and hardship, falls into alignment. In that pinhole of time life makes sense.

Leela must have seen something in my eyes because she gave me her adorable head-tilt and said, "What?"

I turned away from her and said, "Do Leela and I have time to take a quick walk before dinner?"

Our matchmakers spouted effusive assents with big smiles and qualifications like, "the chicken won't be ready for half an hour at least," and sent us on our way.

Leela and I did not take a walk, or at least not a very long one. The moment we got outside my parents' house I said, "I have to share something with you. Can we go to the guest suite?"

There I played the recording for Leela. From the beginning. I paused it after my father shot Roy Hammond in the forehead, and four-year-old me had told him to make the man wake up.

Leela said, "Do you remember any of this?"

"No. Nothing."

"Is there more?"

I hit play on the voice memo.

"You must have seen the terror in my eyes, Joe. You must have picked up on it because you went from thinking I was playing guns to realizing something more serious had just happened. Something terrible.

"My first thought was to cast off from the dock and go back to town, tell the police what had happened, and take the consequences as they came. But the man who lay dead in the sand was Roy Hammond, and the Hammond family owned Beaufort County. If I turned myself in to the authorities they'd own me, too. And so, Joe, I told you the man in the sand could not wake up. He was dead, like when you stepped on an ant or when a bird flew into the window or when we'd drive up to Wisconsin and see deer crumpled by the side of the road.

"You poor thing, Joey. You started crying. You said you didn't want the man to be dead. You wanted him to wake up. You started to scream. 'Make him wake up! Make him wake up!' I told you he couldn't wake up. And that it was okay. Because he was a bad man. He wanted to hurt me. And hurt you. I had to make him dead so he couldn't hurt us or hurt any other people. So he couldn't hurt Mom and Bess and Greta.

"Then I picked you back up, Joe, and we went in search of Roy Hammond's boat and found it on the other side of the sandbar, tied up in a small inlet. I didn't think I could dig a hole deep enough to bury Roy before the tide went out and trapped us there for the evening. If that happened, Mom would call the police or Coast Guard and they'd come looking for us. But I had an idea. We boarded Roy Hammond's boat. It was state of the art with an autopilot navigation system. That's all I needed. We drove Roy's boat over and tied up next to ours. I took you

into our tiny cabin and told you a story and you fell back to sleep. Then I went out and hopped onto Roy's boat.

"It had two gas tanks, one full and one almost full. I had learned how to operate autopilot navigation systems when I worked at the marina. I set the coordinates for Bermuda, then tied Roy Hammond's body to the boat with some heavy fishing line and weighted it down with an old concrete footing lying in a junk pile. There was no DNA testing back then, so the only thing I had to worry about was fingerprints. I got his boat turned in the right direction, initiated the autopilot, and jumped off the back as it started toward Bermuda, dragging Roy Hammond underwater as it went.

"I hoped the sharks would get him. That may sound like a cruel end for a human being, but Roy Hammond raped and murdered Delphi Hill, cinched her into a gill net, and tossed her in the water. And he killed Trip Patterson. Seemed to me no end could be too cruel for that man.

"I expected Roy's boat would be found and his body would be long gone. But his boat never turned up. Maybe thieves got to it before anyone else, or it somehow sank. I don't know. The rumor machine got going, and after a time, people started to openly talk of Roy running from the law because of Delphi's murder. In the end, his reputation suffered the same fate as Roy himself.

"My biggest problem was there was a witness to my crime. And that witness was you. You were a chatty little guy and you had a reputation for telling the truth. Used to drive your sisters nuts when they were trying to get away with something. I could picture you going back to the house on Craven Street and saying, 'Daddy killed a bad guy today.' Couple that with all the attention Roy Hammond's disappearance was sure to receive, and Mom and Grandpa and Grandma would figure out what happened.

"You wanted Roy Hammond to come back to life. I explained he was a bad man, but you knew in your little heart, Joe, he was a human being. And you felt bad for him and kept saying, 'Make him better, Dad. Doctor him better.' I had never hit you, Joe, not once. Rarely raised my voice to you or the girls. But that day, I got down on my knees, placed both of my hands on your little shoulders, and let you feel my strength.

"I said, 'Joey, I had to hurt that bad man so he didn't hurt us. And I had to send him out in the ocean so he wouldn't hurt anyone else.' And you said, 'He got dead, Daddy. The bad man got dead.' And I said, 'Yes, he did. But we can't tell anyone what we did.' I felt sick saying 'we' instead of 'I,' but I was desperate to get through to you. I lowered my voice to a growl and said, 'If you tell anyone about the bad man, he will come back to life, and he will kill us. Do you understand?' You nodded your little head, but I raised my voice. 'Do you promise not to tell anyone?' You said you did. But I wasn't sure I was getting through, so I yelled and shook you. 'The bad man will come to kill us! He will kill Mommy! He will kill Bess! He will kill Greta! He will kill Grandpa and Grandma! He will kill me! And he will kill you! Do you understand, Joey?!'

"You started crying. Crying so hard you couldn't talk."

Leela listened to my father sob. An old man broken. Haunted by his memories with no present to offer relief. Leela instinctively placed her palm on her heart as my father continued.

"I figured I got through to you, Joe, but a minute later you said, 'The bad man got dead. Daddy killed him with a gun.' I slapped you. I slapped you hard and screamed, 'Never say that! Never, ever, ever say that again or the bad man will wake up and kill us all! Never talk about the bad man again! Do you understand?!'"

A fighter jet drowned out his voice. I stopped the recording. Leela wiped her eyes.

I said, "There's a little more, but it basically boils down to my father has felt terrible for four decades. Not about killing Roy Hammond but for scaring me into keeping the secret. And it worked. I've never told anyone. I also have no memory of that day. Not the killing. Not my dad scaring me silent. He said the reason he finally told me is because he's always worried the incident has had some negative effect on me, and he wanted me to know before he died. I thanked him for telling me. Told him it was a brave thing to do. And then he asked if we'd had lunch yet."

Leela said, "My God, Joey. I'm so sorry you went through that."

I felt ashamed, as if now I was damaged goods, and Leela would no longer be interested in me, and I'd acquired a new understanding of myself at the expense of losing the most wonderful woman I'd ever met.

She must have seen the fear in my eyes. She said, "What are you thinking?"

I explained my concern. She smiled the saddest smile and shook her head and reached for me. "I do see you differently now. But it's for the better. What a terrifying experience you had. And now you know about it, which means you can start to heal. It'd be my honor to support you through that."

"Thank you." I reached for her hand.

Leela said, "What is that place, the fish camp?"

"It's a sandbar, like a tiny island. My grandfather was part owner and so is Lawrence. One side faces a tidal creek and the other side faces the open ocean. My family has been fishing there for decades."

Leela said, "Does your mother know what happened?"

"No. She knows about Trip and Delphi and Roy killing them, but she doesn't know my father killed Roy. He was afraid of losing her. He wants to tell her. Says he's getting up the nerve. I don't know how that works with his short-term memory loss."

Leela said, "One thing that makes sense now is why you've been so worried your father may have shot Thomas Hammond. Subconsciously, at least, you know he's capable of it. Did you ask him if Thomas Hammond was involved in the murders of Trip and Delphi?"

"I did. He said no. He thinks that Thomas might have guessed what Roy did or even flat out knew, but Thomas kept that to himself. And for that alone my father never liked Thomas Hammond."

Leela sat still for a minute, then said, "How are you feeling about all of this?"

I began to cry. I don't know if hearing my father's story jarred something loose in my memory, whether in my head or my body, but I cried for my father. And I cried for that little boy, who I saw as someone other than myself.

Leela held me and said, "Can I make a suggestion?"

"Please."

"Delete that recording right now."

32

Leela and I ate dinner with our parents. It was chatty and friendly as our mothers fished for information about our post-Beaufort plans. We answered honestly that we hadn't yet talked about it. My father told stories of his youth. Though he didn't remember our trip that day to his childhood neighborhood, I believe it inspired the stories. Ted talked about an upcoming Civil War artifacts auction in Savannah and asked if any of us wanted to go with him. No one did. He was after another pair of Civil War swords and said they'd probably sell for a fortune because pairs were rare. Leela asked him flat out if he was trying to make a point about the value of marriage, her unmarried status being untenable in her father's eyes. He said no. Pairs of matching swords were truly valuable. End of story.

After dinner, Leela and I went out in search of a drink. We found ourselves standing in front of the inn on Bay Street, where we'd had our first date and one other the night we ran into Virginia and her sister. Odd, how only five days after we'd met, the inn offered us a sense of nostalgia. We went inside, found our favorite bistro table, and ordered drinks.

Leela avoided eye contact. Her forehead wrinkled and her mouth turned down at the corners in a way I hadn't seen before. It was not a warm expression, and I wondered if my father's story had indeed caused her to cool on me. I let her ruminate for as long as I could stand the silence, then said, "Is our honeymoon over?"

It took her a few seconds to react, as if my words had to travel through Jell-O to reach her. She turned toward me and said, "No. God, no. Something about your dad's story isn't sitting right with me." Then her smile and twinkly eyes returned. "I'm sorry," she said. "I was just thinking."

"That was your concentration face?"

"I suppose. I haven't seen it before. I'm too busy concentrating to look in the mirror."

I offered my hand. She took it and we sat in silence until the drinks came.

We made love under the eaves in the Belleroses' guest suite and lay entwined with one another, the sea breeze singing us to sleep through open windows. The next time I opened my eyes, the clock read 3:03 A.M., and Leela was not in bed. I sat up and saw her sitting in a wing-back chair, her eyes wide open.

I said, "Are you okay?"

"Yes. Just can't sleep."

"Do you want to talk?"

"No, sweetie. Go back to bed."

I did. Next time I woke, Leela lay with her back pressed into my chest. I lifted my head to look over hers. The clock read 5:15 A.M., and gray light seeped into the guest suite.

She said, "Good morning."

I kissed the back of her neck.

"I figured out what was bothering me about your father's story."

"Tell me over coffee."

The guest suite had a coffee maker, so we filled a couple mugs with steaming dark roast and carried them toward the water to watch the sun rise and shrimp boats cast off.

Leela said, "Your father said Roy Hammond's words were 'give me the gun' and 'give me the goddamn gun.'"

"Yeah . . ."

"And then your father tried to scare off Roy Hammond like

he had with the would-be boat thieves, but his shot accidentally nicked Roy Hammond's ear."

"Uh-huh . . ."

"And then Roy Hammond pulled his gun, leading to your father killing him."

"That's how I remember what my dad said."

Leela blew a cloud of steam off the surface of her coffee, then said, "If Roy Hammond had wanted to kill your father, he would have snuck up on him and just shot him. Instead, he made his presence known and told your father to give him the gun."

We neared Ruby's bakery, which I couldn't see but guessed was close because we'd penetrated the perimeter of its aroma cloud. I experienced vacation hunger pangs, which differ from everyday hunger pangs because on vacation I rationalize that I can eat whatever I want.

I said, "Isn't that what law enforcement does? Tells the suspect to set down the gun?"

"Yes, but Roy Hammond didn't say put down the gun. He said give me the gun."

"If my father is remembering correctly."

"His long-term memory seems sharp. At dinner he told a story that included the name of every dog in his childhood neighborhood. The thing is, I don't think Roy Hammond was trying to disarm your father as much as he was asking for that particular gun."

I stopped and said, "You think my father's pistol belonged to Roy Hammond?"

"The way Bubba tells it, the night he ferried Trip Patterson over to the Hammond estate so Trip could beat the hell out of Roy, Trip brought a gun but didn't have the heart to use it. But I bet Trip didn't bring the gun. I think Trip wrestled the gun away from Roy, kept it, and gave it to your father without telling him it was Roy Hammond's. If your father had known it was Roy Hammond's gun, he would have gotten rid of it, especially after killing Roy, because your father would have known the gun could link him to the Hammonds. But your father didn't get rid of the gun because he thought it had belonged to Trip Patterson. He probably kept it as a memento of his friend."

We arrived at Ruby's bakery. It wouldn't open for another hour, which, if you ask me, is false advertising—Ruby should keep the vents closed until they unlock their doors.

I said, "What you're thinking is, Roy Hammond wasn't the threat my father thought he was. Roy just wanted the gun?"

"It's possible. But what I'm really thinking is if we can prove the gun originally belonged to the Hammonds, if there's some kind of paper trail that shows that, it could create doubt that the gun ever belonged to your father."

"Even though he identified it as his gun?"

"Yes. Your dad's memory impairment makes his recognition of the gun less credible, especially if the gun technically belongs to the Hammonds."

"All right," I said, "I will admit to being the dumb one in this conversation. And as the dumb one I have to ask, how would we prove that?"

Leela said, "I'm the executor of my parents' estate because of course I am. I'm an only child. And my father's gone over their assets with me, including his collection of Civil War artifacts. They have homeowner's insurance, but they have an additional insurance rider that lists and values his collection separately."

"But if Trip Patterson took the gun from Roy Hammond in 1959, why would the Hammonds still be insuring it? Wouldn't they have reported it stolen over half a century ago?"

"Not necessarily. Listen, I know this is a long shot, but hear me out. When people feel shame over something like being drunk and backing their car into a telephone pole or losing an earring while having sex with someone other than their spouse, they don't make an insurance claim because it leads to embarrassing questions. For Roy Hammond, they'd be worse than embarrassing questions. How do you lose a gun stored in an in-home collection? Why would a thief take just one gun and not the others?

Everyone in the family would be questioned. The staff would be interrogated by police and insurance investigators. And if you're Roy Hammond, and you've recently killed two people, you don't want anyone nosing around asking questions."

"You're saying it's possible Roy Hammond didn't tell his parents or brother that the gun was taken and he just hoped they wouldn't miss it."

"Yes," said Leela. "I don't know how big their collection is, but it's possible no one paid much attention to it in detail. My father shows off some of his collection, but he owns dozens of old swords and pistols and half-burned flags. The items he doesn't have framed are stored in boxes and old chests. If one thing went missing, he'd probably never know it unless he did an inventory and checked it against a list from his previous inventory."

"Okay. So all we have to do is break into Gail Hammond's house, use our safecracking skills, peek at her insurance papers, and photograph them with a tiny spy camera."

Leela stopped and looked at me. The sun rose behind her head, curtained by low clouds infused with smudges of pink and orange. Even silhouetted, I could see a disappointment in her eyes. She said, "Was that sarcasm?"

"Yes. I didn't list sarcasm as one of my faults on our first date because I thought it was an asset, not a fault. Was I wrong? Do we have to go back and start our experiment all over again?"

Leela said, "Why are you talking like this? What's wrong with you?"

"I can't tell if you're serious."

Her eyes shined and her cheeks flushed. "Yes, I'm serious. I was up half the night trying to figure out a way to help your father, and you're making safe-cracking jokes."

"Well, it's just . . ." I trailed off and looked away from Leela.

"Say it, Joey. It's just that my idea is stupid?"

I looked at her and said, "No." But I'd hesitated.

Leela said, "Oh, great. Perfect. You think my idea is stupid."

"I didn't say that."

"You didn't have to. It's crystal clear."

I said, "Are we really having a fight?"

"Apparently." Then she broke eye contact with me, looked out at the boats, and said, "I don't know what we're doing. We're both tired and under stress. We haven't had a moment to ourselves. We're going our separate ways in a couple days. This is ridiculous."

I waited for her to say more, but when I realized she wasn't going to, I said, "When you say *this* is ridiculous. What do you mean by *this*?"

She kept her eyes on the boats and said, "I don't know." Her phone rang. She looked at the caller ID and then at me. "It's my kids." She answered the phone, then told them to hold just a second, muted the phone, and said, "Joey, I'm going to walk back. Can we catch up later?"

I said, "Sure," but instantly regretted it.

Leela unmuted her phone and said, "Hey, guys, sorry about that," as if I'd been a loud plane flying overhead and she was waiting for me to pass, then Leela Bellerose turned and walked away.

33

The dating experiment that had started six days ago, which felt more like a game than an experiment, a game that had begun light and without expectation, had morphed into something heavy. And delicate. I felt the full force of my idiocy.

Leela Bellerose, who I'd known less than a week, was trying to help my father avoid being arrested for murder. She had thrown herself into the deep end to help save him. She knew I'd dropped the pistol in the middle of the Beaufort River. She knew my father killed Roy Hammond and sent Roy's boat and body out to sea. She'd stayed up half the night thinking about my father's story to realize the revolver could have belonged to Roy Hammond, and Trip Patterson might have taken it during their fight and given it to my father without telling him where the gun had come from.

And it was Leela who understood that the Hammonds' insurance rider might offer proof that the family originally owned the gun. She was right. The idea alone could create enough doubt in the courtroom or even with the police to keep my father out of jail. The guilt I felt over my sarcastic quip felt like a gut punch.

I walked down to the water, where sailors untied their boats from the docks and headed out to start their day. A yacht pulled into the marina and three boys ran onto the docks to assist. A blond woman wearing yoga pants and injected lips stood on the bow holding a small dog that barked its chirp-like bark. Defender of the ship. They disembarked and were joined by a man who could not fit into yoga pants. He lacked both neck and waist and waddled more than he walked. The man wore what looked like a captain's hat and a mariner's fat gold watch to ensure no one would question his command. He made a show of tipping each of the boys. A real class act. I imagined he'd earned his fortune selling something ugly like electric chairs or smokestacks and now he was sailing the coast to show off his trophies. One that floated and one that held her little barking dog.

The ugliness of their display was in sync with how I felt after Leela walked away. Boats came and went and the marsh grew more green and gold as the sun rose. The world blossomed with color and people. Shrimpers and tourists. Cafés opening, their patio umbrellas expanding toward the sun like inverted flowers. All sights that should have made me feel better. But they did not.

My post-divorce life began with an insecurity of being single that left me vulnerable to a gravity-like pull toward remarrying. To get back to the familiar, even if the familiar was a destructive relationship, was all I wanted. Somehow I survived that bumpy and dangerous period like a space capsule reentering Earth's atmosphere. A rocky ride that presented the constant threat of bursting into flames.

When I came out on the other side alive and well I questioned whether I could ever marry again. I had worked hard to get my life to where I wanted it, comfortable and happy on my own with no hindrances to my role as parent. I would only let in another person if she added to my well-being. No detractors allowed. When relationships didn't work out, I no longer felt vulnerable and lonely. I felt safe and comfortable in my castle of solitude.

Leela walking away triggered my instinct to return to my fortress and raise the drawbridge. I looked away from the boats and walked with that thought along the seawall, back through town, and to Ruby's bakery, which was now open.

Ruby worked behind the counter and picked up on my mood

just as my mother would have done. She said, "What's wrong, Joey?"

"Marshall's fine."

"Girl next door problems?"

"I wish I knew." I bought croissants, donuts, rolls, and more coffee. Ruby refused to charge me, but I left a twenty in the tip jar then meandered back to my parents' house. They were awake and happy to see me and my bounty in grease-stained white paper bags. After some small talk, I headed upstairs to shower, where I let my mind wander in the white noise.

The ideas swirled and wove in and out of each other to form a tapestry of possibility. I could see it. Almost touch it. And it was all because of Leela. I stepped out of the shower, grabbed a towel, and headed straight to my room, where I fired up my laptop. There, the answers came even faster than in the shower.

I dressed and fifteen minutes later knocked on Ted and Kajal's door with half a dozen sweet, buttery gems from Ruby's. Leela was in the main house drinking coffee with her parents. After twenty minutes of polite conversation, Ted and Kajal excused themselves to go on a walk while the day was still cool.

I helped Leela clean and put away dishes and said, "Total dickhead move on my part. I'm so sorry. No excuses. I fucked up. What can I do to make it up to you?"

Her face faded into something sad. "Move to Boston." There was no sarcasm in Leela's voice. She turned away and dumped the dregs of the coffee pot down the drain.

I went to Leela and pulled her into a hug and we stood like that for a good minute. After we separated I said, "Your idea is brilliant. My uncle David may have a copy of the Hammonds' insurance policy."

Leela nodded, "That's what I was thinking."

"Before I smarted off."

"Yes."

"Thank you."

"For?"

"Caring about my dad." She nodded again. "But I can't involve you anymore."

She looked wounded.

I said, "You know so much. I've already made one mistake by dumping the gun. If I happen to make another one, or worse, if I'm forced to do something like try to steal a copy of the Hammonds' insurance policy, I don't want you involved. You're in up to your neck as it is."

Leela thought over what I'd said, sat with it for a long and awkward silence, then said, "It was not very nice of me to walk away from you at the waterfront, but the reality of going our separate ways is taking a toll on me. Please don't misinterpret that. I am beyond grateful I've met you. Our time together has been . . . well, the word *wonderful* doesn't do it justice. Maybe *miraculous* is closer. I have felt very much alive on this trip. And I value that feeling dearly. Thursday's going to hurt like hell. That's okay. I'd rather experience pain than feel like I'm just existing. Highs and lows are life. I've never been a person who just wants to manage a smooth ride until I die. Intellectually, I understand and accept that, but I'm scared to death. What's happened between you and me is rare. Not in the world but in a person's life."

"Right back at you on all of that."

"So please don't cut me out now. Include me in whatever you're doing. I accept the risks."

I hoped she would say something like that. I kissed her, then said, "I have a thought."

"Oh?"

"It's kind of a radical thought."

"Radical might feel normal in the context of the last six days."

"I like your attitude, young lady."

"Right back at you, Joey Green."

"Take a drive with me?"

34

The police did not invite me to their 11 A.M. interview with my father, but Leela and I met his lawyer at ten o'clock in my parents' living room. Her name was Shayla Kanter, a dark-skinned Jew with spokesmodel height, a take-no-prisoners demeanor, and unsmiling eyes. Her parents attended Beaufort's tiny synagogue after retiring to the Lowcountry after both worked as professors at the University of South Carolina in Columbia. Shayla was number one on Uncle David's list. She'd made the two-plus-hour drive down from Columbia that morning.

I had spoken to Ms. Kanter on the phone the previous day, filled her in on everything except my part in the gun's disappearance before the police found it, and she promised to make the interview an unpleasant experience for the police.

Leela and I left the house at 10:30 and arrived at Uncle David's office a few minutes later. He was in his office, behind a closed door. Virginia sat at her desk in the reception area and greeted us with a smile. She wore her long, gray hair down on her shoulders, a white blouse open at the collar, and a simple silver chain around her neck.

"Hello, you two. Is he expecting you?"

I said, "He is not."

"He's in a meeting, but he'll be done soon. What can I get you? Coffee? Tea? I'm stocked up on chocolate gators, now."

Uncle David's office door opened, and he stepped out with a man in his early thirties wearing a navy suit. Uncle David told the man he'd make a decision by the end of the month. The man thanked him for the interview and left.

"Virginia," said Uncle David, "put Jackson Hassler in the maybe file."

"Done," said Virginia, lifting a résumé from her desk and sliding it into a manila folder.

"Joey. Miss Leela. I wish I had time to chat, but Virginia is leaving me and I'm booked all day interviewing candidates to be my new secretary."

Virginia smiled. "We're called paralegals now. Or administrative assistants. If you ask interviewees about being your secretary, they might think you're old-fashioned."

"I'm not old-fashioned. I'm old. When's the next candidate due?"

"In five minutes."

"You sure you won't stay on until I die?"

"No, sir. The way you're going, I'll beat you to it."

Uncle David grunted at that and asked when I was heading back to Chicago. He promised another get-together before I left, then returned to his office and shut the door.

I said, "What happened? Why are you leaving?"

Virginia said, "I'm retiring."

Leela said, "Congratulations. You should have told us the other night. We would have bought champagne."

"I didn't know the other night. I found out yesterday that Thomas Hammond was quite generous to me in his will. I no longer have to work, so I'm not going to. I care deeply for your great-uncle, Joey, but it's time for me to move on. To travel. I have been almost nowhere, and I can't keep putting it off. No telling when the next pandemic will be. Or war. Or if Venice will be under water. My sister's going with me. June, July, and August. We might even stay through September if we don't get too homesick."

Leela said, "That sounds like heaven."

"Doesn't it? We're going to fly first class, see all the sights, shop like we've never shopped before, and stay in good hotels. I love a good hotel."

I said, "It sounds like you didn't know you were in Thomas Hammond's will."

"I had no idea. The strange thing about it, when David opened Thomas Hammond's letter, he discovered it was a notarized, handwritten will. That makes it virtually incontestable. Please forget I said that. That is privileged information."

"Don't worry. We already knew it was handwritten. Thomas Hammond left some land to my parents and Ruby and Lawrence Hill."

"I heard about that."

Privileged information didn't seem to be all that privileged around here. That was a good omen for the purpose of our visit.

Leela said, "We think Thomas left the land to the Greens and Hills to make amends for the past. Is that why he left you money, as well? For breaking off your engagement?"

Virginia flushed and looked down at her desk. "I honestly don't know."

I said, "When Uncle David and Gail came to the house to present an offer for the land, Gail looked shell-shocked. I thought how is it possible she could be partially disinherited in her husband's will and not even know about it until after he died? That can't be legal. But I did a little research, and apparently in South Carolina and a handful of other states, you can disinherit your spouse from receiving assets that aren't subject to probate, especially assets that exist in only the deceased's name and that predate the marriage."

"Joey, I'm impressed." Virginia smiled. "Maybe you'd like to work for your great-uncle. He takes his coffee with cream and sugar."

I said, "Virginia, I need your help."

"Anything for you, Joey."

"I'd like to see the insurance rider for Thomas Hammond's gun collection."

"Anything but that. You know I can't let you see a client's private information. Even if I believe in the cause."

Leela said, "What do you think the cause is?"

Virginia's smile faded. She did not want to answer Leela's question. Instead she said, "I'm sorry. Showing you anything in a client's file would be a serious violation of ethics and the law. I won't do it, nor will your great-uncle."

I said, "Even if it could save my father's life?"

"What are you talking about?"

I told Virginia about the police finding my father's gun, which they'd tied to Thomas Hammond's murder, and about me leaving him alibi free during the window of time Thomas Hammond was killed.

Virginia said, "Well, that's ridiculous. Marshall would never hurt anyone."

This, I now knew, was not true. But I said, "Of course he wouldn't. The thing is, I think that gun may have come from the Hammonds' collection."

"I am so confused, Joey. How would Marshall's gun have come from the Hammonds' collection?"

I glanced at Leela. We had intended to tell Virginia almost everything, but having just learned that she also benefited from Thomas Hammond's death, I second-guessed that decision. Leela could see it in my eyes and, in what I remember as our first silent conversation—that thing people who know each other well can do—she conveyed to me we had no options.

I said, "In 1959, Trip Patterson gave the gun to my father just before Trip died. My father has always believed it was Trip's. But we now suspect that before Trip died, he took the gun from Roy Hammond." Off Virginia's confused and confounded expression, I recounted Bubba's account of the night he ferried Trip to the Hammond estate.

Leela said, "We wouldn't ask, Virginia, if we didn't think it would help to keep Marshall out of jail."

Virginia shut her eyes. She flushed and held her palm to her chest as if her heart were racing. She took a deep breath and said, "I understand, but I can't show you a client's private papers. I'd be sued for every penny I just inherited."

My phone buzzed. The caller ID showed a local number. I thought it might have something to do with my father, so I answered it.

"Joey Green?"

"Yes."

"Why did your parents and the Hills counter my offer with such a ridiculous and insulting amount of money?"

I mouthed *Gail Hammond* to Leela, then said, "I don't know. You would have to ask them."

"Is my lawyer two-timing me and advising them?"

Uncle David's next paralegal applicant entered the office. Virginia took her into his office.

I said, "The last I heard, Gail, your lawyer strongly recommended they take your initial offer."

Gail sighed her frustration, then said, "Joey, you seem like a sensible person. Would you please have lunch with me today so I can make my case?"

I muted the phone and said, "Gail Hammond wants to meet me about the land offer."

Leela said, "Hell, yes."

Gail said, "Joey?"

I unmuted the phone and said, "I'd be happy to meet you for lunch."

Gail Hammond thanked me, gave me the address, and told me one o'clock.

35

When Leela and I walked into the old house on Craven Street
we found my mother in the living room with the defense attorney, Shayla Kanter. They had returned from the police station.
Because of my father's dementia, the police let my mother sit in
on the questioning. She looked small, frightened, and pale, as if
her hours in the sun playing pickleball had been erased by the
meeting. My father had gone upstairs for a nap. Leela and I sat
down.

Shayla said, "I'm surprised. Shocked, actually. The Beaufort
Police Department seems hell-bent on arresting someone for
Thomas Hammond's murder. I told them I would make fools
of them and hold them financially responsible for any mental
anguish they cause Marshall and Carol, but they did not back
down."

Leela said, "What do you think that's about?"

"I think it's about two things. One, they're desperate to explain how one of their most prominent citizens could be shot
and killed in an exclusive neighborhood. It's bad for business if
citizens and tourists think there's an unidentified killer running
around. And two, it's about the murder weapon. They think
they've found it. And they probably have. Forensic science has

come a long way—especially ballistics. They'll need to present evidence in court and they wouldn't be so brash and confident if their ballistics report wasn't solid. That, coupled with Marshall saying the gun is his, and his temporary absence of an alibi around the established time of death, and the police and district attorney believe they have a case."

I said, "Then why haven't they arrested him?"

"I asked them that and they gave me some b.s. about waiting on a report from a doctor in Charleston who specializes in Lewy Body Dementia. I asked what could be in the report that would help their case, and they declined to answer."

"You think they're making it up?"

"Not necessarily. But I think the real reason they're stalling is to assess how they'll operate post-arrest. Will they release your father immediately after arrest and take his passport? Will they insist on bail first? They're concerned about the optics of jailing a memory-impaired individual—"

Shalya Kanter's phone beeped. She looked at the screen and said, "I'm sorry. I have to get back to Columbia. I'll stay in touch with the DA and let you know what's happening." She stood and slung her briefcase over her shoulder. "Whatever you do, Carol, don't take Marshall out of town. That will only make matters worse."

I walked Shayla to the door and we said our goodbyes, then I returned to the living room to find Leela with her arm around my mother, whose head was down, face buried in her hands.

She took a moment, then looked up with a strength in her eyes I hadn't expected. She said, "We're not going to let them get away with this. Even . . . Even if . . ." She stopped herself and looked at the staircase to make sure my father wasn't listening. "Even if your father somehow got out of the house and into the garage and found and loaded his gun and then went for a walk during a thunderstorm and came across Thomas Hammond and shot him. Even if that happened, he doesn't deserve to be punished. You don't know what Roy Hammond did. You don't understand—"

"We do know, Mom. About Roy Hammond killing Delphi and Trip and about Dad having to leave Beaufort because Uncle David and Grandpa thought Dad might be next. We know that."

My mother looked surprised. "Who told you?"

"Bubba. And Dad. And Ruby and Lawrence, who think Delphi was in love with Dad but she was really in love with Trip Patterson."

"What?" said my mother. "Ruby and Lawrence don't know the truth?"

I shook my head.

"Well . . ." She trailed off for a moment. "I'm not sure what they'd think of that." My mother stood, walked to the window, looked out on Craven Street, and said, "Marshall has dedicated his life to helping people. He gave up financial security. Sometimes he gave up being able to make ends meet. He gave up giving you kids what every other doctor could afford for their kids. It's just who he is and it's one of the main reasons I fell in love with him. I will not let the police or anyone else tarnish his name or reputation or diminish the quality of what life he has left. I will not let them do it, Joey. I absolutely will not let it happen."

I wasn't sure what my mother meant by that. If she'd hire the best team of defense attorneys or flee before the police could arrest him. One thing I did know about my mother—she was at her best, her strongest, when she had to fight for something. She did it my entire childhood, teaching full-time and raising three kids while her husband worked seventy- to ninety-hour weeks at his free clinic while taking home little pay. When my father's memory began to fail, she marched into battle, shuttled him from doctor to doctor until he was correctly diagnosed, administered his meds, changed the locks on the doors so he couldn't wander off.

It was only when she'd done all she could that the stress took its toll. She was a fighter, not a mid-level manager of life. I found her beaten down when I arrived to town. Sending my mother to Florida rejuvenated her not because she sat on the beach, but because she competed in a pickleball tournament. Focused on one point at a time. Then after each victory, she focused on her next opponent.

Now she had a new battle. Fighting the police and district attorney on my father's behalf. But I wasn't sure how much fight she had left.

36

Gail Hammond lived a ten-minute walk from my parents' house, on the Old Point east of Carteret Street, a historic neighborhood with mansions on the water. The house looked like a gigantic version of my parents'. White clapboard, three and a half stories. Giant verandas out front on each level. A lawn sloped down to the water. Three cannons studded the green, left where they were originally installed before the Civil War.

I felt Lilliputian knocking on the door. A man dressed in a white suit opened it and said, "Mr. Green, I presume," as if I'd traveled back in time two centuries. I confirmed his presumption, and he walked me through a house that felt not like a home but a museum. The ceilings had to be twelve feet tall and the windows almost the same. The heart pine floors and rugs, the paintings and vases and furniture looked like an exhibit that might have been installed at the Louvre if Napoleon had conquered and lived in South Carolina.

The man in the white suit led me through a large living room with several seating areas, a library, a billiards room, and another living room with French doors facing the water. That room had a brick fireplace painted white, and over it hung a painting of a young woman. She wore a white dress and sat on a white bench affixed to a white dock and looked off to the side as the marsh exploded in color behind her. She had long dark hair, and though I couldn't see her face clearly, something about her felt familiar. It was a portrait of innocence. Of purity. All of it embodied in the young woman and juxtaposed against the marsh, which was as beautiful as she but far from innocent, a theater for the cruelty of nature. I must have paused to stare at the picture because the man in the white suit said, "Sir?" He broke my trance, I apologized, and we exited the house and stepped onto a granite patio that arched in a semicircle into the lawn.

Gail Hammond sat at a table on the rear veranda. Three silver carts, each covered, waited nearby. Gail faced the house, leaving open the chair that faced the water. She stood as I approached, smiled, and shook my hand, leaving no doubt that this was a business meeting.

"Thank you for coming," she said. "Did you have any trouble finding the place?"

I wanted to say *No. Your house can be seen from space.* But I opted for, "No. It was an easy walk from Craven Street."

"I'm glad," said Gail, who had known the answer before she asked the question.

I was offered an assortment of beverages but chose water. The man in the white suit disappeared and was replaced by one man and one woman dressed in black-and-white uniforms. As they served lunch, Gail Hammond delivered her sales pitch. It began with, "May I call you Joey?"

"Yes, please."

"And please call me Gail. Joey, it is no secret that my late husband left me with a time bomb that detonated a day after his passing."

"You're referring to his will."

"Yes. Strange how a husband can keep such a thing from his wife and do so legally, but that's what he did and that is what I'm dealing with. I don't know if you're aware of this, but Thomas and I were cousins."

"I think I've heard that somewhere, yes."

"We're first cousins, which is legal in South Carolina but frowned upon by most. Thomas and I shared a last name and an ancestor who came to this country before it was a country. Tyler Hammond settled in Virginia and farmed tobacco and fought for American independence alongside George Washington. He later moved to South Carolina to harvest lumber and farm cotton."

I settled into my chair. This, apparently, was going to be a long sales pitch. I didn't have that luxury in the fashion jewelry business. Since Gail Hammond had started talking, most of what I sold would have come into style and gone right back out.

"Some of the Hammonds remained in South Carolina and some, like my father, went elsewhere. He moved to Georgia when he was a young man and prospered in liquid petroleum gas. But the jewel of the Hammond crown remained here in agricultural products, which naturally led to the property development business. Tyler Hammond had a strong gene which he passed to his descendants and that is the gene of shrewd business practices. Many of the men inherited it, and many of the women did as well.

"Thomas's father and his brother, Roy, got a double dose of the gene and they worked hard and without mercy to grow their birthright into a modern powerhouse of business. Naturally, the gene skipped some of Tyler Hammond's lineage, and my husband was one of those skipped. Thomas was a kind man. Extraordinarily kind for a Hammond. I believe if he'd been born in the first half of the nineteenth century, he would have freed his slaves. That is not the kind of thinking that runs in this family."

I said, "That's what we in the north call plain talk."

"Thank you."

"In this case, it's not a compliment."

"I think it's fair to say, Joey, that you and I have different worldviews."

"There's something we can agree on."

"For decades, those of us who are honest about the transactional nature of human interaction were bullied into keeping our views to ourselves. But that no longer is true. We feel no shame in expressing our beliefs."

"There's a second thing we can agree on."

Gail Hammond managed a smile, sipped her iced tea, and said, "My point, Joey, is that after Roy disappeared back in '75, I watched Thomas chip away at what our family had built. Watched it for too many years. My immediate family, my aunts and uncles and cousins, they all went mad about the choices Thomas made. But I'm a woman of action more than a complainer, so I did something about it. I married Thomas."

"And by doing so you took the reins of the family fortune."

"I'd like to think so. Our financials over the last twenty years think so too. But as any honest woman will tell you, you can't change a man's nature by marrying him. It was always an uphill battle. Thomas wanted to sell our land to nature conservancies. Hell, sometimes he wanted to just give it away. I was able to stop that. Or so I thought. I was unaware of Thomas's secret will that superseded our living will and trust."

A yacht-sized sailboat glided across the water toward the old drawbridge, its sails lowering so it could stop and wait for the bridge to open.

I said, "It must have been an unpleasant surprise learning about your husband's will."

"It hurt me on multiple levels. Personally and professionally. Thomas giving those two pieces of property on Hammond Island to your parents and the Hill family halts our development project in its tracks. And yet I reacted responsibly and fairly by making a generous offer for the land, and what did your parents and the Hills do? They countered with double the amount. How much cash do they think I have?"

The hell Gail Hammond wasn't a complainer. She was playing victim, all while dressed and bejeweled in tens of thousands of dollars while lunching at her multimillion-dollar home.

"Because I will let you in on a little secret, Joey. Thomas's will not only gave away valuable land to your parents and Lawrence and Ruby, but he also gave away significant sums to Virginia Rampell and others who Thomas knew I disapprove of. He also gave money away to members of our family who, like Thomas, are missing the gene for hard work and prudent decision making. My God, there's a Hammond who moved to New York City to teach and write poetry. Now, I suppose, she'll just write poetry and live off the hard work of others."

I said, "I don't really know you, Gail, but you seem like a person capable of rebuilding what Thomas gave away."

"I am, Joey, and thank you for saying that. But I need your help."

"You want me to tell my parents and Ruby and Lawrence to accept your offer."

"I want you to convince them to make a reasonable counter. I expect a little back and forth. Anyone who works in property development understands that's part of the process, but their counter is ridiculous. And a deal-breaker. I'd lose money going forward. And my initial offer of two million dollars to each family is life-changing money for them. Especially with your father's health concerns, and Lawrence's recent retirement. My offer gives them real security."

"The deal is about market value, not their security."

"I've done right by them with market value, as well. Will you please help me?"

The old bridge had opened, its middle section rotated parallel to the river so the big boats could pass, cars lined up on both sides waiting for the bridge to become whole again. I kept my eyes on the traffic. I needed a moment to think. Had Gail Hammond just gifted me an opportunity to prove Leela's theory? I was pretty sure she had. Maybe there is such a thing as a free lunch.

I said, "My suggestion, at least for my parents, is sweeten the deal with something unique."

"What do you mean?"

"There's a silver lining to my father's short-term memory loss. His long-term memory seems to have improved. It's become quite vivid, and he's most interested in anything that's old. Maybe if you offered a piece of art from your collection, or something from your Civil War collection."

"Would he like a cannon? I have several." Gail Hammond laughed.

"Maybe. If you could let him pick something himself, that would make him quite enthusiastic. Much more than cash. He can't really grasp what cash means right now. But a historical artifact of some kind would really pick up his spirits. And that would pick up my mother's spirits. If my father got excited about the deal, I promise my mother will counter with a far more reasonable number. And I think Ruby and Lawrence will come to their senses and do the same."

Gail Hammond looked at me with something between curiosity and amusement. "Why would you do that for me?"

"I'm not doing it for you. I'm doing it for my father. I don't want it to leave this table, but he's dying. I want him to enjoy what time he has left. My parents' friends the Belleroses live next door, and every time my father visits, he marvels at Ted Bellerose's collection of Civil War artifacts. Old muskets, swords, powder horns. He really lights up. It brings him back to his childhood when that war was part of the culture down here."

"It still is," said Gail.

"Yes, but he remembers his childhood like you wouldn't believe. It's remarkable. So if you offered something from your collection, something he could see and touch every day, it would make a big difference in the quality of his life."

Gail's eyes sparkled in the sunlight that bounced off the big white house. "What do you think he'd want?"

"You don't happen to have some sort of catalogue of your collection, do you? If I could present something like that to him when suggesting they make a more reasonable counter, he'd be like a kid in a toy store. Seeing him like that would mean the world to my mother and me."

Gail's all-business demeanor melted away and she said, "You

wait right here, Joey Green." She pushed away from the table, stood, and walked toward the house.

She returned a few minutes later with a three-ring binder about four inches thick, handed it to me, and said, "This is an inventory of everything in my art and artifacts collection, complete with descriptions and photographs of each item. Some of the things are in the house, but most are packed away in a high-security, climate-controlled storage facility. I haven't even seen most of these pieces and frankly they mean nothing to me. Even the art. Every painting or sculpture you see in this house was Thomas's doing, most of it he purchased before we married. Thank God, Thomas didn't give these things away too, because I know some are valuable. It must have slipped his mind in his frenzy to break my heart. I will put it all up for auction soon enough, so please, if there's something your father likes in here, I'm sure I'll be happy to include it in the deal."

"Thank you. I'll let him have a look and get it back to you."

Gail signaled the end of our meeting by calling for the dessert cart. I chose a key lime éclair as our conversation wound down to small talk about the costume jewelry business and Beaufort's future.

I left with a promise she'd hear from me or Uncle David by the end of the day, although I had no idea if that was true. On my walk home, I found a bench outside the history museum, sat, and opened the three-ring binder. After ten minutes of searching, I knew I'd keep my promise to Gail Hammond.

37

Uncle David and Gail Hammond arrived at 4:30 sharp while I was upstairs with my father, who had just showered and shaved and stood before his closet, flipping through shirts.

"What do you think, Joe? This one?" He held out a button-down sport shirt of green and navy checks.

"That depends," I said. "What color suspenders are you wearing?"

"I think red."

"Good choice. You don't want them blending into your shirt. Suspenders are a statement. You want people to notice."

"That's right." He laughed. "And khaki pants."

"Perfect."

"Why am I getting dressed up?"

"Thomas Hammond left you some land. You're selling it back to Gail today. They're downstairs waiting for you. All you have to do is sign some papers and you'll be a rich man."

He shook his head, not in disagreement, but in disbelief. "I don't know, Joe. I'm too old to be rich."

"No such thing."

"Will your mother be downstairs too?"

"Sitting right next to you. You don't have to worry about anything. Just pick up a pen and sign."

He clipped on his suspenders and pulled a strap over each shoulder. "How much will we get?"

"Two and a half million."

He nodded and thought for a moment and said, "We'll go see some ball games."

"Let's do that. Fenway. Dodger Stadium. Wrigley."

"No. Not Wrigley. We'll see the Sox. We're South Siders, Joe."

"We can go to both, Dad. You're rich, remember?"

He stared at me blankly, then said, "I'm rich."

"You will be in a few minutes. And you know what else?"

"What?"

"You'll never have to live in a nursing home. You can stay right here."

He said, "I like that." He turned away from the closet and faced me. "How do I look?"

I stepped toward him and said, "Like two and a half million bucks."

"Damn right."

"Uh. You missed a spot shaving."

He smiled. "Get my electric, will you?"

I found my father's electric razor charging on the bathroom vanity, carried it over to the garbage can, and popped the cover off the head. A hundred thousand silver hairs fell into the can like a hundred thousand bits of forgotten information. This, from a man who had cleaned his razor daily since he was fifteen.

When I returned to the bedroom, my father sat on the bed. He looked up at me asked where I'd gone. I showed him the razor, told him to stick out his chin, and buzzed off the spot he'd missed.

He said, "I tried to convince you to use an electric razor."

"I remember."

"But all your friends shaved with a blade so you wanted to shave with a blade."

"An electric razor is more of a lawn mower than a razor. You used to rub me raw when I was little."

He laughed. "You said your face was so smooth because mine was made out of sandpaper." He caught a glimpse of himself in the bedroom's full-length mirror. "I must be going somewhere special to be all cleaned up like this."

"We're going downstairs, Dad. You're going to get some of the Hammonds' money."

"Those Hammonds. Real sons of bitches." He looked away from the mirror and at me and said, "Except for Thomas. He's tried to be nice to me. I just never gave him a chance."

"Thomas Hammond chose his life. Remained loyal to his family. Hell, he even married his first cousin. There are consequences for the choices we make."

He nodded but did not smile. "Sure are." And then, "Joe, how are you doing?"

I didn't know if he remembered telling me about killing Roy Hammond, but I saw concern in his eyes. It must have taken all the courage and strength he had to tell me about that day—I didn't want to put him through it again. I said, "I'm doing well, Dad. Very well."

He nodded and we went downstairs. My mother, Ruby, Lawrence, and Uncle David had gathered around the big table in the dining room, bound stacks of paper and pens laid out. Gail Hammond stood waiting for me at the bottom of the stairs. She wore a white skirt over white shoes, a black short-waisted jacket over a blouse that shimmered like a pearl. She said hello to my father, and my mother helped him to his seat.

I caught a glimpse of Leela, who waited for me in the living room. I turned away when Gail beckoned me deeper into the front hall, where she said, "I can't thank you enough, Joey. You very well may have saved Hammond Island."

"Maybe you can name a lagoon after me or something."

"I just might. Thank you, again."

"It was my pleasure."

She shook my hand with the firm grip of a Hammond who had inherited the gene of ruthless pursuit and then pulled me toward her and kissed me on the lips.

Kissed me like she meant it. That changed everything.

38

I left Leela at the house to make sure all went well with the land sale, then twenty minutes later knocked on the red door of a townhouse. Virginia Rampell opened the door wearing pink sweats and a white T-shirt with Bach's head etched in black.

It took Virginia a moment to recognize me, as if it were impossible I could show up at her house. Then her confusion ratcheted up to alarm. "Joey, is everything all right?"

"Hi, Virginia. Do you have a minute?"

She invited me into her home, her pretty face contorted with worry, and led me into her living room. White leather furniture with clean lines on hardwood floors and a coffee table of weathered green glass, as if a window had fallen into the ocean and been etched nearly opaque by sand and shells. On it were travel agency brochures for Europe.

Virginia said, "Please have a seat. What's going on? Is everything all right with David?" She sat opposite me across the coffee table.

"Yes. I just saw him."

"What's that big binder?"

I set it on the coffee table next to the brochures, flipped it open to a page marked with a Post-it Note, and said, "Is this you?" I turned the notebook so she could see the photograph of a painting.

It depicted a young woman wearing a white dress and sitting on a white bench on a white dock.

Virginia stared at the painting, then a smile crept onto her face. "My goodness. Where on earth did you get this?"

"The actual painting is hanging in the Hammond mansion."

"You're kidding."

"It has a prominent spot above the fireplace. Well, a fireplace. I'm sure that house has a number of them. How old were you?"

Virginia shook her head, but her smile grew. "Eighteen. Wow. Just wow."

"I take it you haven't seen it in a long time."

She laughed. "Joey. I've never seen this painting in my life. Thomas had it commissioned as an engagement present. I posed out there for two days, then the artist went away to finish it, but Thomas and I ended our engagement before it was done. I had assumed he called the artist and told him not to finish it. To just throw it away. But you said it was hanging above a mantel in the Hammond home?"

"Yes."

"Well," said Virginia, "Gail must not know the painting is of me or she never would have permitted it in her house. I can't believe Thomas kept it."

"It does seem a bit odd, doesn't it? Thomas ended your engagement. But keeping this and displaying it in his home makes me wonder if he never fell out of love with you."

Virginia shook her head again. "No, I don't think he did fall out of love with me."

"Thomas ended your engagement because you fell out of love with him?"

"I'm afraid it's a bit more tangled than that."

"Can you tell me about it?"

Virginia pushed back into her white leather love seat and pulled one knee toward her chest and said, "Why do you want to know? It all happened so long ago."

"I want to know because I can't prove my father didn't shoot

Thomas Hammond. I wish I could, but I can't. All I can do is help the police find out who did. That's the only thing that will clear Marshall Green."

"The police must love you poking around in their business."

"The police have no idea what I'm doing. But you know, Virginia, I think I've managed to do what I set out to do. I know who killed Thomas, but I want to go to the police with the full story. I'm just a guy with selfish motives. The police will pick apart everything I say. That's why I need to know some of my guesses aren't guesses but facts. I want no missing pieces."

"And you think I can help you?"

"I'm hoping."

Virginia nodded and thought for a moment, then said, "Joey, would you like a glass of wine?"

I looked at my watch. "Yes, please."

Virginia stood and walked into the kitchen. She pulled two wineglasses from the cupboard and removed a half-full bottle from the refrigerator. She was calm, her movements smooth and unhurried. She poured two glasses of white, returned to the living area, and set them both on the green glass table.

She said, "Thomas Hammond was fifteen years older than me. When we met, he was thirty-two and I was seventeen. The day after I graduated high school, he knocked on the door of my family home and introduced himself to my mother and father. Of course he didn't need to do that. Everyone in Beaufort knew who he was. All the same, he was a real gentleman. Had you met Thomas before last week?"

"No. That was the first time."

"Well, even just meeting him once, you could see he was a salesman. I think he loved to sell because it connected him with people as much as it made him money. And that's what he did with my parents. Connected. Let them get to know him. Thomas was up front. Told them right away that he saw me in town, asked around about who I was and where I lived, and decided he would like to invite me to lunch one day. But he was aware of our age difference—a good salesman always knows what the customer's objections will be—and Thomas understood that age difference might make my parents and me uncomfortable so he wanted to assure us that his intentions were honorable.

"Which they were. About a week later, he took me to lunch. After that, it was walks and boat rides and a month later he took me to dinner. It was all terribly romantic. Thomas was very good to me. Gave me presents and was unfailingly kind and polite and respectful. And yet I knew he would want the relationship to grow more intimate. Physically, that is. He could tell I wasn't ready for anything of that nature. I would let him kiss me, but I'm afraid I failed to return his kisses. I was there, but you couldn't say I was a participant."

I said, "Did he want what he couldn't have, like his brother, Roy?"

"Thomas was nothing like Roy. He showed no frustration and remained an absolute gentleman. Always. One evening, about six months after he first knocked on our door, Thomas Hammond proposed to me. I was in love with him and swept up in the moment. So I said yes."

"You were in love with him?"

"Yes, I was. Definitely."

I said, "Did his expectations change after that?"

"I believe they did. But I still wasn't ready for anything physical. And that led to disappointment, yet he remained kind and patient and adoring. But . . ." She sipped her wine, then set the glass down on the coffee table. ". . . But I was beginning to think something was wrong with me. Oh, Joey. I have never told another living soul this. And I don't know how it could possibly help Marshall."

"It's worth a shot, isn't it?"

"This is terribly difficult for me."

"I promise it'll stay between us."

She sighed and winced and took a deep breath. "Well, all the other girls my age talked about kissing boys and letting boys touch their bodies. I assumed my friends did this as a favor to the boys, but no, they genuinely seemed to enjoy it. They talked about who was a good kisser and who had good hands. My best friend, Annabelle Scott—she told me she was saving herself for marriage, but when she did get married, she was going to do it every night. She said sex was like breathing for her—she needed it to live. And this was before she'd even experienced it. She just knew it in her heart and soul.

"I was just the opposite. The idea of sex felt repulsive to me. I was all for romance. Walks on the water and lovely evenings out. Holding hands with a man felt nice, but anything more than that felt like a violation. I thought I'd develop a taste for it, the way one develops a taste for alcohol or tobacco. But I didn't. And the more Thomas wanted to explore my body, the more revulsion I felt. He asked me what was wrong, and I said I was saving myself for our wedding night, but he knew there was more to it than that. Thomas Hammond was thirty-two years old. He was nice looking and wealthy and had ample experience with a variety of women.

"And so, Joey, I told him I was happy to marry him, but I would not consummate the marriage. Ever. I wanted to. For Thomas and for us. But I couldn't. I had heard some women prefer women over men, but that wasn't the case with me. I preferred no one."

I said, "And you've never told anyone? Not even your sister?"

"No, Joey. I'm . . . well, I'm ashamed."

"You shouldn't be."

Virginia's wineglass had sweated a gray cloud over the wine. She picked it up and ran a finger through the condensation and said, "I hear the rumors about your great-uncle, and I don't envy him. After working over thirty years for him, I would venture to say he is like me. I'm not aware of any contact between your great-uncle and a person that suggests a sexual nature. I have never seen him steal a glance at a woman or man. Honestly, I didn't find working for David Green terribly stimulating. But I've worked for him as long as I have because I feel safe. He never questions me about my personal life.

"I know there are rumors about me and your great-uncle. The few times I've been asked about those rumors by friends or family, I have denied them in a way that is undeniably suspicious because it's far better for this town to assume I'm carrying on with my boss than it is for them to think something is wrong with me."

Virginia couldn't even look at me. How strange for a person to be so beautiful yet feel repulsed by others' physical attraction to her. It must have been terribly difficult. I had not expected to learn anything like this, but it was important in understanding what I'd hoped to learn.

I said, "Are you the person who helped Thomas write his will?"

She hesitated, then nodded.

"So you knew you were a beneficiary. You knew your life would change after he died."

A ship's horn blew low and loud outside the sliding glass doors that faced the river. A tugboat pulled a yacht that must have blown an engine or two.

Virginia shook her head. "No. I only gave Thomas Hammond advice about the wording of the will and the importance of getting it notarized. I didn't know his death would change my life. I don't think anyone knew about that will other than the notary."

"Not my great-uncle?"

"No."

"Not my father?"

"No."

"And not Lawrence?"

"I don't see how Lawrence could have known. Thomas gave it to your great-uncle and told him it was only to be opened in the event of Thomas's death. And that's what happened."

I finished the last of my wine. "What happened to your relationship with Thomas after your engagement ended?"

Virginia removed her wineglass from the coffee table and set it on a side table. She spread her arms and grabbed opposite ends of the green glass slab and slid it until it tipped toward her. She stood and flipped over the green glass so it rested on the couch, revealing the base of the coffee table to be an old steamer trunk.

"Open it," she said.

The hasp of the of trunk was on my end. I flipped it up and opened the trunk. It was full of hand-addressed envelopes.

I said, "How many are there?"

"Over two thousand." Virginia smiled the saddest smile. "Thomas wrote me every week since breaking off our engagement."

39

I left Virginia and saw a message from a number I didn't recognize. It was Gail Hammond. I listened to it, then told Leela I couldn't join her for dinner with her parents. She was disappointed but said she understood. I phoned Gail Hammond and accepted her invitation.

She answered the door wearing a white beaded dress with a neckline deeper than the Atlantic Ocean. A strand of pearls hung halfway down. I'd sold enough fakes to know they were real. Blond hair spread over bronze shoulders. She leaned on the door frame and fingered her pearls.

"Good evening, Joey."

"Good evening. Where's your butler?"

"I gave him the night off. Where's your little friend?"

"Out to dinner with her parents."

She smiled, revealing teeth that matched her pearls as if she'd selected each bead to do just that. "Well, looks like our timing is fortuitous. Please come in."

Gail Hammond led me through her foyer and into the front living room, where a massive donut-shaped chandelier glowed a dim orange-yellow. A bottle of champagne chilled in a silver bucket next to a matching tray of prosciutto-wrapped melon, beef tartare, cheese, olive tapenade, and an assortment of crackers. Chocolate truffles sat on a silver doily next to the hors d'oeuvres.

"I don't know if you've eaten, so in case you're hungry."

"Not hungry at the moment, thank you. But thirsty."

"Good," she said, "because we have plenty of this." She lifted the champagne from the bucket and handed it to me. "Do you mind?"

I peeled the foil and unfastened the wire that secured the cork. Gail said, "Shoot it. We're celebrating."

The cork twisted with a squeak and popped off the twelve-foot ceiling, leaving a mark on a surface so pristine it looked like it had been finished by a professional cake decorator. "Sorry about that."

She smiled. "Don't be. It's something to remember you by."

We sat next to each other on the couch and I poured champagne into two flutes of cut crystal, alternating between them so the bubbles could settle. Gail handed me the first glass and took the second for herself. "A toast." We touched glasses. "You saved me today, Joey. I can't thank you enough."

"No need to thank me at all. It was a win-win deal for everyone." I set my phone on the table and said, "Sorry. In case my kids call."

"You're a good dad. That is a very attractive quality."

"Not why I do it, but I'm glad you feel that way."

"Are you?" She placed a finger on the rim of her champagne flute. "Really?"

"What guy doesn't want to hear that from a beautiful woman?"

Her smile faded. "I've not heard a man say I'm beautiful in . . . Well, I don't remember when."

"That can't be true. Your husband must have thought you were beautiful."

"If he did, he didn't tell me."

"He seemed quite the southern gentleman. Where did his manners go?"

Gail stared off at nothing for a few seconds, then returned to me. "Let's not talk about him. Please."

"It's your celebration."

"It's *our* celebration, Joey. We did this together. Aren't you proud of yourself? Your parents have extra money for the first time in their lives. So do Lawrence and Ruby." She leaned back into the couch cushion and looked up at me. "And it's all because of you."

I turned toward her and did my best to keep my eyes off her bronze chest—bronze all the way down to her abdomen. "It's not because of me. It's because of, well . . . we're not going to talk about him."

"Do you want to know why he married me?"

"I assume the usual reason."

"Which is?"

"Love."

She shook her head. "No, Joey. Not love. Lust. The man, despite his refined appearance and manner, had a hyperactive libido. Even at seventy-five years of age. We ran a business together and shared a bed together. I was his colleague and his sex doll. I was not his partner in life." She tucked her chin to her chest so she could finish the last of her champagne, then handed me the flute. I refilled it as she said, "Strange, isn't it? A man can want you for your mind and your body but not your person. Not your soul. Not even for conversation. Not the essence of what makes you you."

I let that sit and refilled my champagne flute, then turned back toward Gail. "Did you know that going in?"

"I knew he wanted my brain and my body. I assumed that meant he wanted all of me, but over the years my assumption proved incorrect. I learned to live with it." She sighed. "It wasn't that big of an adjustment because marrying Thomas was not easy."

"You mean being first cousins?"

"Yes. There's no shortage of stigma there, but it was so satisfying to reclaim my birthright of the South Carolina Hammond business that I powered through and endured. Thomas got a vasectomy so we knew there would be no compromised offspring. People would not have forgiven us for that. When it became clear we had no intention of reproducing, the gossip and disapproving glances died down.

"The age difference made it worse. He was twenty-five years old when I was born and watched me grow from a baby to a young girl to a teenager. We lived in different states but saw each other most holidays and at family events. I'm sure people wonder if he'd set his eyes on me long before it was appropriate."

"Did you wonder about that?"

She shook her head. "No. Thomas was always kind. Even in the bedroom, sex wasn't about power. It was about sex. And outside the bedroom, he was, as you said, a southern gentleman."

"Still, I'm sure that was difficult."

Gail downed half her flute and separated her knees just enough to press her left thigh into my right leg. "It was. Thank you for saying that." She sunk even lower into the couch and looked up at me. "Joey, we need to have a serious conversation."

"I thought we were celebrating."

"We are. But there's something we need to get out in the open so the celebration can continue."

"Okay . . ."

Gail Hammond placed a hand on my knee and said, "Joey, the police visited me this afternoon."

"Do they know who shot Thomas?"

Gail Hammond looked away from me and up at the chandelier. Even in the dim light her makeup sparkled like fresh snow. "The police brought a gun in a plastic bag and asked if I recognized it."

"Did you?"

Gail Hammond turned her head and stared at me too long, her pupils dilated, the blues of her irises receded like the tide. "Joey. I know what you did at lunch today."

"What's that?"

"You tricked me."

"And how did I do that?"

"Your father never wanted something from our collection. You asked for a list of things I own to see if that gun was on it. When you saw that it was, you called the police."

"Why would I do that?"

"Oh, Joey, please."

"I'm sorry, Gail. You invited me over to celebrate the land sale. Now I don't know what we're doing."

She placed her hand on top of mine. Her other hand found her pearls. "Are you intending to blackmail me?"

I squeezed her hand. "No, Gail. I would never do that."

"Not even for something other than money?"

"I'm not sure what you mean."

Gail sat up then swung her right leg over me, straddling my lap to face me. Her beaded dress rode up, revealing bronze thighs that matched her bronze chest. "Would you quit playing dumb? What is it you want? Me? Do you want me, Joey? Is that why you tricked me into giving you that binder and called the police?"

I placed a hand on each of her thighs but said nothing. They felt smooth and strong and lotion soft. The silence hung until I could hear a clock ticking in another part of the house.

She said, "Why won't you tell me what you want, Joey?"

I reached up with both hands and laid them on her shoulders. "I want to trust you, Gail."

She smiled. "Why wouldn't you trust me?"

I returned the smile. "Because you killed your husband."

Her smile did not falter. "You're sure about that?"

"You didn't know about his handwritten will."

"Of course I didn't. I told you that when David and I presented my offer on the land."

"You wouldn't have killed Thomas if you'd known about that will. He really screwed you."

Gail's smile vanished. "It was a cruel thing Thomas did, giving away so many of our assets."

"I need to know why you did it, Gail. I mean, do you just go around shooting people or did you have a good reason? I don't give a damn about your dead husband or justice or any of that bullshit."

I lacked my father's altruism. But I had one skill he didn't have. I could sell. I could psych myself up to believe the unbelievable and, even better (or worse), persuade others to believe the same. I used that skill daily to unload shipping containers full of worthless plastic baubles. "I'm asking because the moment I met you I felt a connection. Something primal. Like nothing I've ever felt before."

Her smile returned. "Really?"

I was close. So close. I just had to close the deal. I looked her dead in the eye and said, "Yes. And I felt compelled to explore the feeling. It was like I didn't have a choice. I wondered how do I make her like me? How do I get her to leave that rich old man for me? And then he's murdered? Are you kidding? What are the chances of that happening? All of a sudden you're available. It has to be fate, right? What else could it be?"

Gail's eyes twinkled in the soft light. "You think we're meant to be together?"

"I don't know that. It's impossible to know that now. But the connection I feel is powerful. Undeniable. I'm not sure what it means, but I've wondered if you feel the same thing. Then you kissed me at the house. Now you've invited me over to celebrate. And I'm thinking you do."

"Yes, Joey. I do."

"I'm glad." I sipped my champagne and said, "I made up that story about my father wanting something from your collection so you would need me. I wanted to be indispensable to you. I took the binder home and was paging through when I saw the gun the police were taking around the neighborhood and asking if it belonged to anyone. And I thought, wow, the gun that killed Thomas Hammond belonged to the Hammonds, and he didn't shoot himself. Two people in the whole world knew that: you and me. I figured that's my ticket. That's how I get to Gail."

"Then why did you tell the police that the gun is from the Hammond collection?"

"I didn't. You gave me the best bargaining chip I could ask for. Why would I throw it away?"

Our heads were the same height with Gail straddling my lap. Her eyes smiled. "Joey . . . We're the same, you and me. We know what we want and we take it."

"I want to believe that, Gail. I just need to know why you killed Thomas. I need to trust you."

"This is what I hoped would happen, Joey."

"You wanted me to ask you why you killed your husband?"

"No, I wanted to connect with you. Because I've felt what you've felt."

"But you didn't kill Thomas for me."

"No, Joey. I didn't do it for you . . ." She trailed off. I thought I could hear her heartbeat, but I'm sure I imagined that. She shut her eyes and sighed, then said, "All right, Joey. I'll tell you. Because you're like me. You'll understand."

Gail Hammond looked away and said, "A couple of weeks ago, I went into Thomas's home office for some business documents. Thomas locked his upper right-hand desk drawer because he kept a gun in there. The very gun the police brought in the bag. I knew that gun because Thomas felt we needed to protect ourselves. He took me to the gun range and taught me how to shoot." She turned back toward me. "Thomas told me the gun was in that drawer and that he locked it in case someone broke in and we couldn't get to it first.

"That day I went into Thomas's office, his friends at the club called saying they'd had a last-minute dropout and needed Thomas to complete their foursome. He rushed off to join them and must have forgotten to lock the drawer in his haste. And do you know what I found in there?"

"The gun."

"Yes. And something else. An unfinished letter he'd written to Virginia Rampell, his ex-fiancée. From what I read, it was clear he'd been writing Virginia on a regular basis, like he was keeping a journal and mailing her the pages. There was real love in his words, Joey. Love Thomas did not have for me." She shrugged.

"Thomas was still in love with Virginia. Can you blame him? Prettiest woman in town, even at her age. Kind. Good at her job. Single. I'd always figured Virginia preferred women—that's why it didn't work out between her and Thomas. But something else must have been going on. Some other problem that kept them apart. Because Thomas's unfinished letter was written by a man who knew he was loved in return.

"He was going to leave me for her, Joey. I was sure of it. If it were just about love, I wouldn't have cared. But it wasn't just about love. It was about money. I'd lose almost everything. Everything I'd worked for. Everything I'd sacrificed by marrying Thomas."

I took Gail's hands in mine. "I understand."

"Thank you." She exhaled, reached back for the champagne, drank straight from the bottle, and handed it to me. "Thomas was a napper. Napped a couple hours every afternoon because he was always up half the night. So that afternoon while he napped, I took his keys to the hardware store and had a copy made of the desk key."

"You don't have to tell me any more. I know why you did it. You had a good reason."

"No, Joey. Telling the rest will bind us to one another. Forever. You'll know what I'm capable of. And I'll know you hold my most vulnerable secret."

I smiled. "I like that."

She dropped my hands and cradled my jaw. "Thomas loved storms. Said they were God's way of reminding Man of his place on this earth. He liked to walk at night, but he loved to walk in a storm. One night last week, he was awake as usual. Then that storm blew in, and I heard him go out for his walk. I took the gun, headed outside, and walked in the opposite direction of his usual route. I held the pistol in my jacket pocket. With all that rain and wind and thunder, Thomas didn't see me approaching until I was twenty feet away. By the time he recognized me, I had the gun out. I shot him from ten feet away. It felt . . . good. I was done sacrificing for that man. I headed toward home and tossed the gun in a garbage can a couple blocks from the house. I don't know how the police found it."

Gail Hammond kissed me, then pulled back and smiled. "Now you know my secret, Joey. You own me. I am your property."

I said, "I won't go to the police, Gail."

"Thank you."

"And in exchange, you'll become my partner of sorts. You know, after an appropriate mourning period."

She nodded and kissed me again. "I know how this works. I'm good at it. You keep my secret, Joey, and you'll never have to work again. Never have to shovel snow. Go see your kids whenever you want. And you never know, I'm not that much older than you. Maybe we will evolve into something truly romantic. Something—"

The doorbell rang.

"Oh, you've got to be kidding me. It's nine o'clock at night."

I said, "Don't worry about it. I'll get it."

"You stay put. They'll go away. I'm sure it's just kids who come to the rich neighborhood selling candy bars to raise money for summer camp or school band or just for themselves. I swear, half the time those damn kids selling stuff is a scam."

"The doorbell rang again."

"Damn them," said Gail.

A knock-knock-knock on the door.

"Do not move, Joey Green. I will make them sorry they disturbed us." Gail jumped off me and strode out of the room.

40

I stood, picked up my phone from the table, and headed toward the front door. When I got there I saw Gail Hammond facing Detective Chantal Cooper and Officer Doyle. Four uniformed police officers stood behind them. Gail turned back and looked at me. In her eyes I saw the resignation of a creature who understood its time had come to an end.

I said, "There were two guns, Gail. A matching pair. They were both in the Hammond family for a long time, then my father was given one of them almost sixty years ago. He recently lost it, but the police knew he'd owned it and that he was no fan of the Hammonds. That made him a prime suspect for Thomas's murder, and my father's lack of short-term memory and his hallucinations raised even more suspicion. We could not prove he didn't do it. So we had to prove someone else did. We didn't know there were two guns until we looked through the items in your collection. That's when we suspected you."

"I'm not worried. I have the best lawyers money can buy."

"The thing is, Gail, the police found fingerprints on the gun you admitted to throwing in the trash."

Detective Cooper said, "Mrs. Hammond. Come with us, please."

Gail ignored her. "Not my fingerprints."

"No," I said. "Not yours. You must have worn gloves. The

fingerprints belonged to Thomas. He was the only person who'd touched that gun, so it couldn't have been my father's. That's why the police didn't arrest my father. The DA wouldn't prosecute without hard evidence. And guns might look the same on the outside, but no two are alike inside. Each barrel leaves distinct etchings on a bullet it's fired. The gun you used and tossed in the garbage, the one with Thomas's fingerprints on it, is the one that killed Thomas. My father's lost gun couldn't have. Still, we wanted more proof."

"Who's we? Why do you keep saying *we*?"

"The police, me, and my *little friend*. The one who's out to dinner with her parents. Her name is Leela. *We* went to the police and showed them the matching pair of pistols on your insurance rider. And then you called and invited me over to celebrate. Leela was the one who guessed you were onto us and that you may try to cut a deal to keep me quiet." I held up my phone. "So I gave the police permission to activate my phone as a listening device. They heard our entire conversation."

"That's illegal."

"South Carolina is a one party consent state. As long as one party gives consent to record a conversation, it's admissible in court. I gave consent."

"Mrs. Hammond," said Detective Cooper. "We prefer to do this at the station."

Gail turned around and said, "Just. Wait." She turned back toward me, shook her head, and said, "After all I did for your parents. And for you. I would have given you everything you wanted."

I said, "You did, Gail. You just did."

I started the walk back, called Leela to update her on what had happened, then called my kids to say I couldn't wait to see them in a couple days. When I entered my parents' house, I stepped into a party. Ruby and Lawrence Hill; Kajal and Ted Bellerose; Bubba and his wife, Tamika; Uncle David and Virginia; all gathered in the living room with my mother and father. They had no idea where I'd been or what had just transpired. My mother had invited them all to celebrate her hiring of Bubba as my father's full-time fishing guide. She took Bubba off the market for a year to take my father fishing and watch over him. The salary was a pay raise for Bubba, and would allow him and Tamika to spend more time with their first grandchild, who would be born next month. I couldn't think of a better way for my mother to put some of Gail Hammond's money to use.

Leela appeared from the kitchen holding two lowballs of bourbon. I offered my hellos to the group, said I'd be back to tell them a story, took one of the lowballs, and asked Leela to join me upstairs. She followed me up and into my bedroom, where I motioned for her to be quiet while I removed my phone from my pocket, buried it in my bag, and zipped it shut. I kissed her, then said, "I haven't eaten a thing. I was afraid Gail Hammond was going to poison me."

Leela smiled. "Then let's get you some food."

When we got downstairs I said, "Detective Cooper told me they'd delete the listening program on my phone. Fat chance of that happening."

"Joey!" said my father. "Come join us! Bubba made his famous shrimp skewers."

"Be right there, Dad. Save me some." I grabbed Leela's hand. "Detective Cooper wants to meet with us in the morning. She said it's for a post mortem on Gail Hammond, but I don't believe her."

Leela said, "Well, we've got that covered."

"We sure do."

We walked hand in hand into the living room, where my mother (who else?) handed me a plate filled with shrimp skewers, grits, and vinegar slaw, and said, "Now sit down, Joey, and tell us this story you promised."

Of the many differences between my father and me, one of the biggest is our ability to tell a story. He is far more gifted, a man whose words spill like water, punctuated by humor and observations that make the listener wonder if my father managed to travel back in time to re-witness the event to relay it in vivid detail.

But I tried. My audience listened without saying a word, even as I finished by telling them what had happened that evening, how the Beaufort police arrested Gail Hammond in her marble foyer after the realization that there were two matching revolvers with handles of carved ivory when we'd all thought there was one.

My mother cried with relief when she heard that my father was no longer a suspect in Thomas Hammond's murder. Ruby and Lawrence sat silently with elbows interlocked—the end of the Beaufort Hammonds, one by bullet and one by incarceration, gave them at least a sliver of justice for Delphi.

I left out a few key facts. I did not divulge what happened to Roy Hammond at the fish camp when I was four years old. I did not tell of Bubba's boyhood role in ferrying Trip Patterson to the Hammond estate. I did not reveal why Virginia's engagement ended nor did I reveal her long friendship with Thomas Hammond. I did not tell Ruby and Lawrence that Delphi was in love with Trip Patterson and not my father. Those were not my stories to tell. Nor did I mention what happened to my father's gun. That was my story to tell, but I wasn't ready to tell it.

Leela and I were the only people who knew the entire story. Detective Chantal Cooper had one hell of a cop's intuition and sensed that—it's why she wanted to see us the next morning. It was exactly what I'd feared by involving Leela.

After the party, Ms. Bellerose and I spent the night together in the guest suite above her parents' garage. A soft rain drummed on the metal roof, a perfect soundtrack for lovemaking and falling asleep intertwined like co-conspirators.

That's how we walked into the police station the following morning. Detective Chantal Cooper and Officer Jack Doyle led us into a small conference room and shut the door.

Detective Cooper said, "Thank you for coming in. I'm glad we can do this amicably."

Neither Leela nor I said a word. The police officers kept their eyes on us, giving nothing away, but we knew what was coming.

Detective Cooper said, "We would like to know what happened to your father's gun."

I said, "I don't know. I've told you that. I saw it the last time I visited. I haven't seen it since I arrived to Beaufort."

Officer Doyle said, "We don't believe you."

"I can't help you there."

"Ms. Bellerose, do you want to tell us what happened to Marshall Green's pistol?"

Leela smiled. "I have no idea. What makes you think I'd know where it is? I just met Joey last week."

Detective Chantal Cooper looked at Leela and then at me and said, "You two are pretty tight for only knowing each other a week. Seems you enjoy working together. Like cooking up last night's little sting operation. Getting rid of a pistol is easy compared to that."

I said, "You've met my father. You've seen what kind of condition he's in. Not too hard to imagine he lost the gun while fishing or left the garage door unlocked and it was stolen."

"But nothing else has been reported stolen," said Doyle.

"Nothing else is worth stealing. There's a lot of junk in that garage. And why does my father's gun matter? You have the murder weapon. You've arrested a confessed killer. Isn't that a good thing? Pestering us about my father's gun feels like, I don't know, harassment."

Detective Cooper worked a pencil through her fingers and said, "I don't like loose ends. The DA doesn't like loose ends. And your father's missing gun is a loose end. So please, this is your chance to tell us what happened to it."

"Or?" said Leela.

"Or the DA will sit your ass in front of a grand jury and put you under oath. I understand Joey perjuring himself in an attempt to protect his ailing father. But you, Ms. Bellerose? Are you going to perjure yourself trying to protect a guy you've known for one week? I mean, he's not ugly, but still. Is any man worth that?"

Leela said, "You can't make me testify against Joey."

"The hell we can't," said Officer Jack Doyle.

"The hell you can," said Leela, who opened her purse and removed an envelope. "Because Joey Green is not just any man. He's my husband." She handed the envelope to Detective Cooper, who opened it and removed our marriage license. "You can't force a wife to testify against her husband."

I could not have been more proud of my new bride nor more honored to be her husband, even though I knew it wouldn't last. Neither Leela nor I mentioned that South Carolina law permitted us to annul our marriage if we never cohabitated, and that we were off to live in separate homes in separate cities. We had fallen for each other, yes. Our combined ninety-one years of life experience, twenty-some years of marriage, and eight years of post-marriage dating had educated us. We knew what we felt between us was real. We did not know if we could make a long-term relationship work. But we wouldn't have to know. Not for years.

Detective Cooper and Officer Doyle shared a sour look between them as Chantal Cooper returned the marriage license to its envelope and handed it back to Leela. "We'll be in touch. Get out of here."

41

Detective Cooper did not stay in touch. Neither Leela nor I heard from her again. We annulled our marriage in December to avoid lying on our tax returns. But that didn't stop us from embarking on a honeymoon, which lasted a total of twenty-four hours. It began as we stepped out of the police station and continued as we drove forty-five minutes and checked into Savannah's Perry Lane Hotel. It ended when I dropped Leela at the Savannah airport to join her children and ex-husband so they could fly home to Boston together. Our parting hurt like hell even though I knew I'd see her in a few weeks during a weekend neither of us had our kids.

I returned to Beaufort for one last day with my parents. News of Gail Hammond's arrest and my parents' windfall hadn't improved my father's health one bit, but the house felt lighter—at least one of my mother's burdens had eased.

My father couldn't remember the story I'd told the previous night, not in his mind anyway, but his body seemed to know. The guilt he'd felt for killing Roy Hammond in front of me, sending the corpse out to sea, and scaring me silent—a guilt he'd carried for over forty years—seemed to have lifted. His lightness matched my mother's. I witnessed no more hallucinations. The ghosts who haunted him had moved on.

We ate dinner together, just the three of us at my grandparents' dining room table. My mother made a purportedly healthier version of fried chicken that didn't taste healthy and that's just the way I like it. With biscuits and green beans and a peach pie Kajal Bellerose had brought over that afternoon.

"Joey," said my father, as the three of us sat before steaming cups of decaf coffee and peach pie dolloped with vanilla ice cream, "you were just a little guy and wanted to eat the same food as your big sisters. They were adventurous eaters from the get-go, and you wanted to be just like 'em."

My mother smiled, knowing where this story was going. But I did not.

"We had a Saturday-night tradition when you kids were young. We'd make pizzas from scratch—little ones you kids could top with whatever you wanted. Well, one night your sisters put black olives on their pizzas. You peered into the can as if you were looking over a cliff—you'd never eaten an olive before. Greta was the one who said, 'Go ahead, Joey. Try one. See if you like it.'

"Greta spooned one out of the can and handed it to you. And boy, Joey, I'm telling you, you had a sour look on your face. You did not want to try that olive, but you did want to eat like your sisters, so you put it in your mouth, managed to chew a little and swallow." His laugh caught fire, a spark followed by a whoosh, then it roared out of control and spread to my mother. My father removed his trifocals and wiped his eyes and said, "I bet—I bet . . . it didn't take five seconds until you . . . you . . . you threw up all over the kitchen floor." His laughter echoed off the plaster walls. When he caught his breath he said, "And after you finished throwing up you looked up at me and said, 'Do I have to eat another one?' And I said, 'No, Joe, you tried one. You did your part. Now we know you don't like olives.'"

I still didn't like olives.

My mother said, "Marshall, do you remember the gift you wanted to give Joey before he goes back to Chicago tomorrow?"

He looked at her and his laughter faded. "I want to give Joey a gift?"

"Yes, and it's very thoughtful of you. I'll go get it." My mother left the table. She returned in half a minute holding *Carolina Moonset*, the painting of the marsh at night in its gilded frame. "Tell Joey what you told me about this painting."

She turned it toward my father. He grew solemn and wistful. "I've had this painting since before you were born, Joey. Had it since before I even met your mother. It was painted by a boy named Trip Patterson. He was in love with a black girl named Delphi Hill. You know Lawrence. Delphi was his sister. Poor girl was murdered. Trip knew who did it. Roy Hammond. But no one would believe a working-class boy from Pigeon Point. So Trip made this picture as a kind of clue. He painted it in the marsh at night, looking across the river at the Hammond estate. The old big house is dark as night except for one room. See there? Glowing yellow with lamplight. That was Roy Hammond's boyhood bedroom. This painting is Trip Patterson telling us to never forget who killed Delphi Hill.

"Trip drowned in that very marsh at night, so this painting was just too painful for his parents to keep. They offered it to me, and I have made sure it's had a prominent place in my home ever since. Now I want you to have it."

"Thank you, Dad. That's really generous."

"Not at all. It's time I let it go."

The next morning my mother drove to the airport in Charleston. My father sat in the passenger seat and I sat in back. He saw the cranes over Hammond Island and didn't say a word. Nor did he complain once about my mother's driving. I took it as both a good and bad sign. Something in him had let go. He would live the remainder of his life with less anxiety, but the fight in him was gone. He no longer rowed the boat but drifted, resigned to the power of the river. It would take him where it wanted and there wasn't a damn thing he could do about it.

My mother had promised to ship *Carolina Moonset*, so it was just me and my bag standing outside the car as I hugged my parents goodbye. When I walked away I heard my father comment on my luggage, "Green bandana for Joey Green. Smart."

42

Marshall Green died a year and a half later. It was the strokes, not the Lewy Body Dementia, that took him. He spent much of that first year fishing with Bubba. Lawrence often joined them. They'd go out three or four times a week, never more than a half day. Bubba gave my father time on the water he so loved, catching fish and swapping stories and eating Bubba's lunches that always included Budweiser and Goo Goo Clusters.

The fishing outings gave my mother much-needed breaks, though she could afford to hire more help and did. Ruby dropped by the house more often, volunteering herself as my father's personal helper. My father trusted Ruby as much as he trusted my mother. Ruby pulled me aside during one visit and told me my father's favorite thing to do was walk down to the waterfront to see the boats, just like it had been my favorite thing to do forty years ago.

My father and I followed through on our plans to see baseball games around the country. We didn't make it to every park, but took a Southeast road trip that started in Florida, Miami and Tampa, and finished in Atlanta. A few weeks later we rode the train north to watch games in Baltimore, D.C., and Philadelphia. We continued the trip to New York to see the Yankees and Mets, then took the train up to Boston to see the Red Sox play in Fenway Park. In July of his penultimate summer, my mother and father flew to Chicago, where they spent two months with their children and grandchildren. The trip included two trips to Wrigley Field to see the Cubs, and three to the ballpark formerly known as Comiskey to see his beloved White Sox. My kids and I stole him for a weeklong road trip up to Detroit to see the Tigers. Then we ferried across Lake Michigan to see the Brewers play in Milwaukee and drove to Minneapolis to see the Twins, then down to Missouri to see the Royals and Cardinals. But that's as far as we got. We had planned Texas, Denver, Arizona, California, and Seattle for the following summer, but his health was too far gone for that trip. Nor did we make it to Cincinnati, Cleveland, Pittsburgh, or Toronto.

He died in the house on Craven Street surrounded by my mother, Bess, Greta, and me. Our kids were in Beaufort but sound asleep when he passed. He had started hallucinating again toward the end, often pointing up at the corner of the room and talking to whomever he saw. I don't know who it was—he never identified his visitors. But he often smiled when talking to them—I'd like to think he saw them more as angels than as ghosts.

After he died, my mother moved back to Chicago to be near all of us. She lives in a condo in Lincoln Park and attends all of her grandchildren's athletic events, concerts, quiz bowls, and school plays.

My great-uncle David practiced law until he was ninety-three and only retired after breaking several bones in a fall. He still lives in his big house on Lady's Island and writes unsolicited articles to various legal journals and the *Beaufort Gazette,* where he opines about economic development in Beaufort County.

Virginia Rampell and I exchange emails a few times a year. She has done some research and discovered she's asexual. Apparently, one percent of people are. That's three and a half million people in the United States alone. She's now aware of the Ace community and although she doesn't participate, she does feel better knowing she's not alone. Virginia moved to Paris and lives in a small apartment in the Latin Quarter and has never been happier. Some asexual people are also aromantic, but not Virginia. What better city is there for a person who loves romance? She steeps in it every time she leaves her apartment.

After falling in love in Beaufort, Leela and I saw each other at least once a month for the next five years and talked and texted every day. We made no rules about dating other people, nor did we ever discuss it. Later we admitted to each other that neither of us had seen anyone else. We'd both independently assumed that if the other had lost interest, they would say so. But neither of us did.

We each had our kids for Thanksgiving the fall after we'd met. Usually, Leela and her ex split holidays, but he'd met a woman who lived in Los Angeles and said Leela could have them all four days. Leela and I took our kids to see their grandparents in Beaufort and to meet each other. You hear horror stories about those situations, but for us it went well. The next year we visited Yellowstone National Park together, and our new family took root.

Three years after we'd met, Leela's ex-husband moved to Los Angeles to work in a friend's recording studio to play guitar and bass on commercial jingles. We'd worried so much about our exes locking us into our locations, then Leela's just up and left. She stayed in Boston to let her youngest finish high school.

Today I am fifty-one years old. Leela turns fifty tomorrow. Our kids are spread around the country, two in college, one east, one in the Midwest, another kid living the life of a fly-fishing bum in Ennis, Montana, sometimes guiding but mostly fishing and bartending, and the fourth serving in the U.S. Army because she said it seemed like a good direction when she otherwise had none.

I'm sitting in baggage claim at O'Hare. After two years of correspondence, interviews, and near misses, Leela landed her dream job: a position teaching clinical psychology at the University of Chicago. She says she's moving for the job, not me. But she laughs when she says it, and I laugh along with her, a relief valve because for the first time in five years, we will live in the same city. In the same house. Both empty nesters with no one but each other to face day after day.

I cannot wait.

A new shipment of passengers makes their way toward the luggage carousels, and I get up from my plastic seat to watch the first of them head toward the carousel designated "BOS" on the screen. I spot her mid-throng wearing a peasant dress of natural muslin, her dark hair pulled back, simple gold dangly earrings catching the light. I feel like I'm sixteen years old.

The moment Leela spots me I hold up a bouquet of flowers in one hand and wave a tiny American flag with the other as if she's arriving from Kazakhstan because I think it will make her laugh and it does. She is still laughing when I pull her close, and when we separate she has starlight in her eyes.

"So, pal," she says, "are you ready for phase five of our experiment?"

"Phase five? I wasn't aware there was a phase five."

"Oh, yes. It's the most important phase. It tests for viability and efficacy."

"Those are big words," I said, "I am but a mere seller of trinkets. You will have to explain."

And so she does. Leela worked it all out on the plane, and as we wait for her bags to arrive, I think of my father, always the volunteer to get the luggage. And I am so grateful she knew him.

ACKNOWLEDGMENTS

In 1886, Morris Levin immigrated to the United States from eastern Europe and landed in Beaufort, South Carolina, where he lived the remainder of his life. He married Alice Kolikant in 1895. Morris and Alice were my great-grandparents, and they are, ultimately, the reason I wrote this book.

I have visited Beaufort regularly for over half a century. I love Beaufort's natural beauty, rich history, and friendly people. If you've never been there, go. You can thank me in your Goodreads review.

I want to thank Neil Lipsitz. He is mentioned in this book half-fictitiously. He never fished with a goldfish as bait but he did work at his family's shoe store. When I was a child, it really had a talking myna bird. At the time of writing this, Neil sits on the Beaufort City Council. He helped me get a lot of details right. The details that are wrong are not his fault.

Thank you to my family. Being locked down with a novelist can't be fun. "I know it looks like I'm making a sandwich, but can't you see what I'm really doing is writing? Why is that so hard?" And so to Michele, Camille, Carolyn, Elsa, and Riley, I am grateful for your patience and support. Especially my wife, Michele, who puts up with me the most *and* she's my first reader who has nothing but helpful suggestions and an eagle eye for typos.

Thank you to my Monday night Zoom crew: fellow authors Reed Farrel Coleman, Michael Wiley, Charles Salzberg, and Tom Straw. I'm not one of those guys who hangs out with the guys much, but their friendship and their support, personally and professionally, has been invaluable in navigating this difficult time.

Thank you to my agent, Jennifer Weltz, for her hard work on my behalf. I so appreciate Jennifer's long-term view. A wonderful and rare quality in an agent. (I've known a few.)

And thank you to my editor, Kristin Sevick. In an era when editors function more as production managers, I appreciate Kristin's careful reading and thoughtfulness about content, as well as her shepherding of my books through the wolf-infested land of publishing.

And to my parents, who braved my father's Lewy body dementia and short-term memory loss. I thank them for everything from day one.

ABOUT THE AUTHOR

New York Times bestselling author MATT GOLDMAN is a playwright and Emmy Award–winning television writer for *Seinfeld*, *Ellen*, and other shows. Goldman's debut, *Gone to Dust*, was nominated for the Shamus and Nero Awards and was a Lariat Award Winner. He lives in Minnesota with his wife, two dogs, two cats, and whichever children happen to be around.